An Eddie Pannoni Thriller

The Preyers

By

Ernie Lijoi, Sr.

The Preyers © 2015. All rights reserved by Ernie Lijoi, Sr.

W & B Publishers

For information:
W & B Publishers
P O Box 193
Colfax, NC 27235

www.a-argusbooks.com

ISBN: 978-0692366387
 0692366385

Cover Photo By: Ernie Lijoi Sr.
Cover Photo Enhanced By Ernie Lijoi & Greg Parkinson

Introduction

This is a tale based on factual incidents inspired by true events and the career of Detective Ernie Lijoi Sr. This aspect of the case began with the murder of five men in New England sometime during the late 1970's while they were playing cards in a small room above a well known club. You will read excerpts from the news articles that appeared in the news papers during that period of time.

That being said, sometime prior to the murder of six men in the 1970's in New England, there was a wide-spread narcotics raid which spanned several states with numerous arrests and confiscations after an investigation that was started by a deep cover operative known at that time as Eddie Pannoni, drug dealer and gun runner.

This investigation led to the arrest and conviction of hundreds of people. The case was the work of many local police as well as the DEA, ATF and the FBI. Detective Ernie Lijoi Sr. was the (DCI) who infiltrated the suspects while under the guise of Eddie Pannoni.

This same case was followed up by the drug lords of Columbia, who decided to clear the air and eliminate those suspected of being guilty of supplying the police with information and assistance that endangered their world of illicit activity. Step one was the murder of the main narcotics connection in the New England area by blowing up his plane as he returned from Columbia. This man had recently been arrested for distribution of illegal narcotics. The next man to be eliminated, in the opinion of the Columbian drug lords, was his partner Joseph Woodridge, who escaped from the plane explosion and disappeared for a long period of time. Last but not least was the police officer that did the deep undercover work.

The following is the writer's account of what could have happened after these murders, had the opportunity presented itself. The drug lords turned to a New York crime family for assistance to dispose of these liabilities.

Detective Ernie Lijoi Sr. and his partner Detective Jack Wade were contacted and advised of their connection to the case of the 'Card Game Massacre' by federal agents of that time. Follow Detective Ernie Lijoi and his partner as they travel from Boston to New York into the depraved world of illicit dealings where they become soldiers in the world of organized crime, narcotics, robbery, murder, rape and more. Read how the string of evidence leads to the interview of several people regarding narcotics in the Boston and New York area, the connections to the murder of six innocent people and to the confiscation of schooners loaded with illegal narcotics.

All of the names, dates and locations have been changed to protect the innocent with the exception of Detective Ernie Lijoi Sr., who was a real detective doing Deep Cover Investigations (DCI) in a specialized area of narcotics under the guise of Eddie Pannoni.

Much of this story is speculation on the part of the writer, based on his experience and the information that he received during his career as a DCI. The characters in this book are fictionalized versions of individuals that may or may not have had a relationship to real persons.

Other books in the 'Eddie Pannoni Thriller series by Ernie Lijoi Sr. that are available are "Street Business," "Shoveling the Tide," "Chasing Snow," "Destructive Obsession," "Meth or Myth," "The Cash Mule" and now "The Preyers". You can learn more about the writer at his internet site http://www.erniesr.com. Enjoy.

Ernie Lijoi Sr.
Aka Eddie Pannoni

The Preyers

To a deity, they do not pray
It's for the dollar that they prey
On the different
On the meek
This is whom they seek
 They take blood from their lives
Care not for family or wives
 These people that prey
Care not for those they decay.
These People, are the "The Preyers"

Ernie Lijoi Sr.
May 24, 2011

DEDICATION

This book is dedicated to the innocent, those who are preyed upon by the illicit drug traffickers who run these operations strictly for monetary gain.

Definition:
For the purposes of this book:
"The Preyers"

A: To seize and devour prey
b: To commit violence or robbery or fraud
c: To have an injurious, destructive, or wasting effect
<worry *preyed* upon his mind>
— prey·er *noun*
Origin of *PREY*
Middle English, from Anglo-French *preier,* from Latin *praedari,* from *praeda*
First Known Use: 14th century

Chapter 1

Calabria Club

THREE MEN EXITED a vehicle and went to the trunk, where they armed themselves according to the plan. They walked across the street and entered the alley.

Louie led the walk, signaling for everyone to remain very quiet by crossing his lips with his finger. He entered the doorway. It opened into a small vestibule with one set of stairs leading up to a second floor landing and the door to the card room. They quietly went up the stairs and Louie again crossed his lips with his fingers looking at the other men.

The three men were standing outside the door and could hear the laughing and joking going on inside the room, when Louie knocked.

The laughing and joking stopped; "Who is it?" a voice cried out.

"The pizza guy, we made a mistake on the bill," stated Louie.

The laughing and joking resumed as a voice replied: "OK, wait a minute, I'll unlock the door."

A few seconds later they heard the lock snap to the open position. Louie kicked the door, knocking the man that was opening it to the floor.

Everyone was sitting around a circular card table. Piles of cash were on the table. A pile of cash was in the middle, making a good-sized pot. Cards were on the table. All the men looked up in the direction of the commotion. You could see the surprise in their faces when Louie stepped into the room holding that Mac-10 and a few yells when he pointed it towards the men sitting around the table.

The gun roared like a bunch of firecrackers going off one after the other in a small, closed in area. Louie was firing and pointed the gun as he swung it at each and every man, then down to the guy lying on the ground. Wheeze was right in back of him with Ronny behind; Wheeze watching the stairs.

Bullets were penetrating bodies faster than a person could talk. Blood and brains were flying all over the room. After a few seconds of firing, Louie stopped and looked around for movement or signs of life. There were no signs.

The Patriot Ledger

25 Cents   Wednesday, June 28, 1978   West Edition

hotgun believed used   *Site of weekend disco*

5 murdered in Hub restaurant

BOSTON — Five men were found shot to death this morning in the basement of a restaurant in the heart of the downtown shopping district.

Police said the bodies, believed to be in their 30s, were found in the basement of the Blackfriar Restaurant at 105 Summer St., about midway between South Station and Washington Street.

"We got the call at about 8:40 this morning. All of them are dead," a police spokesman said.

Neighbors said the restaurant basement was

used as a disco on Thursday, Friday and Saturday nights.

Reports of the shooting sent hundreds of onlookers into the downtown area. "We're asking everyone to keep away from the area," a police spokesman said.

Initial reports indicated the five were found near the downstairs bar. The discovery was believed to have been made by the manager of the

restaurant, a police spokesman said.

Boston police were not allowing anyone to enter the restaurant and a police spokesman said there would be no official comment regarding the shootings until the medical examiner had completed his investigation.

One detective did say, however, that he believed the shootings had occurred early this morning. One of those shot was found behind the bar, he said.

The restaurant is owned by Vincent Solomonde of 105 Quincy Shore Drive, Quincy.

EARLIER THAT MONTH

In the Brooklyn section of New York, on St. Marks Avenue at the corner of Grand Avenue, there is a bar named the Old Mark Lounge. In the back room of the lounge there are two doors. One door leads to the alley where many a body had been thrown after being beaten and broken for one reason or another. The other door leads to a club called the Calabria Club.

The men went back and forth between the two locations. It helped the bar because of the business that the lounge received on the nights of the card games and it saved the club the expense of making drinks and food for the players.

Both the club and the bar were owned by a segment of organized crime known in the area as a Borgazino family enterprise. This family was headed up by a man known for his viciousness. His street name was Joey (Bats) Borgazino, a burly man, he was 55 years of age, about 5'6," with graying black hair and deep blue eyes, the kind of eyes that see right through you when he stared at someone.

Joey Bats was sitting behind his desk in the office of the Calabria Club when Wally (Wheeze) one of his lieutenants and right hand man, walked in. Wheeze was a man who had enjoyed Italian food all of his life, which showed in his 200-plus pound body. He was 56 years of age, had brown hair and was about 5'7" tall. The wheeze that could be heard in his breathing was probably because he was so overweight, but that didn't keep him from his duties, which he was very good at and enjoyed immensely.

Wheeze was with a man known to him as Louie (The Lark) Mandasa, a hit man, hired out of California and brought in to do a special job. Louie was about 150 pounds, appeared to be in very good physical shape, about 5"10" tall and had black hair and blue eyes. Joey Bats looked at his lieutenant with curiosity. Most of Joey's questions could be read by virtue of his looks and facial expressions. Wheeze recognized these expressions because they had been together for so many years.

"Hey, Joey, I want you to meet Louie the Lark from California. He'll be working on that deal with me."

"Hi, Louie, do you mind if I call you Lou?"

"No, I don't mind at all, Joey. Can you guys fill me in on what's going down?" asked Louie.

"I have no idea Lou. Why don't you wait outside for a few minutes and I'll be right with you," stated Joey Bats.

"Sure, I'll be happy to."

Louie the Lark left the office. Joey looked up at Wheeze from his desk. He was pissed off. Wheeze could see it in his eyes.

"What the fuck is wrong with you, Wheeze?"

"I'm sorry, Boss, I wasn't thinking."

"You're supposed to be my buffer from this shit. I don't wanna know how you get this shit done. I just want it done. If you can't do that, after all these years, we need to find someone that can."

"I'm sorry, Boss I'll fill him in and keep you out of it. I just thought that you may want to meet the guy we hired."

"I don't give a damn. It's not even our money. I have to wait until I get the OK from the Don and then you handle it and speak to me alone. Alone, do you understand?"

"Sure, Boss, I'll fill him in. Hey, boss, here's Don Bodi now with his two body guards."

Don Bodi, the head of the commission enters Joey Bats office while his body guards remain at the door. Joey Bats gets up from his desk chair and greets Don Bodi with great reverence by kissing his hand.

Joey Bats: "Thank you for coming here, Don. I don't mean to rush you, but I need to have the OK on this job."

Bodi: "Joe, why should we go out front for the Columbians? Why should we do their work for them? This guy didn't hurt us in any way. We don't know him and I don't like the smell of the entire operation."

Joey Bats: "If I don't get your OK, I'll have to send the hit man back and cancel the job. But take this into consideration before you make a final decision. The commission will get one hundred thousand dollars for the job. One third of our profit and we make a tighter friendship with them. After all they are our main suppliers at the moment."

Badi: "One hundred thousand you say? That does make a difference and as you say we would be helping out our friends. OK, you have the Commission's approval. Go ahead with the job."

Don Badi gets up and walks out of the room, saying goodbye to Joey and Wheeze.

Joey Bats: "Wheeze, the deal doesn't close until Friday night, right?" asked Joey.

"That's right and I'll take care of it," replied Wheeze.

Wheeze walked into the hallway and joined Louie. They went into a corner office, where they could be alone. They spoke quietly for a while.

"You know something, Lou, to make a long story short it comes down to this. Our suppliers from Columbia want to clean up the matter, that's very important to them."

"When you say, clean up the matter, how many subjects are we talking about?" asked Louie.

"That's not important since the target will be one of several men playing cards on Wednesday night. Our employers want us to do the whole room no matter how many people are there."

"The whole room, what the fuck do they think this is Columbia or Mexico? This isn't the 1920's or 30's." Louie questioned.

"I know, I understand your feelings, but the money is good, they are offering you fifty thousand per head without limits. They wanted the best and you're it as far as we are concerned."

"Wow, that's a lot of money. Who are these guys and how many do you expect to be at the card game?" stated Louie.

"That's unknown except to say there are usually five or six people there every Friday night playing cards. The names don't matter as long as we get the correct location, which we now have."

Louie Asked: "OK what's the story behind the story?"

"As you may or may not know, we had a major hit recently by a pretty sneaky cop who worked his way up the ladder to our level. He got the Jeweler, our main supplier in the south shore and many other suppliers of our products. This made worldwide coverage in all of the news papers."

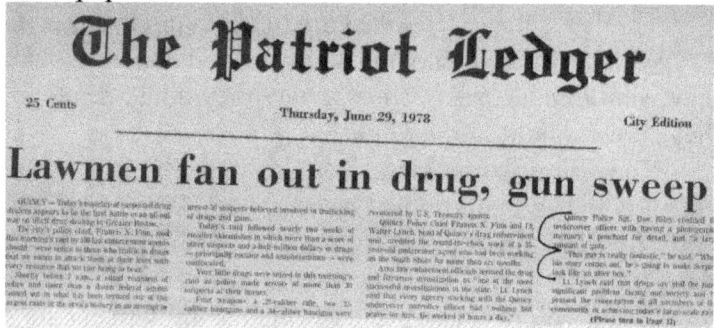

"Yes, I read about the hits you had, the story made national headlines."

"Columbia's main connection here in the US was a David Stewart McQuethy, Junior, who was too careless for his own good, as far as the Columbians were concerned. He was killed on his way back from Columbia where he was doing a pickup of cocaine. They blew up his plane. I have the news article right here. His partner Joseph Woodbridge, also known as Arms, jumped from the plane when the tail section blew up. They were flying very low, under 100 feet, under the radar. They were close to the Florida coast at that time. He got away from the explosion, swam to shore and survived."

"Yeah, I read about that," stated Louie

"The thing is that our connection in Columbia feels that the job is not done until McQuethy's closest friend and partner, Woodbridge, has been eliminated. This subject is a well-known dealer that covers an even larger area than David McQuethy did. Joseph (Arms) Woodridge is one of the people that plays' cards on the second floor of the Green Mountain Lounge at 569 Bridge Street in Brooklyn. McQuethy used to be a major dealer with Woodridge as his partner, before McQuethy was eliminated by his suppliers, the Columbians."

"How do you know that this is the right guy?"

"He's been underground since his partner's murder. Lately he has come out of hiding and made contact with the Columbians to get restarted in his business. In passing, he mentioned the card game."

"I see. So what do you have planned?"

"I'll take you to see the lounge. They play on the second floor and start at midnight on Wednesday. They go right through the entire night and next day or until everyone has had enough."

"Are there any preferences other then finishing them all?"

"You mean do they want a head for proof or something like that? No, none that I know of."

"OK, I really don't want to know anymore than that. I'll take the job. I want a plane waiting for me, ready to leave for Aruba as soon as I'm finished."

"We're aware of your preferences, it is all taken care of, and there is a plane leaving Kennedy Airport at nine on Saturday morning. That gives you plenty of time to make it. I'll get the ticket."

"Make sure it's first class," Louie ordered.

"No problem, I'm not paying for it, the Columbians are. We are simply support and middle men in this deal," stated Wheeze

"Now that brings to mind a question. Why would you even place yourself into this position?"

"I told you, they are our suppliers. I have to keep them happy or they can shut us off, a disagreement like that could start a war. We would have to take the time of finding others to supply us. Of course, in a war like that, we would come out on top in the end, but it's not worth the hassle or the losses. Then there is also the advantage of taking over Arms (Woodbridge) personal business, which will represent quite a bit of additional income to my family."

"OK, I understand. Do you have a preference as to where I stay while I'm here?"

"No, not at all, as long as you're comfortable."

"Good, I have a nice place to stay already, just checking."

"We'll run by the lounge where the job will be handled, so that you have an idea where that is, as well."

"Wheeze, I would like to speak with the boss first."

"Lou, you will speak to me. If necessary, I'll speak to the boss."

"OK, Wheeze, but there are a few points that must be ironed out." Lou explained his position and Wheeze went in to see Joey Bats, the boss.

There were a few men standing and talking in the office.

"Clear the office, men. I need ten minutes with Wheeze," stated Joey Bats.

Everyone left. Wheeze moved closer to the desk area.

"What do you need, Wheeze?"

"Lou wants to make an agreement on the number of subjects involved Wednesday night."

"I don't understand. How can we know exactly how many men will be there?"

"Joey, I think that the best way to do it would be to figure on four people. Those four will represent two hundred thousand dollars at fifty thousand a head. Any more than that will be considered extra to be paid."

"That's fine with me, you can figure any way that you like."

"OK, then his next point is that he gets one half up front to be deposited in Banco di Caribe, an Aruban bank, to his account prior to the start of the job. The rest should be deposited within twenty four hours of completion of the job."

"I don't see that as a problem, make sure that you know his account numbers," stated Joey Bats. "Wheeze, make the deposit on Thursday as long as everything looks good to you. Make it while Lou is with you so that you can show him the receipt."

"OK, Boss."

"Is there anything else that we need to cover?" asked Joey

"No, I feel confident that we shouldn't have a problem," stated Wheeze.

"So do I," Joey stated.

"OK, we're all done here?" stated Joey Bats.

"Wheeze, send in those other men as you leave."

Wheeze and Louie left the club and sent the other men in as directed by Joey Bats, the boss.

"Louie, you're all set. Let's go for a little ride."

***

They drove across town to the Green Mountain Lounge and Wheeze pointed out the second floor location of the card room and the entrance that should be used. Then they discussed strategy.

"Give me a couple of days to look this over, Wheeze, and then we can speak again. By the way do you have the weapon that I requested?" asked Louie

"Yes, all set and waiting for you. There are three of them, since I will be with you along with one more man.

The weapons are as clean as a whistle and can't be traced. We can drop them at the scene as we leave."

"Just out of curiosity, why are two of you coming?"

"You're not dealing with simple assholes here. You may need some help. We'll be there for support. The job is yours."

"How much of my payment do you expect for your support?"

"None, we get our own payment and it's plenty for what we have to do."

"Good. Wheeze, do you mind taking me to Rows Wharf, the Harbor Hotel? I'm staying there for a few days."

"Not at all, I'll make a call and have a package delivered to your room so that you can set up the merchandise as you see fit," stated Wheeze.

"Have all three units sent or brought to my room. I'll check them all out," stated Louie.

"I'll take care of it. We'll probably bring the weapons when we meet to complete the job. Would you like some friendly company?" asked Wheeze

"No thanks."

"Man or woman, it doesn't matter to me."

"No, thanks, I'll be fine," stated Louie.

Wheeze dropped Louie off at his hotel in Rows Wharf.

"Wheeze, meet me here, in room 336, at four o'clock in the afternoon on Thursday. Don't forget the tools and bring the second cover man with you."

Wheeze wasn't asked to come up to the room at this time, so he let Louie go on his own. Louie entered his room and lay down on the bed. He needed the rest after such a long flight.

***

Wheeze drove back to the Calabria's Social Club and walked into the office where he spoke with Joey Bats, the boss.

"Joey, do you have any preference for who I take as a partner on the job?" asked Wheeze

"No I'll leave it up to you, Wheeze. Make sure you pick someone that you can count on."

"OK, Boss, I'll take care of it."

"Tell me, Wheeze, what do you think of this guy Louie?"

"He's OK, smart and doesn't seem to miss anything. He wants to look the place over and get to know exactly where he is when we finally go in. More importantly he wants to know his exit and alternate exits."

"Good, I'll leave him to you; keep me out of it."

"OK, Boss," Wheeze stated. He left the office to walk into the large gathering room where there were several men sitting around the card tables discussing their next caper to make some money. They were bragging, to each other about the last big money maker that each man had.

Wheeze sat down and looked around. He observed three men sitting at another table talking about a bank. He laughed when he heard the subject of the conversation and thought to himself that those three couldn't rob a bank anymore then he could, they were dreamers.

Then he looked over to another table where two men were talking about a job at the airport, something about a guy on the inside who would leave some doors open for them. This he thought was a viable job.

He saw Ronny Surelo, a young man in his late 20's, who seemed to be the quiet type. Ronny's dad was a lieutenant before he passed on. Ronny was a trusted friend because he had been known by most of the men all of his life. Ronny's biggest problem was that he had a baby face and didn't look his age. It was hard for people to take him seriously with the look of a young kid. Everyone treated him as though he was still in high school. They all tried to keep him out of the business, but he insisted and now he was in. Ronny was a 29 years old, 5'10" tall and weighed around 165 pounds. He had brown eyes and bark brown hair. He was a very eager man, wanting to learn about everything. Ronny reminded Wheeze of Ronny's Dad who not only looked like Ronny when he was younger, but he also had that eager to learn personality.

Wheeze called out: "Ronny, come over here, have a seat."

"Hi, Wheeze, what's up?"

"I have been watching you and I think you're ready for a special job."

"What's that?"

"You know better than to ask questions."

"Yes, I do, sorry."

"Let's go for a ride."

Ronny followed Wheeze outside like a baby cat follows its mother outside. They took Wheeze's car.

"Can I ask where we're going, Wheeze?"

"I'm gonna tell you, but never ask questions of me inside anyplace. Wait until we are out riding in the car or in a private setting."

"I'm sorry, Wheeze. I wasn't thinking. It won't happen again."

"OK, Fugheddaboudit."

"So where are we going?"

"You've been on several different jobs in the past, right?" asked Wheeze.

"Yeah, I assisted on a couple of plantings and on a few small things," stated Ronny.

"How did you feel about that?"

"I'm OK with it, but I don't like the stench of the bodies after they have been dead a while. One time we didn't get rid of one guy until two days after he was dead.

Other than that, I'm OK. Why, do you need me for some-thing?" stated Ronny.

"I have a small problem. I need one man to go with me on a job and do back up with me. This will be enough for a guy like you to get his feet wet," stated Wheeze.

"I'm curious, why me? You have several other men that are experienced."

"Out of respect for your dad, I want to try to move you up as long as you are able to do what's necessary."

"If you need me, I'm there, but I don't have a gun."

Wheeze laughed, "Don't worry about that, just be ready at two thirty, Thursday afternoon and expect to be out all night."

"OK, should I meet you at the club Thursday or somewhere else?"

"Yes, at the club".

Wheeze drove back to the club and dropped off Ron-ny.

***

Thursday June 22, 1978

With plenty of time to spare, Ronny walked into the club on Thursday with two coffees and some doughnuts. He walked over to Wheeze's table.

"Wheeze, I bought some coffee and doughnuts for us. I know how much you like those jelly doughnuts."

"Thanks, Ronny"

"Hey, Ronny," someone yelled from the other side of the room. "Why you brown-nosing Wheeze?"

"Brown-nosing? I'm not like you, Spitball," said Ronny

"Wheeze, get up so that he can have his nose back, it's stuck up your ass," said Spitball

Wheeze laughed. "Leave the kid alone."

"Then where's our coffee?" asked Cecilio (Cheech) Tuccio, one of the men sitting at another table.

Cecilio (Cheech) Tuccio was 50 years old, born in Italy and brought to the United States, by his parents when he was a seven year old child. He was 5'8" tall, 160 pounds, brown eyes and graying blond hair. He was well known for his expertise in safes and locks of all types. He had done some time for robbery when he was younger. He robbed a grocery store in the middle of the night and didn't realize that they had a camera running twenty four hours a day. He wound up doing three years, but has been clean since. At least he hadn't been caught since that job.

"Hey, Cheech, I would have gotten coffee for everybody if I knew you were all here."

Cheech laughed and waved his arm as if to show he was joking with Ronny.

"Don't let those guys get to you," said Wheeze. "They're just joking with you."

"I know, but I like to give it back sometimes."

They both laughed and Wheeze placed his thumb between his first two fingers and twisted his hand, a gesture that indicated screwing with someone.

"You ready to go, Ronny?"

"I'm with you, Wheeze."

"OK, let's finish our coffee first."

As they sat drinking coffee, Ronny looked over and saw Cheech (Cecilio Tuccio) and Spitball (Settimio Adamino) laughing and speaking quietly, like a couple of school children, making fun of one of the boys who brought the teacher an apple.

Spitball an Italian male about 5'8" tall, graying brown hair, dark eyes and about 180 pounds was a man who had been working the streets all of his life, with the exception of the last seven years which he spent in prison for armed robbery. He was a nice guy, yet a dangerous man and no one to play around with, according to his reputation.

"Let's go, Ronny. I don't want to be late."

Ronny laughed as he got up from the table to leave the club: "Late, you sound like we're going to a dinner party."

Wheeze turned and looked at Ronny with that stern look of disapproval: "You still have a lot to learn, Ronny."

"Yeah, sorry, Wheeze," stated Ronny with his head down like a puppy that knows he did wrong. He walked out of the club behind Wheeze into the pouring rain and under a sky thundering through the dark cloud, as though they were in a battlefield with hurling grenades and bombs going off above them.

Chapter 2

The Job

Thursday June 22, 1978

"Jesus, this damn rain is gonna ruin the new uphol-stery smell. I just bought this damn car"

"It'll be OK, Wheeze. If need be, I'll clean it for you in a couple of days. They have some new stuff that gives it that new car smell, I'll use that."

"You're a good kid, Ronny. I appreciate that. If things work out for us, you'll be my right hand man."

"That sounds great to me, thanks, Wheeze."

"I said if things work out. I'm not guaranteeing any-thing, not yet."

"I understand," replied Ronny.

"Here we are. We'll be meeting a guy here. This is his operation; all we do is back-up, if needed."

"Understood."

The two men exited the car and entered the hotel and went up to room #336. Wheeze knocked on the door.

A voice came from the room, "Who's that?"

"It's me, Wheeze."

"Oh, OK; come on in."

"Hi, Lou, this is Ronny, he will be working the back-up with me."

"Ronny, nice to meet you, have you put anyone to sleep before?" asked Lou.

"No, is that what this is about? Sorry, Lou, I don't even know what we're gonna do."

"That's good. Wheeze, smart move keeping him in the dark, I thank you for that."

"No problem, Lou. This is your operation. I figured that you would tell him what you wanted him to know when you were ready."

"You're right; I can see why you're in charge."

"Do you have the pieces?" asked Lou

"Yes, I do. Ronny, go to the car, bring up the guitar case that's in the trunk."

"Give me the keys."

Wheeze threw the keys to Ronny and he left the room.

"Wheeze, you have confidence in this kid? He seems very young for this. How old is he?"

"I know he looks eighteen or so, but he's in his late 20's. I knew his father and there wasn't a better man before he passed on. His blood is good. I want to give him a shot."

"OK, as long as you trust him."

A few minutes later Ronny returned with the guitar cases.

"Anyone bother or question you Ronny?" asked Wheeze

"No… why? What's in this case? It's a little heavy for a guitar."

"Place it on the table. Now open the case," directed Wheeze

"Wow, that's some serious shit," said Ronny as he opened the cases.

"Let me look them over," stated Louie the Lark

Louie took the weapons one at a time and went over them with a fine tooth comb. He was obviously a pro because he had them apart, oiled and put back together in just a few minutes.

Mach 10

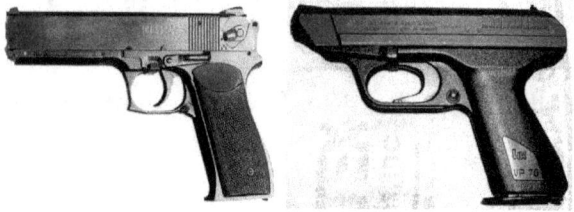

<u>OTS-33</u> <u>VP 70z</u>

"These are nice weapons. I'll take the Mac-10, you guys/ split up the other two pieces of garbage."

"Garbage? What do you mean? They look like good guns to me," said Ronny.

Louie and Wheeze laughed at the question, realizing that Ronny was a cherry at this end of the business. "The guns are fine Ronny, it's just an expression," stated Louie.

"Oh, OK, thanks for letting me know. I was picturing myself needing something to fire and it didn't work."

"They'll work fine," replied Louie.

"Now what?" said Wheeze.

"I hate to do this to you guys, but we stay together until this is over. We'll go to dinner later then tonight, we'll sit and talk. I'll show you what I've learned during my surveillance, how to enter and exit the building and what to look out for and everything I've learned. Do you have any problems with that?"

"No, I'm OK with it, but one question. I understand, but for Ronny's sake, explain why we have to stay to-gether," asked Wheeze.

"Good question," commented Ronny.

"It's simple. That way we all arrive together and no one has any opportunity to speak with anyone outside of this group. In addition, there will be no excessive drinking and no women."

"What are you saying; that you can't trust us?" asked Wheeze

"No, not really, but over the years I've seen some projects go south over a simple thing. I just wanna play it safe. I'll be happy to leave now and you can find another guy to do the job if my way is too hard for you."

"No, not at all. I like the idea of doing it this way," replied Wheeze.

"Ronny, do you have any objections?"

"No, none at all."

"Good, then we may as well relax, it's almost dinner time. We'll eat and after dark go down to the Green Mountain Lounge and you'll see what I'm talking about. No discussion of this job during dinner or anyplace where we can be heard by an outsider."

Ronny and Wheeze agreed.

"I just thought of something," stated Ronny.

"What's that?" asked Wheeze.

"Where the hell will we all sleep?"

Wheeze laughed, "Youth – you guys know nothing. You should have been around in the old days. At least we get to go out for dinner tonight."

"Yeah, I've heard the stories, but that still doesn't tell us where we sleep," stated Ronny.

"The beds have a mattress and a box spring. You can have the box spring. I'll take the couch and Louie can have the mattress. Ok with you, Lou?" asked Wheeze.

"That's fine with me."

"Yeah, that makes sense," stated Ronny

"Wheeze, do you guys know a good restaurant that we can go to for dinner?" asked Louie.

"What do you like?" asked Wheeze.

"I like Lobster Fra Diavolo, (Lobster in spaghetti with a spicy tomato sauce) but that's a little spicy for some people."

"No, that's fine with us and I know just the place, you won't believe how good the food is in this place. It's run by this little old Italian lady, we call her Ma, she does all the cooking; it's like eating at your grandma's house or at home when your mom was alive. She cooks everything to order."

"Sounds good to me, shall we go?" asked Louie.

"Wheeze, you're talking about Mama Frieda's place, right? I can't wait to get there, I love her food. She reminds me of my grandmother." stated Ronny.

"Let's go"

They hid the guns in what they believed to be a safe place and left the hotel. As they were leaving, Louie placed a "Do Not Disturb" sign on the door so that no one would enter the room. Then he took two small pieces of scotch tape and placed one from the door jamb to the door at the bottom with a second piece at the top of the door.

"You're very cautious, Louie."

"Yeah, in this business there's no other way to be."

The three men left the hotel and drove to a small bar at the other end of Brooklyn.

***

Wheeze began to park the car when Louie asked, "Where are we?"

They were parking in front of a bar with a sign that said Mama Frieda's Restaurant "Believe me, this may look like a dive, but the food is fantastic. This is the place where the old lady does the cooking!" Stated Wheeze

"Yes, you'll love it," said Ronny.

"That sounds great; the proof is in the gravy, so to speak," said Louie.

They parked the car and walked into the bar where Wheeze addressed a women standing by the door.

"Ma, how are you doing?" Asked Wheeze, of the owner and cook in the restaurant, an elderly woman in her late 60's. She had combed, but very bushy grey hair, dark eyes and was wearing an apron. You could see the hard work in her face and eyes when you looked at her.

"I'm good, Wheeze. You haven't been around for a long time. What's the matter, my cooking is no good for you?"

"No, your food is always great, that's why we're here now."

"You and your friends take any table you like. I'll be right with you."

"Thanks."

A few minutes later, Ma walked up to the table without a menu: "What can I make you boys?"

"Louie, what's your preference?"

"Ma, can you make me some Lobster Fra Diavolo? I've had a taste for it all day."

"Sure, how hot do you want? Pick from one to ten."

"That's the first time I've been asked to pick the heat. I don't know how to answer."

"Then this is the first time that you'll have it made correctly, a real Italian meal. Do you like a lot of spices or do you prefer mild meal?"

"I enjoy spices when they are made properly."

"Then leave it to me, I'll fix it nice for you. What about you, Wheeze?"

"I'll have the same and make it around a seven."

"And you, young man?"

"The same as Wheeze for me."

"Good, that makes it easy, how about an antipasto?"

"Sure, why not," replied Wheeze as the other men smiled in agreement.

"Wheeze, you know to get your drinks at the bar, right?"

"We'll take care of it Ma, thanks."

Wheeze went to the bar and got drinks for all three men. "We may as well relax; this will take a while. As I said, she makes everything to order."

They drank and Wheeze told the two men some stories from the old days, which brought to mind stories from Louie's past. Ronny kept asking questions because he had heard the original street version of some of the stories, but never from the horse's mouth so to speak. They became so interested in their conversation that they almost forgot about the food that was coming.

Ma walked over with a large plate of antipasto. "Here is the antipasto. I know you boys are hungry so I quickly made this up for you."

"Ma, that's great, how long before the main meal is ready?" asked Wheeze

"Just a few minutes," she said as she walked off.

Wheeze and Ronny laughed. "That's what she always says, but it's worth the wait"

About fifteen minutes later, Ma walked over to the table with two large bowls, each containing about a pound of steaming linguini covered with hot red gravy with large chunks of lobster mixed in. This gravy actually burned the hairs in your nose upon first smell which lingered into a desperate need to dig into the food and savor it. She placed them on the table, one in front of Louie and the other in front of Ronny. "Wheeze, I'll get yours right away."

"Thanks, Ma"

She walked off and returned with Wheeze's bowl and placed it in front of him.

"I was dying here, Ma, waiting for that dish to come after smelling the ones you brought already."

"How does our guest like that dish?" referring to Louie

Louie sat there and looked up at her, "Ma, this is the best I have ever eaten anyplace and I have been to quite a few places."

"Thank you, that means a lot to me."

"No, Ma, thank you. This is a feast that I will never forget."

"Thank you, young man" she replied as she walked off.

The three men ate, drank and enjoyed life as though it was the last night they would be alive. In a way they were also celebrating the death of their upcoming victims. They had no idea how true those thoughts may become.

After dinner they were served a large plate of Tiramisu which was homemade and delicious. They drank and allowed the food to settle into their systems, waiting for dark to drop over the city before they left the bar.

It was 9pm when they left the bar and drove over to Green Mountain Lounge at 569 Bridge Street in Brooklyn. Louie directed Wheeze to where he wanted him to park and Wheeze followed directions.

"We'll wait here until the lounge get's going full blast. Keep your eyes on that first door in the alley. That's the private entrance to the second floor office. Can you guy's see that fire escape further down the alley?"

"Yes, I see it," replied Ronny, Wheeze agreed.

"The window on the fire escape is in that office where we are going; a shitty backup escape, but a backup, if we need it."

They remained there for a couple of hours, watching people go in and out of the lounge. They saw a couple of well dressed people enter through the alley door. A few minutes after the first person entered the door to the upper office, the window to the fire escape opened.

Wheeze and Ronny listened to the procedure that Louie set up for the following night and understood what they were to do. Later that night, they returned to the hotel room and watched TV until they went to bed. The next night would be the night to create a permanent vacation for their intended.

Chapter 3

The Sleep

All three men slept late after a night of drinking and planning. Ronny looked out the window and saw that the sky was clear, blue and sunny. It looked like it would be a good day. He tried to remain as quiet as possible since Wheeze was still sleeping on the couch.

The door to the bedroom opened and Louie walked out. "What time is it?"

"It's one o'clock, be quiet, Wheeze is still sleeping."

"Oh, sorry, good morning."

"Yeah, good morning, I guess we better get him up then we can clean up and go for some breakfast."

"Don't bother, I'm awake, Ronny. A quick shower and I'll be ready to go," said Wheeze.

"I guess we all need showers; go ahead, I can wait." replied Ronny.

"Louie, do you want to go first?"

"No, go ahead, old man. I want to check something on these pieces that I think I saw last night."

"If there's something wrong with one of them, let me know and I'll pick up a replacement. I'd hate to be there holding my prick if my weapon doesn't work properly," said Wheeze.

"I'll check. Something came to me as I was sleeping about one of them, an old, built in problem. I want to make sure that this one doesn't have it," stated Louie.

"I'll be quick in the shower," said Wheeze.

"Oh, Wheeze, when you're finished in the shower, make sure that the plane tickets are ready for me at the airport first thing in the morning, nice and early."

"Will do, Louie."

***

The three men took showers, got dressed and went to breakfast at the hotel. Wheeze confirmed that the tickets for the nine o'clock flight were ready and waiting for Louie at the airport.

"Louie, your tickets are all set for a nine o'clock flight in the morning. How are those items that you wanted to check?"

"They're fine, I just wanted to be sure. What about you guys showing me some of New York today? We have to kill the day somehow, may as well be tourists," asked Louie

"Louie, it'll be our pleasure. By the way, I see that you taped the triggers and the handles for our protection. I should have taken care of that before I brought them to you."

"It's not a problem for me; it's more of a habit. We're better off being safe than sorry." stated Louie

"I always wanted to spend some time just looking around this city," replied Ronny.

"Good, then that settles it. I'll follow you guys around today," stated Louie.

"I have some pull with a few shows in the city, would you like to see one of them? Name it and I'll make a call," said Wheeze.

"I'd rather look around. I don't get a lot of work in this city. I'd like to see things like 42nd Street and Broadway. There's a story I'll tell you guys when we get there about that corner," stated Louie.

"Then why don't we drive into New York City and take a trip on the subway to start, how does that sound?" asked Ronny.

Louie liked the idea. Wheeze said that they would leave right after breakfast.

The New York Subway 42nd Street Stop

Louie stood on the train, fought the crowds and the bouncing of the train as it moved along the underground tracks. The location, the large groups of people struck Louie as being like an indoor bazaar or a large zoo with all of the creatures moving in and out of the cages, not concerned or caring about each other, adding their own little piece of existence to an otherwise mundane life. This was very visible in their faces as they moved through the transit system.

"Now that was a fun trip for me, thanks, guys," stated Louie after the subway ride.

"We're not done yet, Louie. Let's go upstairs," said Wheeze

They went up to the street level and witnessed a sight that is world known, yet rarely seen by people other than those that live and work in the New York area, Times Square.

Times Square N.Y. Traffic

"This is it, the center of the city, the well known Broadway and 42nd Street. Louie, didn't you want to say something about this area?" asked Wheeze

"Yes, nothing special, but when I was in the United States Air Force and leaving my assignment in Germany, a bunch of us agreed to meet here on a certain date and time."

"That's interesting, when was the time and date?"

"I'm sorry to say that I forgot the date, but I remember that it was to be at noon."

All three men laughed and Ronny stated that they probably all forgot the date too.

Louie agreed. "Where do we go now, guys?"

"Just follow me," stated Wheeze as he hailed down a cab.

"Grand Central Station," Wheeze directed the cab driver.

"Yes sir," the cab driver replied

While en route, Wheeze pointed out the famous four faced clock in New York. Then he pointed out the well known Midtown Clock.

The four faced clock The Midtown clock

They finally arrived at Grand Central Station where they entered the massive cave that led to corridors throughout the country.

Near the end of the tour, Louie noticed that it was getting late. "Ronny, Wheeze, would you guys like to go and eat at Ma's restaurant again, this time on me?" Both men eagerly agreed.

They returned to where they had parked the car and drove over to Brooklyn. They enjoyed another great Italian meal together, talking about the day's pleasures.

After dinner they enjoyed a serving of limoncello (Lemon Liquor), which was a common Italian after dinner drink, a gift from Ma to top off the dinner and relax the stomach.

They stayed at the restaurant until nine o'clock when night had fallen and it was time to go to work.

The first stop would be the hotel to stock up on the tools needed to complete the job.

***

"Ronny, here's the key. Go up to the room and grab the equipment while I check out of the hotel," stated Louie.

Ronny did as he was directed, while Wheeze parked the car and waited for them both to return.

Louie came back first.

"All set, Lou?"

"All set."

A few minutes later, Ronny came walking over to the car with the guitar case which contained the weapons. Wheeze got out of the car and opened the trunk, where they placed them for the job.

They took off and drove directly to the Green Mountain Lounge at 569 Bridge Street in Brooklyn, NY. Louie directed Wheeze to park the car in a location that he had previously picked. This location allowed a clear view of the alley doors and the fire escape.

It was now ten o'clock. They waited for the club to fill, the card game on the second floor, to get going and for the people playing cards to relax and with any luck, order some food.

At ten thirty, one man showed up, unlocked the door and entered the building.

"That must be the dealer, getting here early to set up for the game," said Louie.

There was no reply from the other two men.

A few minutes later, another two men showed up, parked a brand new red Cadillac and entered the door to the card room on the second floor.

About a half hour later two more men showed up in another new Cadillac; this one was blue. They parked the car and entered the card room door in the alley.

After another few minutes, a man walked up from down the street, entered the alley and then entered the card room door. There were now six men in that card room.

As the last man walked in, Wheeze spoke, "That's our guy, Louie. I recognize him. I met him four or five years ago. We can do him right now.

"Not now. Look at all the money I would lose, unless you're willing to pay me for the others. Make a decision fast."

Wheeze became tongue-tied and was unable to decide before Joseph Woodridge got inside the doorway to the card game."

"I guess the decision has been made for us," stated Louie.

"I guess so," replied Wheeze. He was counting the people and mentioned that there were six people that had entered the room.

"Louie, you're gonna make a bundle here, that's six and that'll mean that we have to send you another two hundred thousand dollars. I already sent one hundred thousand dollars to your off shore account."

"Yeah, Wheeze, as long as everything goes OK you can send that to my account in the morning," stated Louie.

"Fugheddaboudit, it's handled; it will be there before you arrive, at the latest on Monday morning."

"Thanks, Wheeze, we'll wait here for a while and give them time to relax."

Neither Wheeze nor Ronny replied to the statement.

***

The time was getting near two in the morning when Louie saw a deliveryman approaching the alleyway with three pizzas in his hands. These pizzas were destined for the card game on the second floor. Louie, Wheeze and Ronny watched the deliveryman enter the door to the building and the stairway leading to the second floor card game.

"OK, men, in another half-hour they'll be relaxed, laughing and enjoying the game with their bellies full of pizza. That's when we will approach."

"Anything special that you want us to do, or location to be, that you prefer, Louie?"

"Wheeze, you're with me, Ronny you cover our back and the exit, agreed?"

Both men agreed without question.

"It's time, let's move," stated Louie.

The three men exited the vehicle and went to the trunk, where they armed themselves according to the plan. They walked across the street and entered the alley.

Louie led the walk, signaling for everyone to remain very quiet by crossing his lips with his finger. He entered the doorway. It opened into a small vestibule with one set of stairs leading up to a second floor landing and the door to the card room.

They quietly went up the stairs and Louie again crossed his lips with his fingers looking at the other men.

The three men were standing outside the door and could hear the laughing and joking going on inside the room, when Louie knocked.

The laughing and joking stopped; "Who is it?" a voice cried out.

"The pizza guy, we made a mistake on the bill," stated Louie.

The laughing and joking resumed as a voice replied: "OK, wait a minute, I'll unlock the door."

A few seconds later they heard the lock snap to the open position. Louie kicked the door knocking the man that was opening it to the floor.

All the men looked up in the direction of the commotion. You could see the surprise in their faces when Louie stepped into the room holding that Mac-10 and a few yells when he pointed it towards the men sitting around the table.

The gun roared like a bunch of firecrackers going off one after the other in a small, closed in area. Louie was firing and pointed the gun as he swung it at each and every man, then down to the guy lying on the floor. Wheeze was right in back of him with Ronny behind Wheeze watching the stairs.

Bullets were penetrating bodies faster than a person could talk. Blood and brains were flying all over the room. After a few seconds of firing, Louie stopped and looked around for movement or signs of life. There were no signs.

"Wheeze, take a head count to confirm the number of men," directed Louie.

Wheeze counted out six people and simply replied by stating, "Confirmed, $300,000 dollars total."

"Good" replied Louie, "Now let's get outta here."

Ronny moved into the room and saw all the piles of cash still lying on the table in the quiet room. He was distracted by the sight of at least fifty thousand dollars spread out all over the table with piles of cash at each seat. He was supposed to cover Wheeze and Louie as they left the area.

As they left the room, they heard a shot go off. Louie turned back into the room to watch Ronny fall to the floor.

Louie quickly looked over the room and noticed that one of the men on the ground was holding a handgun. He immediately fired directly into the head of the guy holding the gun making sure he had joined his ancestors. He then went to every single body in the room out of shear madness and fired directly at each one to make sure they were all dead.

"How the hell did this happen?" asked Wheeze as he looked at Ronny.

"That fucken piece of shit must have had just enough life to get his weapon and pull the trigger," replied Louie.

"Let's get Ronny out of here." Ronny was on the floor, lying in a puddle of blood which was seeping out from under his body. They dropped their weapons to the floor as planned.

The two men picked up Ronny and helped him down the stairs. When they got to the car, Wheeze stopped and opened the trunk and got out some blankets and towels that he kept there for just this type of situation.

"What the hell are you doing, Wheeze?" asked Louie.

"Hey, I don't want this prick bleeding all over my new car. He'll ruin the upholstery"

Wheeze placed the blankets on the back seat and the towels all over the body area where Ronny was shot. They laid him down in the back of the car.

Ronny was awake, "Thanks, guys; I didn't see him or his gun."

"That's OK, kid, you'll be all right. As soon as we drop Louie at the airport, I'll take you to our doctor. He'll fix you up," stated Wheeze.

"Thanks, guys," replied Ronny as he passed out

Wheeze drove to the airport and dropped off Louie: "Sorry I can't come in Louie, but you understand, I have to take care of the kid."

"Yes, I understand. I'll call you in a few days to see how he is."

"Good, thanks and have a great trip."

"I expect to."

"Oh, Louie, as soon as I'm done with him, I'll take care of the final payment."

"No problem. Thanks, Wheeze. It was a pleasure meeting you two guys; we have to go to Ma's again, one day."

"It's a date."

"Wheeze, make sure if you have any other jobs that you give me a call first. I enjoyed working with you two guys," stated Louie.

As he exited the car, Louie looked in the back seat at Ronny in an effort to say goodbye.

"Wheeze, he's bleeding all over your seats," stated Louie

"Son of a bitch, let me get him the fuck out of here," said Wheeze "Louie, I enjoyed working with you also, but I gotta go and take care of the kid. I'll be in touch," stated Wheeze as he drove off.

He headed back to Brooklyn where he would drop Ronny off with a doctor who handled these situations for the family.

A half hour later, he drove into the garage of Doctor Robert Coin. The doctor met him and they unloaded Ronny together. The doctor quickly looked Ronny over.

"How will he be Doc?"

"He's lost a lot of blood, but I think I can pull him through all right. I'll take the bullet out, patch him up and you can take him home. I'll have more specific instructions then, including a script for antibiotics."

"Thanks Doc, I'll see you in a few hours. By the way, how much for your expertise?"

"This isn't too bad. A "G" (Grand or thousand dollars) should cover it."

"Done," replied Wheeze

Wheeze needed a cup of coffee after all the running around and went back to the Calabria Social Club.

He entered the main room, where he found Cheech and Spitball still sitting there.

"What's up, Wheeze, what brings you in here so early?"

"Just need a cup of coffee, that's all."

"I'll get it for you," stated Spitball.

Wheeze sat down at a table with the two men, Spitball brought over the coffee.

"Look guys, we did a job tonight and Ronny was hit."

"Is he alive?" asked Cheech.

"Yeah, he'll survive, but he is gonna be a hurt puppy for a while. He took a nine in the upper shoulder, right side."

"Can you tell us what happened?" asked Cheech

"No, I can't, not yet. Tomorrow there will be news articles and then maybe I can give you some specifics," answered Wheeze

"I hope the fuck you made sure whoever did it won't do anything like that again." stated Spitball

"Taken care of" replied Wheeze.

"Do you need us to do anything, Wheeze?" asked Cheech

"Yeah, you guys can come with me to take him home in about an hour. I'll need some help getting him into the house and settled."

"Done," replied Cheech.

"I would imagine that we should check on him from time to time and make sure he's OK," stated Spitball.

"How's about you two guys are assigned that duty, if you don't mind," stated Wheeze.

"Fugheddaboudit, it's done," replied Cheech.

"Thanks, men. Now I have to speak with the boss. He ain't gonna be too happy."

Wheeze got up from the table and walked over to the Old Mark Lounge. He walked through the doorway that led into the lounge from the Calabria's Club.

As he entered the dimly lighted lounge, he observed the long bar to the right hand side of the large room. This bar had been there as long as he could remember. It had gone through two families and was now owned by the

Borgazino family who took over from the Demetrio family years earlier.

The tables were set up along the left hand wall with two booths in the back area. One of these booths was the private seating for Joey (Bats) Borgazino, the boss.

Joey was sitting there with another man having a conversation when he saw Wheeze walk in. Joey whispered to his conversation partner who, in turn, left the table. Joey then signaled for Wheeze to come over, which he did immediately and sat down opposite Joey Bat's.

"How'd it go, Wheeze?" asked Joey

"The contract is completed. I have to send the balance of the funds for six heads."

"You don't sound very happy about finishing the job."

"No, I took Ronny with me, trying to give him a leg up, so to speak. I was forced to take him to Dr. Coin."

"How bad was it?"

"Not too bad. He'll be OK, but we'll have to help him out for a while."

"Take care of it and give him a few grand as a bonus. That will make him feel better."

"Thanks Joe, I'll give him five if that's OK?"

"Fine, he's a good kid, I remember his dad fondly. Ronny reminds me of him sometimes. You know, his dad had the same problem happen to him once. Back in the early 1940's, his dad and I did a thing, three guys in a restaurant. He took one in the chest. He pulled through Ok and so will Ronny. He's just like his dad."

"Anything else, Wheeze?"

"Just one thing; are you taking care of the Columbians or am I?"

"I have a meeting with their contact Monday night at nine; we're having dinner at Ma's. Can you make that meet?"

"I'll be there, nine o'clock."

"See you then. Make sure you take care of Louie's final payment during the day Monday," stated Joey.

Wheeze got up: "Yeah, that's right, I forgot that the bank would be closed until Monday. I'll take care of it first thing Monday morning." He walked out of the restaurant and got into his car. He headed home to get some rest and be fresh for the meeting on Monday night.

Chapter 4

The Payoff

Saturday Morning, July 1, 1978:

Wheeze arose early. He wanted to read the newspapers to see if he and his fellow murderers made any mistakes. He didn't believe that they left any evidence behind, with one small exception that occurred to him as he slept. He and Louie forgot about Ronny's blood on the floor. It was too late to start worrying about the small stuff. After all, they could only get the blood type and gender of the person who bled. Ronny must have common blood. He decided to telephone him to find out.

"Ronny, you sound good."

"Yeah, Wheeze, what's up?"

"You feel any better, kid?"

"Much better Wheeze, a bit of pain though, thanks for asking. I won't be around for a week or two."

"Take your time. I have a bonus for you. I'll stop by with it later today."

"Thanks Wheeze."

"Look kid, you wouldn't happen to know what blood type you are, do you? We left a lot behind."

"Yeah, I'm O-Positive."

"O-Positive, that's great. That's one of the most common blood types, no problem, I'll see you later."

Wheeze finished getting dressed and left his apartment, a small one room unit that he kept in the city for his work. His home was a large two story Garrison that he lived in with his wife and kids. His four children still lived at home with him and his wife. They didn't mind having the kids with them; they had plenty of room in the large six bedrooms, four baths house.

Wheeze hadn't been home in a few days, but kept in touch by telephone. If he was needed, he could drive out to his home in Islip Long Island in about an hour's time.

After checking in at home, he left the apartment and went to his favorite corner restaurant, which was also at the corner of Grand Ave and St Marks Ave in Brooklyn It was on the opposite corner of the Old Mark Lounge.

He picked up the paper as he entered the restaurant. On the front page was the headline: "FIVE MURDERED IN HUB RESTURANT" with the complete story following the headline.

He picked up another paper which had a front page headline of: "FIVE SLAIN IN LOUNGE DOWN-TOWN". There were some pictures of the lounge and the second floor as well as one of the men who were shot; James Kale a former investigative reporter and news commentator.

Another newspaper stated that the head of the narcotics department said that there was a definite link between the south shore narcotics arrest and round up and the massacres in the downtown club.

Another man, identified as Victor Solentie of Quincy, Massachusetts, was also killed. All of the men were pronounced dead by the medical examiner. The place was closed at his orders until a full investigation could be completed.

The story went on to say that the night janitor had entered the building at around four in the morning, cleaning the lounge and restaurant first. After that, he would go and clean the second floor office if no one was there.

He went up the stairs and noticed that the door was open. He entered and discovered the six bodies. The newspaper quoted the maintenance man as saying "The only one alive is me. They are all dead. The bodies are on the floor of the office. They are all dead."

During a telephone interview the maintenance man was asked why the news papers stated five bodies and he stated six. "I don't know why they said five, I saw six dead bodies."

Once the detectives for the New York Police Department arrived they discovered that although it looked like five bodies because of all of the blood and gore, there were actually six people dead. They then called the murders into the FBI office to cover all bases for any information as soon as possible.

* Newspaper article Boston Globe, June 28, 1978

One of the news articles stated that the detectives were questioned by the newspaper people about the sixth body and confirmed that there was a sixth body, but refused to discuss it any further until they received confirmation on all of the identities.

In another newspaper article, the lieutenant in charge of the Quincy Police Narcotics unit stated: * "......There is a definite link between the south shore drug raid and the deaths of the men at the card game massacre down town....."

He further stated that: ** ".......There is enough evidence here to lead us to believe that there is a strong connection between the card game massacre and the south shore narcotics investigation recently completed ......"

Once identification was verified on the bodies, the FBI immediately recognized Woodbridge and tied this shooting into the murder of the major narcotics supplier from the Boston area, named David Stewart McQuethy Junior, who was killed while making a run back from Columbia. Until now, many people believed that Woodbridge was also aboard that plane and died in the crash.

Earlier that same year, McQuethy had been arrested by the Federal Drug Enforcement Administration and the Quincy, Massachusetts Police deep cover investigator, Eddie Pannoni.

The connection between the two was that one of the men killed in that card game was the partner that escaped the plane crash, or so it was believed and indicated to the proper people by the DEA.

The street gossip was that when the plane blew up there was a second man that escaped. McQuethys' partner Mr. Joseph Woodridge the second man in the plane was a marked man because his partner, David Stewart McQuethy, Junior, now dead, had been arrested as a major supplier and distributor of narcotics throughout the United States during the Quincy investigation.

This arrest threatened the stability of the drug lord's corporate endeavors. Because of that arrest, they made sure that his plane blew up on his way back to the US during his last trip to Columbia. The next step was his family and friends, but the Columbian Drug Lords decided to simply handle his partner and hopefully finish the threat at that point.

Based on the connections that the Columbians had in the United States they contacted the Borgazino Mafia, crime family head, Joey (Bats) Borgazino, to handle the job of eliminating Woodbridge. The job was accepted and completed. The payoff was due.

***

Wheeze sat down and ate his breakfast. He read the newspapers with complete concentration, looking for any word or indication of any ties to the Borgazino family. There were none. He was totally unaware of what this hit would cost him and the entire Borgazino family, at a later date.

After breakfast, Wheeze walked across the street to the bank, which in this case was the family bank where he was the only man other then Joey Bats to have access.

A secret room down in the cellar, under the stairs and behind a sliding wall was where they kept the illicit narcotics. In this room they cut the drugs and distributed them with a crew of people that Wheeze had to allow in when it was necessary for them to do their job. This was for small, independent projects. The main cutting area was in the warehouse where they stored the drugs and did the major cutting.

In one corner of the room was a large safe with two doors. It was cemented into the floor and stood about six feet tall and three feet wide.

Wheeze had the combination. He opened the safe and on the second shelf were stacks of cash from the recent distribution. Wheeze had to take that cash and deliver it to the National Bank for deposit into several different accounts that he and Bats had access to. This was done with the assistance of a partner in the bank who received a substantial payment of two thousand dollars each time the family money was dispersed by him.

Wheeze filled two shopping bags with the cash for the bank. He took ten thousand and placed it in his inside jacket pocket, his payment to himself. He took fifteen thousand and placed it in a small bag for Ronny.

He then went to the bank, dropped off the shopping bags with Lawrence Bishop, one of the vice presidents, with a total count and instructions to deliver via electronic deposit the additional monies to Louie.

His next stop would be to pay Ronny and give him the bonus for his extra pain. He entered Ronny's home and threw the bag at Ronny who was shocked and at first thought that he did something wrong and was in trouble. He opened the bag, saw the cash, looked up and smiled. Ronny counted the cash and was thrilled about the bonus, thanking Wheeze for the extra cash. As soon as he saw the money, he wanted to call in a bet on a horse.

"Hey kid, Joey Bats approved that bonus after I asked for it, so you can thank him as well."

"I will. When you see him thank him for me, will you, Wheeze?"

"I'll do that, kid. Shouldn't you at least get some healing in before you spend all that cash on the mules?" questioned Wheeze with a laugh.

"I guess you're right, but what if I die from this hit? We only live once, you know."

"OK, kid, I have to call the boss. Where's your phone?"

"Sure help yourself, its right over there and thank him for me," Ronny stated as he pointed out the phone.

Wheeze dialed the office and Joey Bats answered.

"Joey, I took care of everything. Both people have been taken care of, are we on for tonight?"

"No, that's all been changed. I'll talk to you later about it."

"I'll be right over," stated Wheeze.

"OK, bring some good coffee when you come," said Joey Bats.

"Done."

Wheeze hung up the phone and looked at Ronny.

"Ronny, I have to leave, I may be gone a couple of days. I'll see you when I get back."

"OK Wheeze, and thanks again."

"No problem kid, just get yourself better we have plenty of work to get done."

"I will."

***

Wheeze left Ronny. He went to the restaurant where he had breakfast and bought four coffees. This was the favorite coffee for all the men. He went over to the office where he met with Joey Bats.

"Here's some coffee. I brought some for Cheech and Spitball; I'll give it to them before we talk."

He went to the outer office and handed the two men the coffees.

"Thanks, Wheeze."

"Fugheddaboudit," he said as he returned to the office.

"What's up, Joey, no meeting?"

"Just a change of locations, Wheeze, that's all."

"Oh, OK, let me know when you're ready to get set up for the new location."

"We're all set on the location; we leave at three this afternoon."

"May I ask what our heading may be?"

"South, Key West. We're meeting the rep at that house we acquired from that loser, Jimmy Pimple. Remember him?"

"Yeah, I remember that he owed us three hundred thousand and didn't have the money. I buried him over at the dump."

"Before you guys went on that trip, I had him sign a legal document turning over all of his real estate to me. All I wanted was that house. I let his family keep the rest."

"I didn't know that. That was very nice of you to do that for them," Wheeze stated as he laughed.

"Anyway, that's the plan. We'll stay there for a day or two, do the meeting and come back. By then we should have a new order for him to turn in."

"Great, I'll make up the order and then we'll take some time out for a little pleasure, I can use some relaxation after the past few days."

***

Back at the scene of the shooting:

Detectives from the New York police homicide squad arrived at the scene and looked over the bodies then contacted the FBI which is standard procedure in what appears to be a mob shooting or a hit.

The FBI tied one of the dead men in the card room to a deceased major narcotics supplier for the United States. With that information, they turned the case over to the DEA, who would be working on it with New York.

Agent John Slater of the (DEA) Federal Drug Enforcement Administration was given the narcotics information and case to follow up on since he was involved in the Quincy, Massachusetts case. He was familiar with the Quincy case involving the deceased drug lord David Stewart McQuethy, Junior and his partner Joseph Woodridge, who had escaped death when the plane crashed. Woodbridge was somehow able to get to shore and disappear.

Agent Slater's first thought was to contact the New York detectives and get their OK to brief the deep cover investigator involved in the original McQuethy case.

They agreed, since there was no evidence and nothing to really go on. This was obviously a professional hit and they are hard to solve. Secondly, there was a good chance that if the connection to Detective. Lijoi is correct, he may be next on the schedule of hits.

Agent Slater telephoned detective Ernie Lijoi Sr.
"Hello?"
"Ernie, how are you doing?"
"John, John Slater, I'm doing fine how are you?"
"There has been a little wave out on the street."
"Who did you pick up?"
"No, nothing like that, do you remember the McQuethy case?"
"Sure that was a biggie."

"Remember his partner Joseph Woodridge, the man we could never find, the man who survived the plane crash? He seemed to have fallen off of the earth?"

"I didn't know that much about him, he was more, your thing, than mine, but yes I remember the guy."

"That may be so. He's been killed in New York."

"Not that card game thing that's all over the news?"

"Exactly"

"Wow, somebody really wanted those guys dead"

"Not just somebody, the Columbians. The word on the street is all they wanted was Joseph Woodridge because they believe that he was your informant. My opinion is that they will be after you next. You caused them a lot of grief."

"They killed all those men to get even with a guy that I don't even know?"

"That's the scuttlebutt going around so far."

"I feel terrible about this. You think they'll be after me? What can I do to help?"

"Basically, get your feelers out there, turn over some rocks and let me know if you find anything, no matter how insignificant it may be."

"I'll do that. I'll have to advise the captain about what's going on as well as my partner."

"No problem, get back to me in a couple of days and I may have some more info for you."

"Will do and thanks for letting me know, John. I'm sorry that we have to be talking about this. I hate it when innocent people get killed and for the wrong reason. Not that there is ever a good reason. You know what I mean," stated Ernie.

"Yes I do, I agree. I'll talk to you in a couple of days. Ernie, keep your head high. Be careful. Remember that was your case and if I know these nuts, you're on the list. In their minds, they have no limitations," stated John.

They both hung up the phones.

Back with the Mafia Family:

Wheeze and Joey Bats stepped off of the plane at Boca Chica Field in Key West Florida and were picked up by the Key's Limo Service. They were driven to the house located at 1010 Atlantic Boulevard, a ranch type home, canary yellow in color located on a property overlooking the beach.

As they entered the house, they looked across the street and noticed an unfamiliar family enjoying the day on the white sandy beach, with tall beautiful green palm trees surrounding them and bordering the beach and the greenish blue water crashing softly against the shore.

"We should bring our families down here some day for a vacation; the house is big enough," stated Joey Bats

"My family would love it Joey, just let me know when," replied Wheeze.

"We'll talk about it some more when this is over and we're back at home."

They entered the six-bedroom house that was complete with a kitchen that had a professional stainless steel stove with six burners, a steel griddle for pancakes and a large stainless steel refrigerator. They stopped and looked the place over.

"Man, did I get a deal on this joint. Look at that great big window overlooking the beach. The couches are plush. Everything is perfect. Let's take a look at the bedrooms," stated Joey.

"These beds are comfortable; I'll take this one, if that OK with you, Joey."

"Yeah, we may as well pick our own out for now."

The entire house was professionally decorated, very pretty, yet still felt very comfortable.

"What time is our guy due, Joey?"

"He'll be here first thing in the morning, probably around ten."

"Want to go and look around downtown, maybe get some dinner?"

"Good idea, let's go."

Wheeze called a taxi cab that picked them up and dropped them at the Blue Haven Restaurant where they enjoyed a dinner.

After dinner they strolled along the gulf walkway to Malory Square where they watched the entertainers performing along the walkway. They stopped and spoke with some of the venders and discussed all the young men and women enjoying themselves from all over the world.

After walking around the town and viewing some sites, they went back to the house to rest for the remainder of the night. They were looking forward to the meeting in the morning.

***

Wheeze got out of bed and went directly to the kitchen to make some coffee for Joey and himself to go along with the donuts that they purchased the night before. It was seven in the morning and they had a meeting at ten. They both had coffee and some donuts for breakfast. They got dressed and ready for the meeting.

It was about ten when they heard a car pull up out front. Wheeze and Joe looked out the front window and saw a well-dressed dark-haired, dark- skinned man, who appeared to be Columbian, exit the vehicle carrying a briefcase. This person walked up the driveway to the front door. They heard the door bell ring. Joey Bats sat down in the brown high wing backed chair located in the living room, while Wheeze answered the door.

"May I help you, sir?" asked Wheeze

"Yes sir is Mr. Borgazino available?" asked the stranger.

From the living room came a voice: "Come on in, Paolo," stated Joey

Paolo stepped into the house and put his hand out to shake with Wheeze.

"I'm Paolo Cristino the rep from our friends the Soldado family, with their thanks."

***

The Soldado syndicate was headed up by Roberto Soldado a well known drug lord and murderer. Soldado was responsible for thousands of deaths in Columbia, as well as a large contingent of people in Mexico.

Wheeze shook his hand and exclaimed that it was a pleasure to meet him. He then directed the 5'7" man, about 40 years of age, weighing about 165 pounds with black hair and dark brown eyes, dressed in a blue suite with white shirt and tie into the living room where Joey bats was waiting.

Joey rose from his chair and walked over to shake hands with Paolo: "Good to see you again, Paolo. Would you like a drink or some coffee?"

"Coffee would be nice."

Joey looked at Wheeze, who immediately stated that he would get the coffee.

"Paolo, I want you to become familiar with Wheeze since he will be at any further meetings. I'm getting older and tired of the traveling. You understand."

"We all have to start looking forward to the golden years of retirement" said Paolo

Wheeze walked into the room with the coffee and placed a cup in front of each man, then sat down with the third cup.

"Wheeze, you will be handling all future meetings and orders. This place will become familiar to you in time. Paolo will be your contact. You will have a number to contact him and we will give him your number. Agreed?"

"Of course, whatever you want, Joey."

Joey looked at Paolo who laid the briefcase on the coffee table, opening it to show the cash payment due to the Borgazino Family for the card game hit.

"I believe this is the correct figure we agreed upon Joey, six hundred thousand dollars," stated Paolo.

"Yes, that's correct. I was a little worried that the newspapers may cause a problem where they only mentioned five instead of six bodies," Joey said.

"At first, it did cause a little confusion until we received the official reports which cleared it all up," stated Paolo.

"I'm happy that the air is cleared. Wheeze has some requests for you. Can you handle our order at this time?"

"Sure what do you need, Wheeze?"

"I need one thousand bricks of ganja at your wholesale price of two hundred dollars per brick and two thousand keys of blow at your wholesale price of fifteen hundred dollars each. The total amount due to you will be, three million two hundred thousand dollars."

"Maybe I should take this money back with me, as partial payment, to cover the order?" asked Paolo.

"I don't think so. We'll send the cash via our normal electronic channels, through the bank, to your accounts as directed in the past," stated Wheeze.

"You're right, Wheeze, that's the way we always handled things and we'll continue in that fashion," stated Joey Bats "But, I don't blame you for trying, Paolo."

"No problem, men, my boss didn't instruct me to collect any money, but to simply pay our bill and see if there were any further orders. All will be handled accordingly," stated Paolo.

"Now we're talking the same language, Paolo," Wheeze responded.

"I have to go, you men are paid and I have your new order which will arrive here in Florida at an agreed upon time and location. You understand that we deliver to the shore or dock of your choice and the problem is yours from there?"

"Yes, we understand: standard procedure. Do you know if there is a diversion set up or shall we arrange for that after we know the exact dates and time?"

"We will arrange for a second smaller ship to have a few bails aboard, but we will discuss that at the appropriate time," Paolo indicated.

"OK, it was great seeing you again, Paolo. As I said, Wheeze will make any further contacts; you have his numbers, correct?"

"Yes, I do and here are my numbers so that he can contact me. Wheeze, I will call you next week with the delivery information," stated Paolo.

Joey walked Paolo to the door. He left the house and drove off. Wheeze was in the living room counting the money and getting it ready for the deposit.

***

After Paolo left the area, Joey walked back into the living room to assist Wheeze, after which they left the house and returned to New York.

Chapter 5

The Ship

Monday July 3, 1978

The Deep Cover Investigator or DCI who had worked the original case was Detective Ernie Lijoi Sr. He is a clean-shaven Italian male, 5'8" tall, 185 pounds with short brown hair and brown eyes until a case comes up that required his alter-ego, Eddie Pannoni, to reemerge. When Eddie Pannoni is needed, Ernie changes his appearance by adding a mustache and sometimes a full beard and a very curly afro or a stylish hairdo whatever he needs to do the job right.

While working undercover, he had arrested the same people on several occasions. Due to his ability to change his looks, he was unknown to them each and every time.

His partner, backup man and good friend, Detective Jack Wade, is a white male, dark complexion, half Spanish, 5"8" tall, 180 pounds, with black hair and brown eyes. Jack didn't require changing his look. He did a great job backing Ernie, getting the files and information needed for each individual and each case.

These two men made a great team; they were highly respected throughout the police world and feared throughout the criminal world since no one ever knew what Ernie really looked like.

Detective Ernie Lijoi and Det. Jack Wade arrived at the office at about the same time that morning.

"Jack, we have to meet with the captain and tell him what has happened. There may be some trouble, and we want to be ready."

"Trouble, you mean from the Columbians because of what Slater told you?"

"Yes, I think I have an idea that may nip this in the bud before it goes any farther or at the very least, will get us on the inside."

"Well, let's hear it," stated Jack

"No, it's just an idea. I'm still working it out. Give me a day or so, then we can all talk about it."

"OK. I'll call the captain and set up a meeting time."

Jack telephoned the captain and asked that they meet at a coffee shop in the square, after hearing some of the background from Jack. They agreed to meet in an hour.

***

At ten am the two detectives walked into the coffee shop on Quincy Ave. called the Mug and Jug Coffee House. They joined Captain Donald Richards at his table. He was a grey haired man about 59 years of age, 5'7" tall, with blue eyes and had a slight belly protruding over the belt of his pants. A man who had seen it all in his 30 years as a police officer, he was well liked by his men and highly respected.

"Ernie, Jack told me the basics and said that you would fill me in. Is it true that those innocent men were killed in that New York club because it was believed that one of them was your informant?"

"As far as Agent Slater is concerned. He's believes that to be true."

"I read what the lieutenant had to say in the papers; it appears that he believes it also. What do you need from me?"

"I need a bit of a free hand to investigate, for me and Jack if he wants in on this," stated Ernie.

"What do you mean, 'IF'?": "You couldn't run a thing like this without me," injected Jack.

"Thanks, Jack, I was hoping you would say that," replied Ernie.

"What about our connection to this, do you think we'll have problems down the road?"

"That's why I wanted to meet with you. I have an idea that may help out the situation, but it may require some officer swaps or something like that."

"You want to get assigned to temporary duty in New York don't you?"

"No, not really, but the situation requires that we get ahead of the Columbians, if we can. I would rather go after them. I don't want to wait until they come after me."

"Why not speak with Slater and see if you can go under their authority?"

"Yes, I thought of that also, but it will still require the authorization of both you and the chief."

"There will be no problem with me. The chief has complete confidence in your ability to do what's best. You should be OK. If that's what you want, you have our complete confidence."

"It's not just me, it's Jack, also."

"Yes, I understand. Give me a report with all of the particulars after you speak with Agent Slater. Include his phone numbers. I think I have them, but just to be safe include his contact numbers."

"Will do, Captain"

"OK, men, I have to get back to the office. You stay and finish your coffee. You two men make sure that you keep me in the loop on this thing, no matter where it may take you and don't worry about approvals. That's my job, I'll handle it."

"Thanks, Boss," replied both Ernie and Jack.

The captain left the restaurant and Jack suggested that he and Ernie cruise around town and check out some interesting locations while they both thought about what to do next in the Brooklyn murder case or if they should do anything at all.

***

The two detectives were cruising down Sea Street through an area known since the Second World War as 'German Town', a section of the city that was once a camp for German prisoners during the Second World War.

Jack and Ernie noticed that there were three very well dressed men standing on a corner like a group of kids. This seemed odd to them for this section of the city. They were passing the isolated corner of Rock Island Road and Edgewater Drive. There were no businesses, only private homes, a great view of the ocean and the Boston Harbor Island called "The First Street Park," from the spot where the three men were standing.

"Let's go down the street and park; we can see what they're doing," said Ernie.

Jack was driving and did as requested.

They noticed a black limo parked just around the corner on Edgewater Drive as they drove by and two Cadillac's, one blue and one red parked along Rock Island Rd.:

"You don't see many limos or new Cadillac's in this section," stated Ernie.

"Let's hang out and see what's up. These three men look like they're having some sort of a meeting, they don't seem to belong here, they don't fit into this area," stated Jack.

"I agree we'll see what happens. Our key guy is the limo if we have to choose," stated Ernie.

Jack agreed.

They parked the car and Ernie took a pair of binoculars out of the glove box to try and get some numbers off of the plates of the Cadillac's that they could see, but the view of the plates was blocked by poles. They decided to wait and see what happens. They didn't have long to wait.

The three men standing on the corner talking were looking out at the open ocean toward the island. They soon began pointing at a sail boat that was crossing their view and looked to be about 50 feet long with three masts.

The men had some discussion and all returned to their cars. They drove off with the limo leading the pack.

"This is a damn delivery, Jack. This could be from Columbia or one of the Caribbean Islands. We'd better get some help."

As they followed the limo and the two Cadillac's, Ernie radioed the station for assistance and then the Coast Guard for possible assistance later.

The cars that the detectives were following drove over to a small marina that had been empty for several years. They waited for the ship to arrive. Just inside the gate were two trucks with their engines running. The limo pulled up behind one of the trucks and the two Cadillac's parked behind the limo.

Ernie and Jack drove past the marina and made what observations they could.

"November 7 to headquarters."

"Go ahead Nov. 7."

"Go over to Chanel #4, please."

"Dispatch on Chanel #4"

"Dispatch, we'll need assistance. No sirens or lights and no one is to come any closer than three blocks to the old run down marina on Venus Road. It appears that we have a case here. Also, please contact the Coast Guard and advise them that we want to allow the birds into the nest to check their chickens and eggs. Do you understand?" asked Ernie

"Understood, Nov. 7"

The dispatcher then gave several cars locations to stand and wait for the orders of Nov. 7, Det. Ernie Lijoi and or Nov. 5, Det. Jack Wade.

"Dispatch, be advised that we have two very large cargo trucks here waiting on the egg delivery as well as several other vehicles. We estimate six, plus the ship's crew. This is gonna be a busy day."

"Understood"

Ernie had to speak to the dispatcher on the private channel to keep the public from knowing exactly what was going on and where. He asked the dispatcher to patch him through to Agent John Slater of the DEA.

"John, are you there?"

"Yeah, Ernie, what's up?"

"I'm looking at a marina with a limo and two Cadillac's parked here along with two trucks waiting for what I believe to be a ship loaded with drugs. Have you heard anything?"

"You son of a gun, you got it. We heard on the street that there was a shipment coming in from the Soldado Columbian drug syndicate. We were not able to get anything further on it nor did we know it was going to be a ship," stated John Slater.

"Well, you're welcome to join us once we have it. We can use the help unloading."

"We will join you, but I have to tell you something first."

"What's that?"

"That's the same family that arranged for the Green Mountain Lounge murders in New York, if I have the information correct."

"I've never heard of this Soldado family. OK, we'll take this group as soon as the ship lands and they start unloading. You and I will have to talk later," said Ernie.

"Deal, we'll be there in about an hour, sooner if we can. By the way where the hell am I going?"

"Just contact the dispatcher via radio on Chanel #4, he'll advise you."

"OK, see you soon and be careful there's a lot of money at stake here. They don't like to lose money," stated John.

As Ernie and Jack watched, they saw the ship dock in a rundown dock and slip. Two men walked out with a ramp and attached it from the dock to the ship. The three men that arrived in the limo and the Cadillac's walked on to the schooner, each of them were carrying a briefcase.

"I can't believe what I'm seeing," Ernie stated.

"What are you talking about?" asked Jack.

"I think those briefcases may hold the payments, which is very unusual they usually do it a different way at this level," said Ernie.

"Maybe it's a special trip," stated Jack.

"Yes, maybe, John said that his group heard on the street that a shipment was due, but didn't know it would be a ship," Ernie said.

"We'll find out soon enough," stated Jack.

"As soon as they step off the ship we'll close in and confiscate the ship, money, drugs, trucks and cars. We'll arrest everyone and sort it all out later."

"You know what I dread, don't you?" asked Jack.

"The unloading, right?" replied Ernie.

"Yes, I hope it's not grass, that shit is heavy when it's in bails."

"We have plenty of help coming; we've done it before and we can do it now," said Ernie.

"I know, but sometimes I feel like it would be nice to just turn the whole thing over to the Fed's and walk away," stated Jack.

"I know how you feel, but just think of all the lives saved by stopping this one ship. That thought makes the work easier."

"I can't argue with that. Here come the buyers, they're walking off the ship now."

"Yes and there are two guys walking behind them with dolly's full of bails of grass and some boxes on top. I bet those boxes are full of kilos of cocaine," stated Ernie

Ernie notified all of the cars and people waiting for the OK to move into the area that they were needed immediately. He instructed the cars to block the gate and cover every person on the property and the schooner. The front gate closed in a large yard which led to the slips for the ships.

While he was finishing his instruction, cars began to pull up. Police officers and detectives went in all directions, covering the entire area.

Captain Richards pulled up next to the car that Jack and Ernie were in: "You guys seem to have everything under control. Good observation."

"Thanks, Captain, we have to talk later; this may be connected to that New York case we were discussing."

"OK, men, let's clean this up," stated Captain Richards as they drove to the front gate of the marina where the other cars and officers were waiting with guns drawn, holding everyone at bay from a distance. The suspects were out in the open and had no choice, but to capitulate.

In the background was the grey and white sail ship with its sails down. The ship was quiet, no one was moving on board. No one was moving on land. It was a stand-off.

Ernie and Jack pulled up behind the cars, blocking the gate with the captain's vehicle and exited their vehicle when a shot rang out.

A second shot rang out, but the police didn't return fire because they couldn't see where the shot came from. Ernie yelled as loud as he could, "The ship, the firing is coming from the ship. I saw a flash."

All the guns turned toward the ship, but still did not fire. They could see no one.

Another shot whizzed through the gate, hitting one of the gate poles, ricocheted and struck Captain Richards in the chest. Captain Richards fell to the ground. Jack went over to check him while Ernie covered him. The wound was not bad, more of a light penetration then a full damaging hit. Ernie called the dispatcher for medical assistance.

The suspects, by this time, were running in different directions trying to hide and get out of the way of the shooting that was going on. It looked like a group of clowns running all over the place without a place to hide.

The police didn't try to stop them in any way because they were closed in by the gate surrounding the property. The cruisers were also surrounding the property. It was a standoff at this point. They had to stop the shooting from the ship before the men inside the perimeter began shooting in return.

Ernie looked over the situation and decided that someone had to go in. He started to walk inside the gate while the other officers covered him. Jack was right behind him.

Because of his movement into the yard area, he had a better view of the ship. He could see a man at the top of the stairway that leads down into the living quarters of the ship. This man was a darkly tanned individual who appeared to be Columbian. He was holding a gun and stuck his head up and over the opening from time to time.

"Can you see him, Jack?" asked Ernie

"Yeah, you're a better shot then I, you take him."

"Do you have the bull horn?" asked Ernie

"Yes here, why?"

"I want to try something first. Call one of the guys that speaks Spanish to come over here."

Jack called in the request and Officer William Valenti joined them.

"Bill, you speak Spanish, right?"

"Yes, what do you want me to say?"

Ernie replied, "Tell him as I tell you: 'Sir, you have no way out, throw out the gun and walk out with your hands over your head'."

"OK."

Bill began to translate: "Sir, usted no tiene ninguna salida, lanza hacia fuera el arma y camina hacia fuera con su entrega su cabeza"

The man answered: " I can' t va a encarcelar, yo está haciendo simplemente una entrega"

"What did he say, Bill?" asked Ernie

He said: "I can't go to jail; I'm simply making a delivery."

"Tell him that he should not go to jail unless he shoots someone. He will be deported most probably."

Bill answered the man with Ernie's words in Spanish: "Usted no debe ir a encarcelar a menos que él los tiros alguien, él esté deportado lo más probablemente posible"

They then heard the man say, "OK, OK I comea out, but I go back to Columbia, OK?"

"Son of a bitch, he speaks English," stated Jack to Ernie.

Ernie replied to the man on the ship: "Yes, we'll do all we can to get you back to Columbia, but you must straighten this problem out first."

The suspect seemed to accept Ernie's statement and stepped up onto the deck with his hands over his head. He was taken into custody. The truck drivers and the two man crew didn't give the police any problems. The three men that originally gained the interest of Ernie and Jack while standing on the corner speaking with each other were quiet and peaceful. Everyone was taken into custody, brought to the police station and booked.

Ernie and Jack went over to check on Captain Richards while the other men cuffed and handled the prisoners.

The ambulance was there and said the captain would be OK, he was very lucky. They placed him in the ambulance and drove him to the hospital for treatment.

"We'll stop by and see you later or tomorrow, Captain," stated Ernie and Jack.

Just then Agent John Slater arrived with his team and assisted in the unloading of the ship as well as the counting of the cash.

The entire case consisted of one fifty-eight foot sail boat, two trucks, two Cadillac's, one limo and eight prisoners. Also confiscated were four tons of marijuana, five hundred kilos of cocaine and three briefcases containing a total of three million dollars in cash.

The entire cash value of the case was not immediately figured out because it was believed that the trucks, Cadillac's and limos were rentals and would eventually be returned to the rental company. That would be after a court battle by the state to try and keep them.

The confiscations were being transported. The prisoners were being booked at the station. All of the cash and the briefcases were placed into the evidence locker. The illegal drugs were turned over to the DEA Agent John Slater and his team for analysis and destruction. Capt Richards was in the hospital being taken care of.

Agent John Slater, Detectives Ernie Lijoi and Jack Wade decided to have a meeting in the morning at the office of the DEA to analyze all of the points that they knew about and hopefully come up with some decisions that would help them to clear up the case.

Chapter 6

Sit Down

Tuesday July 4th, 1978

Det. Ernie Lijoi was a family man with a wife and two children. Because of his work it was hard to spend a lot of time with his boys, although he tried to get away with them every chance he got. One of the favorite places that they loved to visit in the summer was a private park named Hale Reservation in Westwood, Massachusetts.

Ernie would take his wife and two boys there on weekends. They could play, swim in the lake and would spend an hour or two on some of the visits fishing in the back sections of the lake, where they caught plenty of cat fish and bass.

The first time that they went fishing together, the kids wanted to keep the fish, take them home and eat them. Ernie told them that the fish were too small. If they agreed to put them back in the water, the fish would grow up and next year they would be bigger and some day big enough to eat. The boys agreed with their Dad and it became a custom to place the fish back in the water after they were caught. This was long before catch and release came about.

Ernie got out of bed and went into the kitchen where his wife Teresa had breakfast waiting for him.

"That was some arrest you guys made yesterday," stated Teresa.

"Yes, it was a stroke of educated luck."

"Luck, what do you mean?"

"Jack and I saw something out of the ordinary, stayed with it and it grew into the case you saw on TV. That case is now the bottom or start of a much larger case involving those murders in New York."

"Larger case?"

"Yes, Teresa, I may be going back undercover if we can find a way in."

"I don't understand why it's always you who has to go. Can't you settle for just the little guys?"

"I take out a little guy and he is replaced before I can book him. I take out a big guy and it is not as easy to re-place him. Besides my New York accent helps out the cases in this state when I'm undercover."

"Yes, I understand. I've heard your opinion before many times, but you're not getting any younger and these cases seem to be getting larger and harder. Where will this one take you?"

"Probably to my old stomping grounds, but there is nothing in stone, we don't even have a connection yet. Only some minor connections that don't sound like they will be helpful."

"Are you going into the office today, after putting in fourteen hours yesterday?" asked Teresa

"I have to go into work. We're having a meeting this morning. I want to stop by and see how the captain is do-ing. Jack and I have a few points of interest that came up after we counted all the cases we confiscated and began analyzing the evidence."

"Call me before you come home and I'll have dinner ready for you."

"OK, but I should be home at the normal time of about four thirty in the afternoon, barring any unforeseen incidents, as you know."

"That's why I ask that you give me a call if you can."

"I will" Ernie stated as he kissed his wife Teresa goodbye and left the house for the day.

He walked out to the car in the driveway and as soon as he started down the driveway he could hear that familiar sound of the mockingbird singing away. He didn't answer the bird at first. The bird kept repeating the same tune that he always sang. Finally, he whistled the tune. The bird replied and they swapped tunes of music until Ernie started the car and drove off.

Ernie arrived at the office at about 8am and Jack was already there. He had started the reports that were needed for the District Attorney John Hageman.

"Jack, what are you working on, the reports?"

"Yeah, I figured that we should have the preliminary one ready for the meeting at ten and we can send a copy over to the DA with the rest of the reports this morning so he has an idea of what's going on."

"That's great, thanks. I'll call the DA and advise him of what he'll be reading and that the reports are on the way."

Ernie picked up the phone and dialed the district attorney's office.

A young lady answered.

"Alice, this is Det. Lijoi, can I speak with John Hageman please?"

"Stand by, Ernie. Great job yesterday, the whole office is abuzz about it."

"Thanks, we're happy about the way it turned out."

"Stand by; I'll transfer you to him."

Ernie heard the phone ring again: "Ernie, that was some job you guys did."

"Thanks, John, is there anything special that you need?"

"I need a couple of questions answered, if you don't mind?"

"Not at all, shoot."

Ernie proceeded to answer the questions, explaining why he and Jack noticed the suspects and what made them tie the suspects to the ship passing the shore. It all came down to that sixth sense that a police officer may have because of his special experience and knowledge in specific fields. This idea of knowledge from experience was called or referred to as a sixth sense by the United States Supreme Court in several cases.

After the questions, Ernie asked if John thought that they would be able to keep the vehicles.

"I doubt it; if there's a mortgage, the bank gets the vehicle and, in some cases, sells it back to the suspect. If it's owned by a rental company, which is what I suspect, the rental company gets the cars back. I wouldn't count on getting those vehicles. That does not mean that I will not try like hell."

"We have three million dollars in cash. How do you want us to handle that?" asked Ernie.

"Do you have any suggestions, Ernie?"

"Yes, I'd like to send the cash to the lab for finger-prints. That will tie the whole thing in nicely if we can get any matching prints to the men carrying the money," Ernie replied.

"If you don't, then that may create an issue of owner-ship, but I think you should do it anyway. I can handle any issues that may arise."

"You said you're having a meet this morning with the DEA. What will that accomplish?" John asked.

"I'm not sure yet. We may be looking at a much larger case. We'll all get together in a few days."

"OK, let me know when and I'll be there to help in any way I can."

"Thanks, John"

Ernie walked into the office where Jack was typing away on the electric typewriter finishing up the preliminary report.

"Could you hear that conversation, Jack?"

"Only your side of it."

"He'll need the report that you're doing and we probably will not get the vehicles. We'll test the cash for prints and go from there. You ready for the meeting?"

"I thought they were coming here?"

"No, we're going to their offices. On the way back, we'll stop in and see the captain."

"I forgot to tell you I called. He's OK, he'll be up and around in a couple of days."

"Great to hear, he was always a tough old dog anyway."

"He sure is."

The two detectives left the office for the federal building in Boston to meet with the DEA.

***

They arrived at the meeting and were met by Agent John Slater, a white male about 6' tall, thin, with long dirty-blond, thinning hair and brown eyes. He was clean shaven with no scars or distinctive marks. John directed them to a meeting room with a large table and seating for eight men. There were four agents drinking coffee and sitting at the table, one of which Ernie and Jack did not know. The other agents were known to the Quincy detectives because of the cases they worked together in the past.

"If everyone has coffee, let's sit down and start this meeting. You all know each other, I believe," stated Agent John Slater.

"John, you're correct with one exception. We don't know this gentlemen sitting across from us."

"Ernie and Jack, meet Agent Paul Saunders, a DEA agent assigned to New York. He drove up last night to attend this meeting and try to help us out."

"So there is a definite connection to the New York thing?" asked Ernie.

"We think so, but we'll get to that later. Have you or Jack come up with anything more?" asked John.

"Yes, I think we screwed up yesterday," stated Ernie.

"How the fuck could you screw up, you got three million of the mobs money, the boat, the vehicles and eight bodies as well as all the drugs," stated John Slater as the other men suddenly became very interested in the statements being made, instead of their coffee.

"I believe there were more ships and we missed them," stated Ernie.

"Please explain that statement, Ernie," asked John.

"We confiscated three million dollars cash, correct?" asked Ernie.

"Yes," replied one of the people sitting at the table.

"Then how come we only have one million dollars wholesale price worth of illicit narcotics from that ship?"

"Good question," answered one of the men, "Why?"

"What got me thinking was that when we cleared the area, there were four other trucks parked down the street by the diner and four men standing on the sidewalk drinking coffee in front of the diner. They were all watching what was going on at the ship yard where we were."

"And you concluded that there must have been more ships," stated John.

"Not right away, but when I started counting the cash, estimating the amount of drugs confiscated along with what I observed, I put two and two together. I thought there were two ships that we missed and four trucks, two trucks for each ship like the two we already had in custody. That does make sense, doesn't it?" asked Ernie.

"It sure the hell does," said Jack. "I couldn't believe that Ernie figured that out so quickly."

"That's very interesting, Ernie. We would have caught that in time, you beat us to the punch, another good job."

"Yes, that's very impressive and it leads me to believe that what John tells me is extremely accurate," stated Agent Paul Saunders the New York Agent.

Ernie looked at him with curiosity in his face. "What do you mean, Paul?"

"John stated that you would be the best man to work the New York case with me. I agree" stated Paul.

"Jack would have to be included in that," replied Ernie.

"Is he a DCI (Deep Cover investigator)?" asked Paul.

"No, but he is my team member, my right hand and a good friend. I trust him implicitly," stated Ernie.

"I understand, you two are a team and trust each other. Including Jack is not a problem."

"Then would I be wrong in assuming that you guys tied one of the current suspects into the New York thing?" asked Ernie.

John laughed: "You're correct, we did and you will not believe how far in we're talking."

"OK, let us in on this, will you?" asked Jack.

"Do you have the booking sheets on the men you arrested yesterday at the ship?" asked John.

"Yes, I do, what's the connection?" asked Ernie.

"The guy that was in the limo was a William Surelo right?"

"Yes, that's correct," stated Jack as he went through the paperwork in front of him.

"Paul, will you finish this for him?" asked John Slater.

"Sure. Ernie and Jack, there was evidence that one of the assailants at the shooting in the Green Mountain Lounge was shot. We found blood by the door and drips going down the stairs and out the door to the street. Someone was shot and taken out of there."

"OK, so how does that tie into this?"

"Investigation and information received indicated that we were correct and that a guy named Ronny Surelo was present at the shooting and may have been shot. That's the gossip on the street."

"Then you're saying that our limo guy, William Surelo, is related to Ronny Surelo?"

"Yes, that's what we are saying. Not only that, but Ronny Surelo is one of the Borgazino family headed up by Joey (Bats) Borgazino. Bats is a known associate of the Soldado family, which is a Columbian drug syndicate headed up by a mad man known as Roberto Soldado. Soldado was also the supplier to your guy, David Stewart McQuethy, Junior, who Saldado killed by blowing up his plane," stated Paul.

"Wow, what a vicious circle that is. They murdered those innocent men in New York to get one guy, Joseph Woodridge, the partner of McQuethy, right?" asked Ernie

John Slater replied: "That's right, now all we have to do is prove it in a court of law and that's the hard part."

"What do you suggest?" asked Ernie.

Paul immediately answered, even though the question was directed at John Slater:

"I think we should try to flip the limo guy, William Surelo, Ronny Surelo's cousin, but it's your call, Ernie, he's your prisoner."

"I don't mind flipping him it we can, but who will work the case in New York?" asked Ernie.

John Slater answered: "I thought we already addressed that issue; you and Paul out front and Jack with the back up team."

"We just wanted to be sure we were all on the same page, John, thanks," replied Ernie.

"The issue is how to flip him. He's no slouch. He's been around and will wait till the last moment to agree to anything," stated John.

"Guys, if I'm going to be under with Paul based on how this turns out then I believe that we shouldn't offer him anything. We shouldn't talk to him. Let him sweat. He'll wonder why no one is coming over to speak with him, to get him to turn and that will eat him up," suggested Ernie.

"We don't usually do things that way, but it's worth a try. I like it," stated Agent John Slater.

"Then you'll leave it to me to know when to approach him and everyone will stay out of it until then?" asked Ernie.

"I agree, as long as you keep me in the loop," stated agent Paul Saunders.

"Then we are all in agreement?" asked Jack.

All of the men present agreed to leave the turn to Ernie and Jack. They would make the decisions as to when and where to act. It could work. They were all hoping that it would.

"Now that this is settled, I want you all to agree that I have complete control. I don't want anyone doing anything in connection with any of the eight prisoners without checking with me first," stated Ernie.

Everyone agreed to the conditions and left the case to Ernie's judgment.

They covered a few strategic moves and the meeting broke up with the agreement that Ernie would call the next meeting and would keep Paul appraised of what was going on.

The next stop was to stop at the hospital to see the captain and advise him of the outcome of the meeting.

Ernie and Jack entered the hospital room where Captain Richards was laid up with bandages across his chest. He smiled when he saw Ernie and Jack walk in.

"Looks like that idiot got lucky, guys," stated the captain.

"Not really, he'll pay for what he did," replied Ernie.

"You guys know my wife Jeannie, don't you?"

"Yes, we do. Hi, Jeannie, sorry about the captain's injury," said Jack.

Jeanie, a women of her mid 50's, brown eyes and hair with a dash of grey replied; "Oh, he's not a complainer, not here in the hospital. When I get him home he'll start."

"When are you due to leave, Captain?" asked Ernie.

"The doc said that if I'm OK, I can leave here by Friday, as long as there's no bleeding and my vitals are good."

"Glad to hear it. Can we talk for a moment?"

"Sure. Honey, can you go and get me a cup of coffee?"

"Sure, I'll be right back. As Jeannie left the room, she gave Det. Ernie Lijoi a sly look as if to ask why he had to bother her husband with police business now while he's injured. There were no words, but Ernie got the message.

"Captain, she's pissed that we are having this meeting with you and I'm sorry about that. I don't blame her, but it's necessary."

"Don't worry about her, she'll get over it. How did the meeting go?"

Ernie and Jack explained all the particulars and what the outcome of all of the preliminary investigative techniques had created.

The captain was happy to hear that there was a good connection. After a few questions and answers the captain told Ernie and Jack that they could count on him for whatever assistance they may need.

"Thanks, Captain, now we have to let the DA know what's going on and get him on board."

"Give me that phone, Ernie."

Ernie handed the phone to Captain Richards.

The captain told him to dial the district attorney's office, which he did. He and Jack listened to the conversation from the captain's end.

"Hi, this is Captain Richards. Let me speak with John Hageman, please."

He paused for a moment while she put him through.

"John?"

"Captain, how are you feeling? Sorry to hear that you got hurt."

"Yeah thanks, I'll be Ok. I'm calling for two of my men, Ernie and Jack. They really fell into something here. I can't speak of it over the phone. They will explain."

"Yes I'm aware of some of it. We spoke this morning."

"I know, but a lot more has happened and I want complete cooperation with Ernie from your office. To begin with no one speaks to the suspects without Ernie being present and he will take the lead in any conversation. I need you to go along with him on this. He'll explain. They are coming to see you as soon as they leave here."

"John, you know I respect and have full confidence in those two men. I'll agree to whatever you need. Let me speak with them and I'm sure there will be no problem."

"Good, they will be on their way to you in few minutes. Thanks for your cooperation."

The captain hung up the phone and looked at Ernie and Jack: "Do you need an explanation of that call?"

"No sir, thank you for the confidence, we'll let you rest and apologize to your wife for us, please."

"Go ahead get out of here. I'll explain to my wife for you."

"Thanks" The two detectives left the hospital and drove to the town of Dedham, Massachusetts, the county seat, where the district attorney's office was located.

They entered the offices of the district attorney. As they entered, they saw the D.A. John Hageman, who looked at them and waved them into his office saying, "I'll be right in, men."

A few minutes later the DA entered his office and stated: "I spoke with the captain; he was very excited about what you guys are doing. Please, fill me in."

"You know some of it, but there have been some additional developments. We'd like to keep you in the loop."

"OK, I'm here and waiting."

Ernie and Jack filled the DA in on all of the developments in the case and advised him of the master plan.

"That sounds great; when do you want to speak with William Surelo?" asked the DA.

"Not until we are almost at a conviction, as long as you can tell me that there will be one," stated Ernie.

"I can assure you that he's looking at about thirty years at the very minimum and maybe more."

"Is he being held on a large enough bail?" asked Jack.

"Each and every one of the suspects is being held on ten million dollars bail. We can use that to loosen their tongues as well as to the sentencing, if need be," stated the DA.

"Thanks, I was hoping that you would say that. Then I want to start with the truck drivers who were hired just like the trucks and may not have even known what they were about to carry."

"I think I know where you're going and I like it. I'm in. You can count on my cooperation and support. Just make sure we discuss any offers first."

"Thanks John, for now let's keep this between us. Jack or I will be in touch."

After the meeting, Ernie and Jack left the DA and returned to their office. They each took their own car and drove home.

Ernie stopped at a phone booth to telephone his wife and let her know that he was on his way home.

***

The rest of the week would be the confiscation paperwork and reports on the vehicles, the schooner, the arrestees and the narcotics. Preparing the paperwork on the entire case for the numerous trials that will come in time for each and every separate confiscation and prisoner.

The next thing would be to do reports on the meeting that they had with the DEA and the outcome of that meeting for the captain and the district attorney. This has been a busy week.

Chapter 7

Diversion

Saturday July 8, 1978 in Brooklyn

Wheeze got up, had breakfast and headed out to the office because he was in a hurry to speak with Joey Bat's.

"Joey, it's Saturday and I haven't heard from Paolo. Did you hear anything?"

"No, when we were in Florida, he said that he would call in about a week, you'll hear from him, don't worry."

"I hope so we're getting low on supplies."

Just then the phone in Wheeze's office next door rang. Wheeze went into the office to answer.

"Hello"

"Wheeze, this is Paolo."

"Paolo, we were just speaking of you."

"Oh, meet me tomorrow at the same location, same time."

"I'll be there," stated Wheeze as he hung up the phone.

Wheeze then walked back to Joey's office and advised him of the situation.

"OK, Wheeze, you handle it."

"Joey, if the kid is OK, maybe I'll take him, if you have no objections."

"I have no objections, but I would give him some more time to heal. Take him next time."

"OK, you're the boss."

"Have a good trip; I'll see you when I see you."

"Fugheddaboudit," replied Wheeze as he walked out of the office and into the main room of the club.

"Hey, Wheeze," yelled Cheech

"Yeah, Cheech, what's up?"

"Did you forget?"

"Forget what? Ronny's OK, right?"

"Fugheddaboudit, the delivery, our monthly delivery."

"Oh shit, thanks for reminding me. We better take care of that. I'll run down and get the cash. Take a ride, then you can set it in place."

"Sure."

They left the club and walked down the street to the bank. They withdrew five thousand dollars in small bills, took the cash and placed it in a brown paper bag.

"OK Cheech, here's the payment; you can take care of that now."

"On the way back I'll place it. They're due to arrive in twenty-five minutes."

They walked back to the club and Cheech took the bag of cash down the street to the front of 388 St Marks Avenue, where he placed the bag on the sidewalk side of a parked car under the rear wheel. This was a location that they commonly used for the drop. Cheech walked away.

As Cheech was walking away, a pretty little girl, about six years old with straight brown hair and beautiful brown eyes named Anna was playing with a ball on the sidewalk. The ball got out of her hands and went under the car into the street.

A child playing on the sidewalk was a common site in Brooklyn. There was always someone watching the children. It didn't matter if the child was yours or not, there were so many women watching out the windows that a child sometime felt like he or she had a hundred moms. There was never a disagreement when someone corrected a child. Everyone in the neighborhood worked together. The most common words coming from the adults to the children were: "If you keep on the way you're going, I'll call your mother."

The ball kept going and rolled past a couple of cars where it rested right next to the paper bag. Anna picked up the ball and the paper bag. She looked in the bag and her first thought was to show Mommy all of the money she found. She ran into 388 St. Marks Ave.

By this time, Cheech arrived at the club and waited to see that the bag was picked up. He had his back to Anna as he walked away from the bag, never seeing that she had found it.

A few minutes later, a police cruiser arrived at the location where the bag was supposed to be.

A uniformed captain got out of the cruiser and looked around. He checked under the wheels of three different cars; the one in front of 388 St Marks Ave., the car behind that one and the car in front of the original car.

He got back into his cruiser and drove off with no bag of cash.

Cheech was watching from the club and could not understand why the captain was looking under other cars. He would soon find out.

Three cruisers pulled up to the front of the club and the officers entered the club.

"Captain, what's wrong?" asked Cheech.

"I didn't find the package."

"You didn't? I put it there myself," replied Cheech.

They went on arguing about the bag.

***

In the meantime:

Anna had arrived at her mom's apartment after climbing the eight flights of stairs to get to the fourth floor where the apartment was located. She opened the door yelling for her mom. "Mom, look what I found."

"What do you have, my baby?"

Anna lifted and stretched out her arms, holding the bag open for her mother to see in.

"Where did you find that?"

"It was in the street, under a car where my ball went."

"Oh, my little love, you go back there, put the bag back. That belongs to someone and they will be looking for it. I'll watch you from the window. Here's two cents, go to Louie's candy store and get yourself some candy after you return the bag."

"OK, Mommy."

Anna returned the bag and her mom watched, she then left the area and went to the candy store."

Her mother, Mary, had a good idea who owned the bag and wanted to protect her child from making a mistake.

Mary went to the window and watched Anna as she place the bag back under the rear wheel of the car.

This all happened within a time frame of about ten minutes.

Soon after Anna returned the bag, the captain, some officers, Cheech and a couple of men from the club all walked over to where the bag was supposed to be.

"What the fuck are you doing, Captain, getting senile?"

"What are you talking about?" asked the Captain.

"What's this, a watermelon?"

"I can't believe it. That wasn't there a few minutes ago," said the Captain.

"I don't know what happened, but don't pull this kind of shit again. Driving up to the club with all those cars and rushing in like that, it looks bad for us" stated Cheech as he threw the bag of cash across the car to the captain who caught it, got into his car and drove off.

Cheech was standing there with Spitball and another man who started to laugh at the police captain as he drove off.

"You know, Spitball, there was a little girl playing ball here when I made the drop. There she is now"

Cheech and Spitball saw Anna walking down the street towards them, eating some candy.

"Little girl, what's your name?"

"Anna, that's my mom up there, in the window."

"OK, dear, did you find a bag?"

"Yes and it had money in it, a lot of dollars. I brought it to my mom and she told me to put it back. Are you the owner?"

"Yes, I am and this is for you for being a good girl." Cheech handed Anna a dollar. "Now I'm going to speak with your mom, do you want to come with me?"

"No, I'm going back to the candy store."

"OK."

Cheech and Spitball entered 388 St. Marks Ave and went up to the mother's apartment and knocked.

"Hi, Cheech"

"Mary, is your husband Joe home?"

"No, Cheech, what can I do for you?"

"Do you mind if I speak with you for a moment?"

"No, what's wrong?"

"Nothing, I wanted to thank you for having your daughter replace the bag."

"Oh, no problem, Cheech, I knew it had to be something that you or your guys did."

"Well, if you ever need anything, don't hesitate to let me know."

"Thanks, Cheech, but it was a small thing."

"By the way Mary, you have a son Bruno, don't you?"

"You always call him Bruno, Cheech, maybe because you grew up with my brother-in-law Bruno. My son's name is Ernie, after his grandfather."

"Yes, I'll try to remember that. He's a good boy, he runs for cigarettes for me whenever I need them."

"Yes, he is a good boy."

"Mary, say hi to your husband Joe for us," stated Cheech as he and Spitball left the front door of the apartment.

***

By this time Wheeze was at the airport and getting onto a plane for Florida to meet with Paolo. Later that day, he arrived in Key West, Florida and went directly to 1010 Atlantic Boulevard, the house at the beach.

His first move was to telephone Joey Bats and let him know that he had arrived.

"Joey?"

"Yeah, Wheeze."

"I'm here and I'll call you tomorrow afterwards."

"OK, have you arranged for the equipment?"

"No I'll do that tomorrow once I know how far north they can deliver."

The equipment that Joey was asking about were the truck's to transport the illicit narcotics to the warehouse in Brooklyn from the delivery ship in Florida or wherever the drop may be.

"Then get back to me after you meet and know the arrangements."

"I will," Wheeze stated as he hung up the phone. He left the house and went out for some dinner. Upon return to the house he went to bed for the night. Tomorrow would be a busy day, he thought to himself.

***

The next day, Wheeze got up, showered and dressed. He made coffee and toast; it was almost ten in the morning and Paolo was due to arrive at ten.

He heard a knock at the door and answered. It was Paolo.

"Come on in, Paolo, I just made coffee."

"Yes, I'll have a cup, but we will drink our coffee outside, across the street, on the beach."

"What are you worried about, the police?"

"Not the police, the competition, our competition in Columbia who would not hesitate to wire this house to learn, our plans."

"Oh, I see. OK, here's your coffee. Let's go."

The two men walked across the street, where they sat on a bench at the end of the sand and talked quietly and safely.

"Wheeze, I have two ships coming to meet you and a diversionary ship just ahead of the first two."

"OK, how far north can you get them for me?"

"Because of your cooperation in our most recent venture, we have decided to help you out. As you know, we usually deliver to Florida. In this case, we can go as far as Cape May in New Jersey. From there you will accept the products and the responsibility for its safety."

"That's fine with me; what about the diversion?"

"That will cost you an extra one hundred thousand dollars to pay the crew, who will disembark as soon as they notify the police and to cover the loss of the smaller ship with the diversion stock aboard."

"That sounds acceptable, but let me be sure that I have it straight. You will deliver the two ships and I will meet them. The third ship's crew will call the police as the first and second arrive at the meeting place. The third ship's crew will disembark after notifying the police that they see a ship loaded with drugs. The police will follow up on the call and take that one while we unload the other two ships. Is that correct?"

"You have the idea perfectly."

"Good. Then all we have to do is locate a perfect location on Cape May for the drop, unless you already have one."

"There is an old military tower and a stream that comes off of Cape May on the western side of the cape."

"Yes, I know the area," said Wheeze.

"Good. There is an old abandoned roadway there to the right as you go upstream and my ships will pull into the area where the stream and the roadway meet. You can unload there and the stock is yours."

"Agreed," stated Wheeze "What time and date do you think is acceptable?"

"The ships have left; they will arrive on the eighteenth at about midnight. That night should have a three quarter moon, giving plenty of natural light. Is that OK with you, Wheeze?"

"Yes, that gives me plenty of time to make arrangements."

"Then our business is completed except that you will owe us one point eight million instead of one point seven million dollars."

"That will be taken care of immediately upon receipt via the normal channels."

"Thank you."

"Will you be at the drop, Paolo?" asked Wheeze

"No, my friend. I rarely show up at deliveries, although it has been known to happen for good friends. I like to be sure that all goes well. This concludes my official part of the deal, until the next time. Simply telephone me and ask to meet. I will meet you here from now on."

"That's fine and thank you for all of your cooperation. Shall we return to the house?"

"Yes, let's do that."

The two men returned to the house and Paolo left the area making sure that Wheeze had everything straight.

After Paolo left the house, Wheeze telephoned Joey Bat's to advise him.

"Joey?"

"Yeah, Wheeze, how did it go?"

"Much better than I expected. I am on my way back. I'll speak to you when I get in. say around seven tonight at the office?"

"I'll see you then," replied Joey.

Wheeze packed up his few belongings, telephoned for a cab and went to the airport where he took a plane back to New York.

***

Upon arrival, he immediately went to the Calabria Club to meet with Joey Bats. The two men met and Wheeze filled Joey in on the particulars of the meeting with Paolo.

"I told you that guy Paolo was OK," said Joey.

"Yeah, you did and you were right."

"It's great that we only have one state to cross with the stock. From now on they can't say no to that location for deliveries. It really helps us out. We can use our own men and you'll get the trucks," stated Joey.

"Yes, I'll take care of that tomorrow," answered Wheeze.

"OK, Wheeze, get some sleep you've been doing a lot of traveling"

"I will, I'll see you in the AM."

Wheeze left the office, went to dinner and returned to his apartment where he slept the entire night.

***

The next morning, Wheeze made a few calls notifying the men to meet him at the club at around noon.

Noon at the Calabria Club

Wheeze arrived at the office. As he entered, he observed six men sitting, drinking coffee and talking.

"Hi, Wheeze, what's up?" asked Spitball

"Look, I just want to make sure that you all know to keep the seventeenth, eighteenth and nineteenth clear. I will need everybody and I don't want any fucken excuses."

"What about Ronny?" asked Cheech?

"Ronny should be Ok by then so he is included, unless he's not feeling any better."

"He's feeling fine. He wanted to come in today, but I told him to wait a few more days," stated Spitball.

"That's good, Spitball," stated Wheeze.

"OK, does everyone have that straight?" asked Wheeze.

The men all shook their heads in agreement or replied OK.

"Good and I don't want any speculations on those dates. No one speaks of them at all to anyone except you, Spitball. You tell Ronny and no one else. Any questions?" asked Wheeze.

There was no reply. They knew better then to ask questions until the appropriate time.

"OK everyone can go ahead with what you were doing and I'll meet with you again before the dates mentioned," stated Wheeze.

Some of the men went back to their coffee, while others left the building, saying that they had a job to do.

Wheeze made arrangements for the trucks which were a gift from a man that ran a truck rental company. He owed Wheeze and Joey Bats for some help that they gave him about a year ago.

Mr. Adolpho Granolini, an Italian male and owner of the Venus Trucking Company in Brooklyn, New York, ran into a problem with some people that were trying to take over his business. The main man was a Robert O'Rielly, who had threatened Granolini with his life if he didn't sign over the papers and front the organization for his Family.

Granolini went to Joey Bats and Wheeze. He told them what was going on and requested their help.Soon thereafter, O'Rielly dropped the pushing of Granolini and friendships were made instead of partners and enemies.

Granolini never knew how it was done, but he was satisfied, so satisfied that three or four times a year when Wheeze or Joey Bats needed some trucks, he supplied them free of charge. That was the least he could do to re-pay them for their help.

***

Wheeze was ready for the delivery on July 18th; he had his men and his trucks ready. The next step would be to go over to 2659 Knapp St in Sheepshead Bay in Brook-lyn where the warehouse was located and make sure that the warehouse people would be ready for the delivery.

The warehouse had only one man on duty at all times. He was an old friend of the Borgazino family. His name was Alfonzo Durangani, a grey-haired elderly man who dressed like a street bum and did his job at the age of 80 years old. At one time, before his retirement by the family, he was a capo, always dressed to the tees and as sharp as could be. A caporegime or capodecina, usually shortened to just a capo, is a term used in the Mafia for a high ranking member of a crime family who heads a "crew" of soldiers and has major influence in the organi-zation.

Wheeze drove over to the warehouse and walked in to find Alfonzo making himself some coffee. Wheeze spoke to the old man in Italian since Alfonzo had lost most of his English from his old age.

"Alfonzo, come siete, esso; s buona vederlo il mio friend."

"Abbiamo una consegna entrare presto. Potete avere vostra gente pronta?"

"Certamente, possiamo essere pronti ogni volta che li avete bisogno di finchè riceviamo lo stesso pagamento"

"Grazie Alfonzo che saremo qui con due camion sulla mattina del diciannovesima. La nostra consegna è fissata per la mezzanotte sul eighteenth"

"Allora saremo pronti da uno di mattina sul diciannovesimo il mio amico"

"Grazie, io non può rimanerlo deve lasciarlo hanno cose per prendere la cura" del dichiarato di Wheeze.

"Non neppure una tazza di caffè?"

"Il tempo spiacente e prossimo."

"GIUSTO, il mio amico, sia sicuro."

In English:

"Alfonzo, how are you? It's good to see you my friend. We have a delivery coming in soon. Can you have your people ready?" asked Wheeze.

"Certainly, we can be ready whenever you need us as long as we receive the same payment."

Thank you, Alfonzo we will be here with two trucks on the morning of the nineteenth. Our delivery is set for midnight on the eighteenth.

"Then we will be ready by one in the morning on the nineteenth, my friend."

"Thank you. I cannot stay, I must leave, I have things to take care of," stated Wheeze

"Not even a cup of coffee?"

"Sorry, next time."

"OK, my friend, be safe."

***

Wheeze left the area and returned to the club for the time being to go over everything and make sure that he didn't make a mistake on any part of the operation. He would then wait until the seventeenth to prepare everyone for the job that was coming up.

Chapter 8

Interviews

Massachusetts, Tuesday July 11, 1978:

Ernie was in his office early to finish up the reports with Jack. "Man, that is one hell of a pile of reports," stated Ernie.

"Yes," said Jack, "That will keep them busy down at the DA's office for a while."

"You hungry, Jack? We'll go over to the coffee shop and get some eggs or something?"

"A little, I was up at five this morning and its eight now. I haven't eaten since yesterday at five in the afternoon."

"Let's go."

They arrived at the coffee shop, ordered breakfast and talked while they ate.

"You know, Jack, it would definitely be, different for me to return to New York as a cop working a case after growing up there as a kid."

"Yeah, that Brooklyn accent helps you out here, but there you would be just another guy. Maybe they'll detect a Boston accent from you after all these years and you can reverse the story that you use here on the street."

"Yes, I thought of that, but shit, I could run into people that know me. Who knows if they would recognize me, after all this time?"

"Ernie, there is nothing written in stone; you may not be asked to go. We may not be able to flip the people that we need. They may not need a deep cover man on this one. There are too many things up in the air right now. I wouldn't even concern myself at this point."

"You know me, Jack; I'll go over and over it, in my mind, until it feels right to me just in case they need us to participate. Of course, New York has many qualified men that can handle the job."

"I'm sorry that you're made that way, Ernie, but then again, look how many cases that concentration and thought has helped us with."

"Yeah, I guess you're right, but don't put it all on me. You think the same way. It takes one to know one," stated Ernie as he laughed Jack joined in the laughter.

"Jack, did I ever tell you about an area in New York called Sheepshead Bay bridges in Brooklyn, New York?"

"No, I don't think you ever mentioned it."

"When I was just a boy of about twelve years old, my friends and I used to go to an area called Sheepshead Bay where there were three walking bridges that crossed the one hundred and fifty yards of water. You could walk from one side of the bay to the other and see the boats docked under the bridge. We used to take a train to get there from our section of Brooklyn. The reason for going was to make some money. We would dive from the bridges, about forty to fifty feet in the air, down into the water. We believed that the people who walked the bridge were rich because they would throw dimes, nickels and sometimes quarters into the water. My friends and I would dive for the money. People threw the change just to watch us dive. This was in the 1950's and those were great days. The water was so clear that at thirty feet you could see the clean sand and pick out a coin from a distance. Once in a while someone would throw a half dollar, that was when the guys that could do the flips got real rambunctious and all the tricks came out, I learned to do the flips, at least then. I couldn't do them now. Jack, let me just say one more thing, in those days we could make two or three bucks a day diving and that was a good day's pay," Ernie laughed as he spoke of the money they made diving at Shepsheard Bay

"That's a nice story, have you been back since?"

"Yes, I was there a couple of years ago standing on one of the bridges and wanting to throw some change, but there was no one diving. Then I noticed the water was not as clear as I remembered it and realized that it was dirty, actually filthy. It's a sin what's happening to our oceans."

"That place is on the ocean?"

"Yes, some day maybe we'll go there and I'll buy you some clams; the area is known for them."

The two men finished breakfast and headed out to drop off the copies of the reports to the DA for his files, and to get some particulars on how the case was progressing.

***

After speaking with D.A. John Hageman, Ernie and Jack found that the cases were all set to be tried before the courts for the week of the eighteenth, next Tuesday. It was time to start speaking with the suspects.

They returned to their office where they telephoned the county jail and made arrangements to speak with each of the truck drivers, the crew of the ship and the captain, leaving the three buyers for last.

They would start the interviews the next day. The day had flown by it was just about quitting time. Ernie told Jack that he would see him in the morning and left the office. Jack headed home also.

***

Wednesday July 12, 1978

Ernie got out of bed, had breakfast and drove to the office. The weather was perfect, the sun was shining and the sky was blue, with a perfect air temperature in the seventies.

Ernie and Jack met with the two truck drivers, one after the other, in the morning at the county jail. They were mirror interviews; both men had the same answers and were very much in the dark about what they had to transport in the ship.

"Jack, they both have families and they both needed the work so they didn't even ask what they were hauling. They simply needed the money to feed their families."

"Yes, but that doesn't legalize what they were involved with."

"You're correct, but it does take into account that they were just a couple of slobs having a bad time and needing work. Let's call it the Economic Syndrome."

"Let's see, they agreed to testify that William Surelo, the man driving the limo, hired them. Surelo offered them one thousand dollars each to drive the trucks," stated Jack.

"Yes, and he hired six men and six trucks at the same price. That would include the other four trucks that we noticed at the diner, down the street from the marina, as we left the marina area," Ernie stated.

"Yes, you're right, that's an important point also," stated Jack.

"He told them that they would follow him to his warehouse which means that they didn't know where the warehouse was. As long as they testify to those points, I'm sure that we can give them a break," Ernie said.

"I agree, we should speak with the DA when the interviews are over."

"Agreed," said Ernie.

"Let's have lunch and we'll talk with the crew this afternoon," stated Jack.

"That sounds like a plan. You know we have a big advantage with the crew and the captain of the schooner," Ernie said.

"What's that?"

"They would rather get deported than go to jail," Ernie indicated.

"That's very true," replied Jack with a big smile.

"Jack, before we go to lunch we should contact that officer, Officer William Valenti, the man that speaks Spanish. He should be with us to be sure that we get the stories straight."

"I'll take care of it," replied Jack.

***

They went to lunch and returned that afternoon to interview the schooner crew that knew only that they were to be paid one thousand American dollars for the trip which, in their country, was enough to live on for a year.

When asked if they knew what they were carrying aboard the ship, they replied by stating that they did know what was aboard. They stated that they had no knowledge about the laws in the United State. They stated that they were not told that they would be delivering here.

When asked who would pay them they replied that the captain was the man that hired them and he would pay them upon return to their country.

After the interview, Jack and Ernie knew that the two men were lying. They were aware of the distribution system and had worked it before, although the detectives could not prove it. The detectives had them on this ship load and would push for deportation as long as they testified that the captain hired them and would pay their salary.

"That was a waste," stated Jack.

"No, not really, we can use their testimony and then they'll be deported. It's the captain that we want; the crew is just extra corroboration."

"Yeah, you're right," said Jack.

"Tomorrow morning we'll start on the captain, then the Cadillac men and then William Surelo who was in the limo. He will be last," stated Ernie.

"You know, Ernie, we keep referring to those guys as the Cadillac men, but they do have names," Jack said.

"Yes, I know they do, but I don't expect much from them. They're hardnosed, experienced dealers. I'll check the files before the interview. I'll be courteous. Instead of just calling them assholes, I'll call them by their names, don't worry."

"OK, Ernie, the captain of the schooner is first tomorrow. I'll see you then."

The two men left the jail house and headed home for the night.

Ernie went into the guard office at the jail and telephoned his wife Teresa. He told her that he would be home in a half hour.

"OK, I made eggplant, do you want some parmesan style?" asked Teresa.

"That sound great to me, see you in a little while." Ernie hung up the phone, went to his car and drove home.

***

That night after dinner, Teresa asked about the case that Ernie was working on and whether or not he would be going into deep cover as Eddie Pannoni.

"Teresa, it's too soon to tell. I'll make sure that we discuss it if it looks like I may take Eddie out of moth balls," Ernie laughed to lighten the conversation.

Teresa smiled back at him and replied, "OK, I would appreciate discussing that before you do it."

"You know I always discuss it with you before I start."

"I know," Teresa replied.

That night they watched TV for a while. Then they sat out on the porch watching the evening moon shining off of the lake.

***

Thursday, July 13 1978

As soon as he stepped out of the door way of his condo, Ernie heard the mockingbird singing. It seemed as though this mockingbird was waiting for him each morning to have their friendly, musical conversation, but it was misting and Ernie didn't want to waste time standing there, in the rain, talking to a mockingbird. He quickly replied with a couple of tunes and drove off.

At the office he parked the car, entered the building and walked up to the top floor where the office was located. This was a separate building from the police station which was used to house the Special Services Detectives.

Each of the men that were authorized to use this office were considered specialists in their field of expertise. Jack was an expert photographer, Ernie in narcotics and five other men who all went by the call sign of November. Ernie was November 7 and Jack was November 5.

These men also had their own channel which was channel 4 on the police communication system. This channel could not be picked up be any outside listeners with electronic equipment.

As Ernie entered the office, he saw Jack: "Hi, Jack, ready to go to the jail house and interview the captain of the schooner? Maybe we can get the two Cadillac guys in today?"

"I don't see why not. Should we take Valenti with us?"

"Yeah, want to give him a call? We'll pick him up, go for coffee and then to the jail."

Jack contacted the dispatch and asked to have Officer Valenti call in to the office. A minute later the phone rang.

"Bill Valenti?" asked Jack.

"Yes, sir, you wanted me to call?"

"Yeah, you're with us today. Why don't you get your car and drive over to our office? We'll meet you down in front of the building."

"OK, sir, I'll be right there."

Ernie and Jack locked up the office and waited for Bill to show up. When Bill pulled up, they went over to his car.

"Bill, follow us. We're going for coffee, then to the jail to do some interviews again, but you can go after the first one. We'll cover your afternoon."

"Thanks, guys."

Bill did as instructed and followed Jack and Ernie. They all went for coffee, then drove over to the county jail.

The three men entered the jail and were directed to a room where the captain of the schooner was waiting to be interviewed. Jack, Ernie and Bill walked into the room.

"What do you need to get me the fuck outa here and back to my country? You promised me that I would be deported."

Ernie, Jack and Bill's faces took on a surprised look. Ernie spoke to answer the captain.

"I am Detective Lijoi, this is Detective Wade and this gentlemen is Officer William Valenti" Ernie introduced everyone in the room before he answered the captain.

"Captain Andrea Dolbini, you transported and illegally imported a ship loaded with illegal drugs, shot a captain of the Quincy Police and now you want me to just open the door and let you go back to Columbia?"

Captain Dolbini, a grey-haired man about 5'6" tall, 180 pounds with dark brown eyes looked up at Detective Ernie Lijoi, then back down at the table where he was sitting and stated, "I really fucked myself this time."

"Captain Dolbini, your English is much better than I expected. Why didn't you speak plainly at the ship?" asked Ernie.

"I was afraid and thought that if I played stupid I would be better off. As for shooting that guy, it was an accident. I was aiming in the air to scare everyone away from the boat. I don't know how he got shot."

"It was a ricochet that got him, but you still pulled the trigger," stated Jack.

"Is he OK? I'm sorry about that."

"He'll be Ok, but I doubt that he will be coming to your defense," Ernie said.

"I understand."

Ernie turned to Bill Valenti, the translator: "Bill, you can go, he speaks great English. Have a great day, call the duty sergeant and let him know that we have you covered."

"Captain Dolbini, what can you offer us that may change our opinion of your present situation?"

"I can tell you this; the ship, although hidden in companies all over the place, is owned by the Soldado family in Columbia. If this gets out, I am dead."

'It won't get out, don't worry."

"Who were you to meet at the dock?"

"That same man that I have met on three other occasions, Mr. William Surelo. He was supposed to give me three million and I was to return with the cash."

"Why didn't Surelo send the cash through electronic services?"

"I don't know he's the only one that does it this way. I have picked up and delivered to him before."

"OK, as long as you testify to that part of the story, we will not stand in your way, nor keep you from being deported."

"Not the Soldado Family information, right?"

"Correct, only the Surelo information as you just told us."

"I'll do it, but what about your captain, will he oppose me?"

"Let us handle that part of it."

"OK, thank you, Officer Lijoi. I guess I'll owe you men after this."

"You never know who may show up on your doorstep needing some help, Captain," Ernie replied.

"If this works out, you can count on me."

"That's good to know," stated Ernie.

The detectives left the room and Dolbini was returned to the population.

They would next meet with one of the two Cadillac men.

"Ernie, let's get a cup of coffee before we meet this guy."

"OK, let's go."

***

A half hour later they returned to the jail to meet with Mr. Andrew Sanchez and Mr. Enrique Rivera the two drivers of the Cadillac's. They would meet them in the same room where they met the other men. They would speak with them one at a time. Mr. Sanchez was first.

"Mr. Andrew Sanchez, how has the county been treating you, sir?" asked Ernie.

"I'm OK. What do you want and why don't I have my lawyer here with me?"

"Sir, you have every right to have your lawyer present, but we had hoped that we may be able to talk man to man for a while," stated Jack.

"Speak, I'll listen for now," replied Sanchez.

"I hope you realize that you're looking at about thirty years and that's only if the court doesn't decide that you were a co-conspirator in the shooting of the police captain," Ernie indicated.

"Shit happens, they gotta do what they gotta do," replied Sanchez.

"Then you're not interested in cooperating with us and possibly reducing the charges or time in jail?" asked Ernie.

"No, I'm just a delivery man and my lawyer will bring that out plainly. I didn't even know what I was carrying in that briefcase. I'm not worried," stated Sanchez.

"Oh, you were unaware of what was in the briefcase? Are you sticking to that story?"

"Yes, and nothing that you can say will change my mind. Now the meeting is over, Leave or get me my attorney before we talk anymore."

"Your wish is our command, sir. See you in court."

The detectives left the room and a few minutes later returned to that same room to interview Mr. Enrique Rivera, the second Cadillac man.

The interview went almost exactly the same as the interview with Sanchez. There was no convincing these men that they would not get off. They could if Ernie divulged a certain piece of evidence. He was not ready to do that, not yet. He wasn't really sure that he had all of the parameters covered yet.

The two detectives left the interviews with no surprises. They didn't expect any cooperation from Sanchez or Rivera and they didn't get any.

"Jack, no surprises there. Why don't we call the DA and meet with him in the morning?"

"I'll call his office now."

"OK, while you do that, I'll call and check on the prints from the cash."

Jack picked up one phone in the guards' room and Ernie the other.

"This is Detective Lijoi checking on the report from the three million dollars cash. We were looking for prints that match the print cards that we sent with the cash. Of course we would not turn down any other prints."

The man at the other end of the line asked him to stand by.

"Det. Lijoi?"

"Yes."

"You have different sets of prints on the cash, in each of the briefcases. The first identified as Mr. Sanchez case were the prints of Mr. Sanchez and Mr. Surelo. On the cash in Rivera's case were the prints of Mr. Rivera and Mr. Surelo. On the cash in the third case was Mr. Surelos prints alone. I'll send you a copy of the report through channels."

"Thank you, I'll expect it soon. You've confirmed my belief that they all knew what was in the cases and they all handled the cash."

Ernie hung up the phone and turned to Jack.

"Are we all set for the meeting with the DA in the morning?"

"Yes, we'll meet at ten."

"Good, did you hear that conversation with the lab?"

"I heard you say that they confirmed what we were talking about."

"Yes, they did, we'll have the report in a day or so."

"These assholes don't realize how much ot a hole they're in."

"Fuckem, they want to play hardball, let them. We'll play it a little harder."

***

Friday morning at ten Ernie and Jack walked into the district attorney's office with Captain Richards.

D.A. John Hageman was standing next to a secretary's desk and saw the men enter the office. He looked at them and walked over to Captain Richards to shake his hand:

"I'm happy to see you, Captain. You must be feeling better."

"Yes, I am. Ernie and Jack filled me in and I wanted to be here at this meeting."

"You're always welcome here, Captain. Why don't you men go into my office and I'll be right in. I have to finish up with Sue, my secretary."

The men walked across the room and entered John's office. They sat, talked and waited for him. John walked in.

"How did the interviews go?" asked John.

Ernie and Jack proceeded to update John Hageman on the interviews.

"That's great; I can use the drivers, the crew and the captain as witnesses. These guys are finished. We'll deport where appropriate and the drivers will get a short sentence. Of course, this is all after I run it by the judge and get his approval, but I doubt that there will be a problem."

"You understand that we have not put this all in writing yet. We haven't had time. You'll have the reports in a few days," stated Ernie.

"As long as I have them a day or two before the trial so I can give the defense all of the particulars on the evidence and the list of witnesses."

"You'll have them," said Jack.

"What about that limo guy, Surelo? You didn't mention him."

Ernie smiled and looked at the captain: "Do you want to tell him, Captain?"

"You should tell him, but if you don't mind I'll at least get it started?" Captain Richards stated.

"Go ahead," stated Ernie.

"John, a while back, Ernie and Jack came to me with an idea that is only now ready to hatch."

"Oh, what was this idea?"

"To wait until the case was almost over before approaching Surelo, to make him sweat and wonder why no one had approached him. I agreed to the strategy," stated Captain Richards.

"That could be dangerous; what if he gets a break in the case and beats us?" asked John.

"Ernie, you take it from here."

Ernie replied to John's question. "John, it will be hard to beat you. I would say impossible, now that we have those witnesses. On top of that we have Surelo's fingerprints on the cash in each of the briefcases along with the prints of the other two men. They are claiming that they were only delivery men and knew nothing about what was in the cases."

"You're right that makes a big difference. Make sure I get that lab report along with the other lab reports on the quality of the narcotics that were delivered," John said.

"No problem, you'll have the reports in a few days," replied Jack.

"I also approve of the strategy now that I am aware of the entire situation. I assume that you are going to present him with alternatives at the appropriate time," stated John.

"Yes, exactly."

"Great, a good meeting, we're all on the same page," stated Jack.

As John got out of his seat he stated, "Ernie, I will be using you as an expert witness. You know the procedure, you've testified in that fashion before."

"No problem, John, it will be my pleasure."

The meeting broke up and the detectives all returned to the office in Quincy. The next step for them would be to wait for the trial unless something happened before then.

***

It was Friday afternoon; Ernie, Jack and the captain went back to the office where Ernie and Jack began some of the reports while the captain spoke with the chief of police on the phone.

At about four in the afternoon, they decided to call it a day. They went home for the weekend feeling satisfied that they did a good job, so far, on the case.

Chapter 9

The Call

Friday July 14, 1978

Ernie arrived home on Friday afternoon and as he walked into his home he asked his wife if she wanted to go out to eat.

"Where do you want to go? I was just going to put a couple of pieces of fish on for dinner."

"I was thinking that we have that camp in Maine, we haven't been there for a while because I've been so busy with work. We have a whole weekend ahead of us. We can eat at the restaurant in Kittery, Maine on the way up. What do you think?"

"I can be ready in a half hour if you pack a bag for yourself."

"You realize that we won't be eating for at least two hours, right?"

"I don't mind, if you don't mind," stated Teresa.

"Good, sounds like we have a plan; let's get going."

They got packed and left the house for the weekend.

On the way to the camp in Augusta, Maine they stopped at the Weather Vane, a restaurant on Rt. #1 in Kittery, Maine to eat and then Ernie visited the Kittery Trading Post across the street.

They arrived at the camp on Togus Pond in Augusta at about nine that night. Ernie started a fire in the stove that they used to heat the house. This was mostly to get the dampness out because the house had been empty for so long.

"It's really damp. The heat will dry everything out and we'll be fine by morning. We haven't been here in about a month. I kind of miss this old place."

"Yes, me too," stated Teresa.

They went to bed looking forward to the morning, the view from the back porch and the fish that Ernie hoped to catch.

***

The next morning, Ernie woke with all kinds of energy. He got up at about five in the morning, got dressed went down to the dock and turned the twelve foot boat over. He went to the shed and got the seven horse motor and gas tank then placed them in position on the boat. He got into the boat and started the motor. As the motor warmed up he went into the house to get his fishing rod, tackle box and a cup of coffee. He was off fishing for the morning.

He was rigged up with lead line to get down to the depths where the deep water trout hang out. He was trolling for about an hour when he got a hit and landed his first fish, a five pound brown trout. He was thrilled and placed the trout in the large cooler that he had on board to keep the fish fresh.

After catching the trout, he changed rigs and fished for his favorite fish, the smallmouth bass and the largemouth bass. Togus Pond had plenty of both as well as many other species. He had great time fishing and was catching lots of bass.

He looked towards the house and saw Teresa sitting on the deck by the dock at the edge of the water.

She saw him look and waived.

He started the engine and headed back to the dock.

"Look at this trout, Teresa."

"That's a nice one; we can have it for dinner. I'll call the neighbors. I saw you catching bass; you don't keep them, do you?"

"I only keep what we will eat. Bass is not on the menu today, not with a trout like this."

They both laughed as Ernie took the trout. He cleaned it, making it ready for cooking that evening.

It was eleven in the morning by the time Ernie finished with the fish and washed up.

"Teresa, would you like to go out to get some breakfast?"

"Yes, let's go to Holloway; I can look in the antique shops after we eat"

"OK, I'll change"

Ernie changed his clothing and they left for the rest of the day.

***

That evening they had the trout for dinner and were joined by some neighbors.

The next day, Sunday Ernie went out fishing in the morning. He fished for bass. He didn't try to get any trout because he knew that they would be leaving for home that afternoon.

They left later that day, stopped for dinner and arrived at their home in Massachusetts by seven that evening. Monday would be the start of an important week in the case that Ernie was investigating for the DA, the Federal Drug Enforcement Agency (DEA) and the New York Police Department, who were still in the dark on who killed the men in the card game. They had some great ideas, that Ernie and the federal agents came up with, but proving them in a court of law was another story.

Monday July 17, 1978

It was a warm sunny morning with blue skies and the scent of flowers all around Dedham, Massachusetts, where the District Attorney's office was located.

D.A. John Hageman entered the office and was greeted by the other assistant DA's who were preparing for their upcoming day at the court house.

John walked into his office, took off his suit jacket and sat behind his desk. As soon as he sat down, the phone rang. It seemed to him that someone was watching to see when he would be ready to take calls. He smiled as he heard the phone and the thought passed through his mind.

"Hello"

"Mr. Hageman, this is attorney Joshua Cohen calling about the William Surelo case. You may remember that I am his attorney."

"Yes, Mr. Cohen, I remember you well. That representation of the twisted facts, especially the facts about the cash was very well done; not successful, but well done" stated John Hageman. He pictured the heavy-set, balding man that was about 250 pounds, sporting a mustache, holding a large cigar in his hand as he stood in the hallway of the court house.

"We try, gotta make a buck, you know how it works."

"Yes, I understand. What can I do for you?"

"I went over all of the new facts with my client. No one has been to see him about cooperation. He is willing to testify against the other defendants if we can make a deal."

"No, thank you, I don't need him."

"He can add to what you have," stated Cohen.

"No, thank you, I don't need him. We'll get them all, including your client. Every one of them will do thirty years without his help, but I'll tell you what I can do."

"What's that?"

"I can send a couple of my ace detectives, Lijoi and Wade, to speak with him. Maybe we can do something in another area depending on how the meeting goes"

"OK, this guy doesn't want to do any time so I'm sure that we can come to some agreement. I would like to be there for the meeting."

"That's fine. They will be at the prison this afternoon at about one. Is that OK with your schedule?"

"I'll be there."

"I'll try to be there myself, but I can't guarantee it."

"OK, I'll look forward to meeting these two men."

John hung up the phone. He immediately telephoned the dispatcher in Quincy and asked to have Det. Lijoi or Wade call his office.

"Hi, John, what's up," asked Detective Jack Wade.

"You two guys have an appointment at the jail at one this afternoon with William Surelo and his lawyer a Mr. Joshua Cohen."

"What happened?"

"Exactly what you and Ernie wanted to happen; he's worried that no one has been to speak with him. He's afraid of thirty years, which is what I told his attorney I was going to ask for in the court case. He offered to testify against the other defendants. I refused, stating that you two men would like to speak with him and maybe we could do something on another front."

"That's perfect, no one is better at figuring these guys than Ernie. Do you want to be there? We may need your assistance."

"I will do my best to be there, but if I'm not, don't make any promises that I can't keep unless we speak first."

"We are well aware of that fact, no problem."

"Good, I'll try like hell to be there, if not I'll see you here after the meeting."

"Agreed," stated Jack

Ernie entered the office as Jack hung up the phone.

"Hi, Ernie, you'll never believe what that call was about."

"Surelo wants to give up everything." Ernie laughed thinking he was making a Joke.

"Did you hear the conversation or something, how did you know?"

"I was making a joke. You're kidding, who was that?"

"I'm not kidding that was the DA," Jack stated as he went on to tell Ernie what John Hageman stated.

"Wow, I didn't expect him to cave so quickly," said Ernie.

"The cases start tomorrow so he's not being too quick. He's trying to head off the trial, that's all."

"Yeah, I guess so, but we have to keep one hand high. He could be trying to pull the wool over our eyes in some way."

"I agree. Let's go get some coffee."

The two detectives left the office and went to their favorite coffee shop.

After coffee, they decided to return to the office and review all of the completed reports and discuss the case of Surelo. They wanted to make sure that they were in agreement as to exactly what they wanted from Surelo, what they wanted him to do for them and the other agencies involved.

***

At twelve noon they started out for the jail to interview Surelo. They arrived at almost one in the afternoon. They were directed to the meeting room where all parties could sit and talk about the case.

Present in the room was attorney Joshua Cohen, DA John Hageman, Det. Ernie Lijoi and Det. Jack Wade. The defendant, William Surelo handcuffed to the chair and the table.

Mr. William Surelo was 5'10" tall, about 40 years of age and weighed 190 pounds, with brown eyes and thick black hair. He had a scar on his left cheek that ran from the left eye down to the bottom of his face, which added to the creepiness of his features. His file indicated that his nickname was Scar.

"Guard, I think you can remove the cuffs before you leave," stated John Hageman. There are enough of us to keep this meeting peaceful."

The guard removed the shackles and left the room, stating that he would not be held responsible for any problems.

"Don't worry about it, we'll be OK," said Jack.

"Ernie you take the lead on this. I'll jump in along with Jack if and when it becomes necessary," said John.

"OK, thanks John. I have one question. Mr. Surelo, what is it that you think you can do for us? After all, it's you that wanted this meeting."

"I didn't ask for this meeting," stated Surelo.

"Your attorney contacted the DA. He stated that you wanted to do something to help yourself. You must have something in mind."

"No, not really, except that I can testify against the others that were with me."

"We don't need your testimony, we have them for thirty years at least, not counting the shooting, and you for even more," answered Ernie.

"More – why more?" asked Surelo

"Because, we have your statements on record where you state that you didn't know what was in the brief cases, you were only a delivery boy. Contrary to that statement, we have evidence, finger prints, that indicate, you were the only one that handled all of the cash that was in each of the three brief cases. We have much more than that, but you get the drift of where we are and why we don't need your lying statements any longer."

"OK, OK, what do you guys need? I would really prefer not to go into state prison for thirty years, not even for three years."

"Let's talk about where the drug order originated."

"I'm Mr. Cohen, gentlemen; I do not recommend that my client gets off topic unless we have an agreement."

"We can't have an agreement unless he is willing to help us," stated Jack.

Mr. Hageman stood up: "Here's what I am willing to agree to and only on the basis that your client is acceptable and useful to the Detectives. I will recommend leniency, so you may be looking at ten years instead of thirty, plus the shooting which could add another twenty years."

"Not enough," stated Cohen, "he can give you a lot of help, but he has to remain at large to do it"

"Let's see what he may have, then we can talk. He has to make the first move and it has to be a good one," stated John.

Cohen looked at his client, Surelo and nodded his head in an effort to give Surelo the OK to talk.

"You want me to tell them what I know without any firm agreement?" asked Surelo

"Someone has to talk up first. They don't have years hanging over them. You do and they have you." replied Cohen

"OK, I hope you know what you're doing?" Surelo stated to his lawyer.

"Before you say anything, Mr. Surelo, I want to start the tape recorder so that our conversation can be written properly and we'll have it for the record," stated Jack

Surelo look at Detective Ernie Lijoi, Det. Jack Wade and DA John Hageman. He looked down at the table; you could tell that he was thinking, trying to come up with a way of giving as little as he could. He then looked up at Ernie.

"My drugs come through a group in New York. I have a cousin, named Ronny Surelo. His father, who was my uncle, is now dead. He was very high in the Joey (Bats) Borgazino family. My cousin Ronny is with them now and he arranged for this separate run as a friendly gesture for me and to make us both a few bucks on the side," stated Surelo.

"Is that why you had to pay cash instead of the usual mode of money transfer?" asked Ernie.

"Yes, Ronny is not high enough to approve me for the credit. One day he will be, but not now," answered Surelo.

"What can you do for us?" asked Ernie.

"What can I do for you? Nothing, my cousin is hurt, he took a hit in the back and is recovering. He's in New York so there is really nothing that I can do along that front," answered Surelo.

Ernie looked at Jack and they both looked at John. They were all thinking the same thing. Could his cousin Ronny be the hit man that was shot at the card game?

"How did your cousin get hurt?" asked Jack

"Why would you care?" Surelo asked.

""We don't care, just curious, trying to break the ice," said Ernie.

"Oh, I see. Can we go off the record on this?"

"I don't see why not, it has nothing to do with us in Massachusetts, does it?" asked Ernie.

"No, nothing; turn the reorder off," required Surelo.

"Jack reached over and turned the recorder off for the moment.

"He was involved with a job in Brooklyn and got tagged as he left the job. It was his first job so I feel for the guy."

"Yes, I can understand that. What I don't understand is why you deal with these depraved preyers of life. I expect it's the money that keeps you involved. Please, don't tell us anymore, we don't need to know," responded Ernie.

Surelo smiled; he liked the fact that Ernie was not interested in his cousin. When in actuality Ernie was playing a game that he had used many times on the street. The more you tell people not to say anything about a certain subject, the more relaxed they are about talking.

"I know you guys don't want to know about that, but he is really hurt. He said that he had a hole in his back from a nine millimeter that you could put a quarter through," Surelo continued.

"I'm sorry to hear about your cousin, I hope he pulls through OK," stated Ernie.

"He'll be ok, it's mostly a flesh wound, but it is painful he said."

"I think we have done enough to break the ice, let's go to a late lunch and come back in an hour or so," stated John Hageman.

Everyone was in agreement and they broke for an hour.

Later, Ernie, Jack and John were having coffee when Ernie asked Jack to call the feds and find out what type of gun was used at the card game by the victim that shot the assailant.

Jack made the call, asked the question and hung up the phone after he received the answer.

"It was a nine millimeter," this Ronny may be our key."

"Then our goal is to get next to him and possibly learn exactly what's going on," stated Ernie.

"That means that Eddie will have to reemerge and you will have to team up with Surelo to break into the

New York family," stated Jack as he and Ernie looked at John Hageman.

John was looking down at his coffee, deep in thought as he took in all that was stated.

"You're right, guys; let me make a call before we go back in," stated John.

"Who are you calling, if you don't mind my asking?" asked Jack.

"The case judge, I want some court agreement on what we're contemplating. We're talking about convicting his friends and letting him out on the street. To do that we need a cover that the court will agree with, then we can go forward."

John telephoned the court house and then was connected to the judge who was reviewing the submissions by the defense and prosecuting attorneys before the trial so that he was up to date and had his decisions on whether or not the prosecution should go forward.

John explained the case and the connections to the New York mob, the card game and the importation of illicit narcotics. The judge agreed to delay the trial if John and the defense attorney, Mr. Cohen, were in agreement.

"We're all set, as long as Cohen agrees," stated John to Jack and Ernie after finishing on the telephone.

"Good that gives us an opportunity to do something here. I'll call the Fed's before we go any farther," stated Ernie.

Ernie spoke with the DEA Agent John Slater who was happy to hear from him. John was even happier to hear about Surelo and the progress that had been made. He offered all the support necessary to do the job.

"John, one question, do you have someone in New York that can do this job?"

"Are you kidding? Between my agency and the New York Police Department there are no better people to do this job. I figured and so did the New York detectives that since this was originally your case, you would want to be out front. After all, the mob killed those guys because they thought that one of them was your informant. The New York Police can understand what your feelings are. They offered the option of you coming in as lead with my agency and the New York Police doing backup with Jack."

"OK, that's good of them, but for now I'll keep it generalized so that anyone can fill in that cover spot. I haven't even spoken to my wife about it yet."

"Ernie, you have the option and that includes Jack. It's up to you guys to make a decision. The job will get done in time, but you already have a stake in it. Let's face it; you know all the players and you have a Boston accent to New Yorkers."

"I have always been told that I have a strong Brooklyn accent," stated Ernie.

"Agent Paul Saunders of Brooklyn, New York couldn't believe that you were originally from Brooklyn because of the Boston accent that you developed over the years."

"That's interesting, maybe Jack is right. He said that I could reverse my story and be from Boston buying in New York, instead of the other way around."

"I know you and I know you can pull this off."

"OK, let me get back to you."

After lunch, which was spent mostly on the telephone, Ernie, Jack and John Hageman went back to the jail house.

They met again with Surelo and his attorney, Cohen. Ernie and Jack had a good idea of what they wanted to do. The job was to get Surelo to do his part; it would not be easy to convince him. Ernie would have to get Surelo to offer his services without telling him too much.

Mr. Joshua Cohen was sitting with his client talking as the three men walked in. Cohen sat there looking towards Ernie, Jack and John Hageman. He asked if they were able to come to some kind of an agreement on the case that was currently on the table. Surelo simply sat there quietly.

Ernie answered, "I don't think we will be able to use your client. He has nothing that we can use, unless he can come up with something."

Hearing that statement, Surelo looked up and you could see the fear of jail in his face and eyes: "Hey, I can do a lot of things, but I don't know what you want or need."

"We don't want and we don't need. It seems like it's up to you to come up with something more important than your ship load of drugs and we haven't heard anything that is even interesting."

"What about the Columbians?" asked Surelo?

"What about them? That's another country, not the United States. I can't swim that far," stated Ernie.

"I think we're done here, we're wasting time, that's all we're doing," stated Jack.

"Wait a minute, what about the family in New York? They're responsible for ten times more drugs than I am. Drugs that are coming into this country."

"What about them? You don't have a way into them or do you?"

"What do you mean by, 'a way into them'?"

"We may be interested in meeting some of them and making our own deals, but that's a long shot and may not be worth giving you your freedom," stated Ernie.

"That's it! I can bring you in as one of my major people. All we need is a good story that can be confirmed by the documentation. These people are not stupid, they have their ways of finding things out," stated Surelo.

"I don't know. What do you think, Jack?" asked Ernie.

"It doesn't sound bad."

Surelo jumped in stating: "Look, there's one thing that I must insist on."

Ernie asked, "What's that?"

"My cousin, Ronny Surelo, we have to protect him in some way."

"We're not here to negotiate with you. You either want to help out and save your fat ass or you don't. Make a fucken decision. Don't waste my time," stated Ernie

"I have to look out for my blood," insisted Surelo

"OK, then we're done. I'm not wasting any more time on this asshole. I'm here out of courtesy to your attorney, Mr. Cohen. By the way, I don't see your cousin here looking out for you, Mr. Surelo. Sorry we couldn't come to some agreement," stated Ernie.

"No, no wait a minute. OK, forget about my cousin, he never did anything for me anyway," indicated Surelo.

"If we do this, I don't want to hear any bullshit about your cousin William Surelo. If he goes down he goes down and that's the way it goes. We will protect you as an informant, no guarantees for anyone else," Ernie stated.

"I agree," Surelo replied.

"Then we're back to where we started from," stated Ernie.

"What about you, John? After all, you're the one that has to deal with the court."

"It won't be easy, but with the agreement of Mr. Cohen, I think I can pull off my end," state John Hageman.

"John, can you hold off the trial for a few days so that we can set up some strategy?" asked Ernie.

John looked at Cohen before he answered Ernie and waited for Cohen to say something. Cohen simply looked back at him and shook his head "Yes," indicating agreement. John turned to Ernie to reply to the question.

"Yes, I believe that we can do that, Ernie," stated John.

"Good, let's meet in a few days and put this together. Mr. Surelo, I don't have to tell you to keep this to yourself for your own safety, do I?"

"Detective, I don't even know what you're talking about. This meeting never took place as far as I'm concerned."

"OK, we'll be in touch soon."

The meeting broke up and they all left the room. Surelo was taken back to his cell until the next meeting.

In the hall way on the way out Ernie suggested that they all go home and think about what to do and how to do it. They would meet the next day and make some decisions.

"Ernie, Jack, I want to complement you two on how well you handled the case and wish you the best in New York." John stated

They both thanked John for his support.

Chapter 10

Delivery

Tuesday July 18, 1978

On Monday night Ernie arrived home, had dinner and told his wife what was going on in the case. She didn't like him going to New York or placing himself out in front by being the deep cover man on the case. They decided to sleep on it and discuss it the next morning.

The next morning, while having breakfast Ernie and Teresa spoke about the case.

"What can you tell me? I know you have to keep it all very close and are not supposed to discuss it. After all, we've been through this before, but what can you tell me about it now?"

"Teresa, you know that the less you know the better off we are when it comes to my work."

"I know, but we have a decision to make or have you already made that decision and only trying to get my approval?"

"No, I want your agreement that what I am about to do is the best thing to do in this situation," Ernie answered.

"But, I don't know the situation," stated Teresa.

"All you really need to know is that there are six men dead because of my case. One of them was believed to be my informant. That puts me in the hot seat. They could come after me or you or they may think the job is complete and leave it alone. That doesn't make killing six men OK. They did it because of my work. I have a need to correct that by getting the people responsible."

"So you feel as though you're in the middle?" asked Teresa.

"Yes, kind of, I want to get these guys before they try and go after us."

"They wouldn't come after me, would they?" asked Teresa.

"No, they wouldn't. I should not have said that. I guess I have made a decision on this thing. I'm gonna do it; you with me on this?" asked Ernie.

"Ernie, I will always be with you, no matter what you do. That doesn't mean that I agree with what you're going to do. I don't think you should do this, but I'm talking to the walls. Do what you feel you have to and don't worry about me. I'll be here when you need me."

"Thank you, Teresa. I have to get to the office. I'll see you this afternoon," Ernie started out the door.

"Call me later and we'll decide what to have for dinner."

"I will," Ernie stated as he left.

He walked to the car and noticed that the air was clear and dry, the sky was a beautiful blue and the flowers were glowing with beauty from the different colors of the plants. As he opened the door to enter the car; he heard the mockingbird saying good morning with the whistling tune that they had learned from each other.

Ernie returned the sound by whistling back to the bird. He remained there admiring his surroundings and talking with the Mockingbird for about two minutes. He felt peaceful and happy. He entered the car and his thoughts went back to the case and the surrounding problems that needed attention.

He arrived at the office and met with Jack.

"Ernie let's get outa here; I know you'll want to go over all of the possibilities and contingencies involved in this case."

"So, you think I've made up my mind to do this?"

"Ernie, you made up your mind at the first meeting when you found out that this is all connected to our regional case. I could tell back then. If it makes you feel any better, I agree with you."

"I didn't realize that I was so obvious, Jack."

"You're not, except to me and maybe Teresa. We both know you very well. After all you and I live together all day, every day, remember?"

"Yes, I guess you're right. Let's get outa here."

They left the office and spent the day discussing the possibilities of the case, what if this or that happened? How do we handle it? The entire day was spent discussing the subject of the cousins William and Ronny Surelo, as well as the Borgazino family.

The next day would be another day of discussions with the DEA and the DA. They were ready for any and all questions.

***

Brooklyn
Tuesday July 18

It was twelve noon. Wheeze decided that he should check on the trucks that he needed and make sure that the men knew what they had to do.

He telephoned Alfonzo Durangani at the warehouse, who indicated that he was ready to receive the product and begin cutting it up, creating a street acceptable and saleable product for the dealers to deliver to their customers. Durangani had his entire crew of eight men ready and waiting.

Wheeze then checked with Ronny Surelo, who was feeling much better from his gunshot wound. Ronny was placed in a position of authority to handle all of the men for this job. His job was to make sure that the delivery was covered, that there were enough men to unload and drive the trucks. He also needed armed men to cover everyone that worked on and around the ships when they arrived.

Wheeze had one call left to make. He picked up the phone to call Paolo Cristino at the number that he was given by the representative of the Columbian, Soldado family. They needed to discuss the time of delivery and diversionary tactics.

"Paolo, it's Wheeze, are we all set for our outing?"

"Yes, all set; the second outing will go well, I'm sure."

"Same time then, no changes."

"Correct, I may be in the area and if so I'll stop by for a moment to say hello."

"Good, looking forward to it."

Paolo was talking about the second diversionary ship. This ship would be placed in a position to keep the police busy while Wheeze and his men unloaded the actual shipment.

Wheeze sat back in his chair, going over everything in his mind and making sure that he was ready on all fronts. Now he would wait until the meeting at the Old Mark Lounge to advise his men.

That evening at seven, Wheeze met with all of his men at the Old Mark Lounge. He bought everyone a drink and spoke in general with the men. They then followed Wheeze through the back connecting door into the Calabria Club and then to Wheezes office.

"Grab a seat or a piece of floor, guys."

"Hey, Wheeze, I've been hearing rumors about tonight. You're not setting us up for something, are you?"

asked Freddie Amarolt, aka Freddie the Clam, a small man, thin, with blond hair, about 29 years old. He always worried about the worst things that he could worry about.

"Freddie, get off my back. Don't get my fucken Brooklyn up. You irritate me more than anybody I know. You'll be safe, don't worry. Who the fuck ever named you the Clam? You should have been named the mouth; it would have suited you better."

"The Clam comes from my father, you knew him and sorry, I have a habit of worrying, that's all."

"Yes, I knew your dad, good man. He was as quiet as a clam. You should have been more like him," stated Wheeze.

Jimmy Apples spoke up: "Yeah, clam, you worry too much."

Jimmy Apaolitano, aka Jimmy Apples was a ladies' man; he loved the ladies and they loved his blue eyes. He was a large-framed man, about 220 pounds, well-built at 5'11" tall. He had a thick beard, black hair and blue eyes. Jimmy was a second story man who got some sort of a kick out of doing breaks. He started with house breaks as a kid. Now he planned and led major art robberies throughout the New York, Pennsylvania and New Jersey areas.

Willie the Wimp spoke up with his stutter: "Ji... Jim, Jimmy, Don, don't be so ha... har... hard on him."

William Roundara, aka Willie the Wimp, was the last important man in the organization. He was the son of a very good friend of Joey Bats by the name of Joe the Mo, a hit man from the 1950's. Joe the Mo was murdered by one of his targets who was a little smarter than Joe was at the right moment. After that hit, Joey Bats took Willie under his wing and he became like a family member, although Joey Bats grew to dislike Willies' stuttering.

Apples replied to the wimp: "Wimp, don't get your balls in a stir, you'll never be able to pronounce the problem." Everyone laughed.

"OK, guys, can we get down to business here?"

The men all kept quiet and listened to the instructions that Wheeze was in the process of delivering. He was the mentor for all of them.

"As of right now, there will be no phone calls and no contact with anyone outside of this room. If anyone has anyone to call, do it right now, not after the briefing. Are we in agreement?" asked Wheeze.

The men all sat there waiting for the information. No one replied.

"Here's what we need to do: Apples, Wimp and Clam, at nine tonight you three go down and get the trucks at Venus Trucking Company; see Mr. Adolpho Granolini he is a good friend. Treat him right."

"We will, Wheeze, where do we take them?"

"I'll get to that."

"You three will take the three trucks and drive them to this location on Cape May," stated Wheeze as he pointed to a map.

"No... no... no problem," stated Wimp.

"Ronny, you have a machine gun, a Mack 10, right?"

"Yes."

"You cover the entire team from the top of this small ridge. You should be able to make everything out from there. This is almost a full moon night."

"I'll be there."

"Tuccio, you take two soldiers and cover the right side and the back," directed Wheeze.

"I'll take care of it," stated Tuccio.

"Spitball, you take two soldiers and cover the left side and the front of us," directed Wheeze.

"No problem, Wheeze."

"Once the ships arrive, Spitball, you will take all of the cover men from Tuccio along with your men and unload the ship into the trucks. The trucks and all of you men will meet me at the warehouse. Don't all take the same route to the warehouse. We'll unload at the warehouse and we'll be done for the night. If anyone needs directions, let me know."

"Understood, Wheeze," the men replied.

"You all have weapons, right?"

They all shook their heads indicating that they did.

"I'll meet the trucks there and wait for delivery at the dock," stated Wheeze.

"Are we doing anything about the cops?" asked Apples.

"That's being handled by the distributors and we will have a cover team in place," answered Wheeze.

"By the way, there may be one Columbian guy there, don't shoot the prick. It will cause us all kinds of trouble. I will need to speak with him if he shows," stated Wheeze.

"You can still talk with him. We'll just take his arms off and break his legs," stated Clam as they all laughed.

"If you see the guy, leave him alone," stated Wheeze.

The men all started joking about this unknown party and stopped as soon as Wheeze yelled: "What's wrong with you fucken assholes? Don't you realize that this is what's paying your income for the next three or four months? Let's stop the fucken around."

Wheeze was beginning to feel the pressure; this happened with every delivery. He wanted everything just right. He wanted no problems. He would worry until he got the delivery to the warehouse and out of his hands.

No one answered Wheeze. They all simply kept quiet. They could tell that the pressure was building.

"No one leaves until we all leave. The teams stay together. No telephone calls and no speaking to anyone outside this group. We want this thing to go safely and peacefully. Do you all understand?"

The men agreed and the meeting broke up. It was almost nine and they were getting ready to leave. It would take almost three hours to reach Cape May and get set up for the delivery.

***

Cape May, New Jersey

It was almost midnight and each man had his spot staked out. The trucks were in place, Wheeze was in his car and the moon looked full. So far everything looked good.

Suddenly, one of the men knocked on the window of Wheeze's car. "There's a car coming."

Wheeze got out of his car and watched as the car came in closer until he could see the driver. It was Paolo.

Paolo exited his car. "Wheeze, I see you're all set."

"Yes, I think so, where are the ships?"

"They will be here in a few minutes; here comes one around the point now."

They both looked and saw a second ship turn the point and then a third.

"How did the diversion go?" asked Wheeze.

"Perfectly, they telephoned the coast guard and the local police before abandoning the ship. Right now the police are all over the diversionary ship. That ship had only two kilos and ten bails on board. They will be busy all night confiscating the ship and unloading it. They'll be happy because they'll make big headlines for themselves. We have plenty of free, safe time," stated Paolo.

"They're docking now," indicated Wheeze.

Wheeze directed the men to their jobs and the ships were unloaded while Wheeze thanked Paolo for his support and interest in the delivery. Paolo left the area knowing that the job was completed. From his point of view, the delivery had been made.

The men loaded the trucks and the ships left the area. It was four in the morning when they started out for the warehouse. Wheeze took one route and the others went in several different directions once they got out of the pickup area.

***

Wheeze arrived at the warehouse at seven in the morning. He opened the garage doors to the storage area so that the trucks could pull in and were out of the view of the public and especially the police.

They arrived and the men unloaded with the help of the men that worked for Alfonzo Durangani, the man that ran the warehouse and the cutting operations for the Borgazino family.

"Alfonzo, how long will it take to complete the cutting and packaging process?"

"I can finish in four days; then it will all go back to you for distribution to your dealers."

"OK, I think I may place Ronny in charge of that part of the operation and I'll oversee it."

"He's very young for that much responsibility, but who am I? I'm an old man now and maybe I don't know what I'm talking about."

"No, your counsel is very valuable to me," stated Wheeze.

"Thank you, I just think he's a little young for so much responsibility," stated Alfonzo.

"Remember, Alfonzo, I was only 25 years old when you started me out as an assistant consigliore."

"Yes, but you were an exceptionally knowledgeable young man at that time."

"And I feel that way about Ronny; you remember his dad. He was a good man for us and Ronny will be good for us also," stated Wheeze.

"Yes, but his father was a little slow at times, that's why he's dead. Nothing like you," stated Alfonzo.

"Well, I'm gonna give him a shot and we'll see how it goes."

"It's your decision, I have nothing to do or say about it. I have a lot of work to get done. I'll see you in a few days, Wheeze."

"OK, I'll see you then."

Wheeze gathered the men together and thanked them for a good job while reminding them that no one should talk about what had happened.

"This was an as usual job, men. It's secret between us and our people only, understood?"

Everyone understood and agreed they all knew the consequences of being caught distributing illegal narcotics.

It was Wheeze's personal worries, not the men that were bothering him. Things that he could not talk about to the men. "OK, all of you take off, return the trucks and I'll see you guys tomorrow at the club," Wheeze stated to the men.

Everyone left the warehouse and went off in different directions.

Chapter 11

The Cover

Monday July 24, 1978

Ernie awoke from a sound sleep. They had a week-end of enjoyment and pleasure out at their camp on Togus Pond in Augusta, Maine. He sat out on the porch with his wife Teresa, having breakfast when she asked about the case.

"I'm still not one hundred percent sure that I will go under cover, Teresa. As soon as I make a final decision, I'll discuss it with you, but you may as well know it looks very positive right now."

"I'm not happy to hear you say that, but I do understand that you have to do what you think best on this," said Teresa.

"It's not so much that I think this or that is best. We have a team that will make the final decision and then I get to agree or disagree about going into deep cover. Right now I am not opposed to going under, but I'm concerned about you and your feeling on this."

"I understand, all I ask is that we discuss it, that's all," said Teresa

"We will; I have to get going." Ernie kissed his wife goodbye and left the house.

As he walked to the car there was a large cloud over his head, no rain, but it looked like it may pour at any minute. Then he heard his buddy singing.

He returned the song by whistling and the symphony went on and on for about three minutes. Ernie had to leave the area, but he carried a big smile that the mockingbird gave him.

He arrived at the office and Jack walked in right behind him.

"I was just noticing that it may rain, Jack, what do you think?"

"All I know for sure is that we have a few days ahead of us filled with meetings with the DEA, ATF and the New York Police department, not to mention the captain. Am I missing anyone?" stated Jack.

"No, I don't think so," Ernie answered with a slight laugh to his voice. "How do we get ourselves into this shit anyway?" asked Ernie.

"You're too good at what you do, that's how."

"Yeah, thanks, it's all me. I suppose you don't feel the need to take this case?"

"Yeah, I guess we are both to blame, but it looks like we're in and I wanna stay in, if we can."

"I agree," answered Ernie.

"What's first?" asked Ernie.

"I was thinking, why can't we have a group meeting and do it all at once. We have all the information that we need."

"I don't know why not. I assumed that you already tried to put something like that together."

"No, I didn't, but I'll get on the horn now," replied Jack.

Jack telephoned all the agencies and people involved and set up a meeting at the SSU offices (Special Service Unit) for that afternoon at one. They went out to the coffee shop and relaxed for a while, knowing that the meeting was going to be interesting and contain a lot of information. This was the meeting where the final decision would be made along with plans for the future.

After the coffee they stepped out onto the sidewalk in front of the coffee shop. The two men stood there watching a pretty young lady walk across the street.

Ernie noticed two young kids about sixteen walking fast behind the girl.

"Jack, she's a very pretty girl."

"Yeah she is, but too young for us. That's the girl from the laundry up the street. She must be going to the bank."

"Yes, I can see the blue bank bag sticking out of her pocketbook. That's a lousy way to carry it," stated Ernie.

"Those kids are pushing hard to catch her."

"Jack, they're gonna take her deposit bag."

Ernie and Jack calmly walked over to the edge of the sidewalk so that they would be in view of the girl. They stood there talking, watching and looking in a way as to not seem like they were paying attention to the kids.

As the girl pasted Ernie, the two kids tried to take the bank bag. Ernie grabbed one kid and Jack the other.

"Hey, what the fuck are you doing, man?" said the kid to Ernie.

He was holding the girl's bank deposit bag in his hands and trying to fight off Ernie at the same time.

The girl started screaming for help.

Ernie yelled, "We're police officers, you two are under arrest."

As Jack was cuffing his prisoner, Ernie took a punch to the face from his and he returned the punch with two slaps, spun the suspect around and cuffed him.

They called for a car to take the prisoners into the station. Jack then called for two other detectives to take the arrest and do the paperwork. If they completed the case themselves, it would make them late for their meeting.

By the time everything was cleared it was almost one and they had to leave for the meeting. Detectives Rick Bradshaw and Carl Robinson of the SSU (Special Services Unit) took over the case and handled the reports and the victim.

Ernie and Jack left the area and went back to the office. Jack went over to make coffee for everyone and Ernie went to the files to pull all of the reports, along with the listed information that they had gathered.

Just then the door opened and Captain Richards entered the office. Behind him was the DA John Hageman.

"Hi, guys, we just saw the DEA (Federal Drug Enforcement Agency) and the ATF (Federal Alcohol, Tobacco and Firearms agency) parking, they should be right up," stated Capt. Richards.

Jack: "Good I'm making a large pot of coffee."

Capt: "That sounds good. I can go for a cup."

DA Hageman: "Count me in on that."

Jack: "Two cups coming right up."

As Jack handed the coffee to the captain and the DA, the door opened and in walked the Agent John Slater of the DEA, Boston, Agent Paul Saunders of the DEA, New York and Agent Peter Starling of the ATF, representing Boston and New York.

Jack: "Guys the coffee is all made, help yourselves. We can talk in here," as Jack directed them into the back office where there was a table that would seat everyone comfortably. They all sat down and the first comment came from John Slater of the DEA.

"Ernie, I know that you'll be giving us copies of the reports, but give us a brief rundown of what happened at the interviews with your suspects."

"Sure, I'll be happy to and Jack, you jump in if I miss something."

Jack indicated in the affirmative by nodding his head.

Ernie went on to tell everyone what happened at the interviews and they were all interested in the information.

Ernie: "There was one thing that sticks out about the interview with Surelo."

Slater: "What's that?"

"I didn't say anything, but he indicated that his connection was his cousin Ronny Surelo and that Ronny had been shot recently. I'd love to try and match his blood with the blood found at the scene that did not belong to the victims."

"That's what we heard on the street and your conversation with Surelo confirms, in my mind, that his cousin Ronny was there at the card game. Doing what exactly is unknown at this time," stated Slater.

John Hageman stood up and asked: "We know everything that has been going on, but we have to be able to prove it in a court. How do you men propose that we get the evidence that I would need if I was the prosecuting attorney?"

John Slater: "I think that we should offer Ernie the opportunity to work with Paul Starling and finish the job that was started when he did the David McQuethy case."

Everyone looked at Ernie, waiting for his reply while he looked at Jack.

"Jack, what do you think?"

"I told you what I thought. You've made your decision."

"You're right. Gentlemen, let me talk with my wife. I'm sure you can understand that request. Then I'll make a final decision by morning. Can we meet here tomorrow, at say noon, and finish up?"

Everyone agreed and some wished Ernie luck with his wife while others told him that they really wanted to see him finish this. He agreed with them all.

The meeting broke up. That afternoon, Ernie telephoned his wife Teresa and asked her if she wanted to go out for dinner.

"Yes, I'd like that," she replied

"OK, I'll see you in a little while."

Ernie got home, cleaned up, changed his clothing and took his wife out for dinner.

"So you've made a decision on the case?"

"No, not yet, but I'm very close. I wanted to talk with you about what it will involve and make sure that I'm not overlooking anything or underestimating anything."

"OK, so do you want to tell me what you can and I'll ask you some questions if I have any?"

Ernie agreed and told Teresa as much as he could without allowing her to know all of the particulars.

"Then you will be required to work in New York?"

"Yes for a few weeks, maybe a few months, I don't know, but if I start, I have to finish."

"Will you be home at all?"

"Yeah, I'll come home every so often. As often as I can."

"I don't like it, but knowing you, you'll never feel right if you don't do it and I can tell that you seem to need to finish this job."

"Thanks, Teresa. Jack said almost the same thing. I must be projecting something to you guys."

"Ernie, I'll do anything I can to help you and you know I will support you, but you also have to know that I don't like it. I am worried about you doing this. You will be dealing with some extremely dangerous people."

"I can't be worried about you worrying. You have to promise me that you will not hound me while I'm doing this."

"I will not hound you, have I ever hounded you?"

"No. I have to give you credit, you have been a good partner and friend in all of this. Just try not to worry."

"That I'll do, now let's finish dinner and get home. There's a TV show on tonight that is supposed to be interesting. Hopefully, it will take my mind off of this case of yours."

That night they stopped talking about the case. Ernie knew that Teresa would have additional questions later.

***

The next morning Ernie got up, had breakfast and left the house. He spent a couple of minutes with the mockingbird and then drove off to his office.

He was ready and wanted to get his thoughts down on paper, along with the outcome of the meeting from the day before so that he had all of his options in front of him and available for Jack, as well as the other men.

He arrived at the office and Jack was right behind him

"Ernie, I think we should get all the options down on paper so that we have everything available to us."

"I was just thinking the exact same thing on my way in here."

"Let's go for coffee and then we can come back, put it all down on paper and be ready for the meet."

They left the office and were going down the stairs when they heard the phone ring. Ernie went back up to the office to answer the telephone.

"Hello"

"Ernie?"

"Yeah, who's this?"

"Bob, Bobbie Melons."

"Bobbie (Melons) Maloney, how the hell are you? I haven't heard anything from you in a while."

Bobbie (Melons) Maloney was a connected wanna be, Irish Mafia type guy. He was a white male, about 6'1" tall, well built at 240 pounds with light brown hair and hazel eyes. Bob was an informant for Ernie in the past, but his primary work was being a thief. He would steal the nose off of your face if you let him. Ernie always kept one hand high with Bob.

"What's up, Bob?"

"Ernie, I know this guy that's trying to do the 'Scarab Scam'. At least I think it's a scam. He's offering an Egyptian scarab artifact for one hundred thousand dollars."

"So don't buy it, what do you want from me?"

"This is a good arrest for you," stated Bob.

"What's in it for you, Bob?"

"Nothing, I may need a favor later."

"Bob, you must need him out of the way or something. We're not in that business. You know that I don't play those games."

"He's committing a crime. Why not take him? Maybe if I need some help later you can give me a hand."

"Bob, I'll meet the guy, but I make no guarantees about later. Remember that."

"Yeah, I understand. I don't want anything in reality, but it's always good to be on your good side, as I've learned in the past," stated Bob.

"When can I meet him?" asked Ernie

"Right now, I'm just down the street at the coffee shop and he's at the table waiting for me; I told him that I may have a buyer."

"We'll be right there."

Ernie called Jack back to the office and told him what was going on. He then changed from his street clothes into a suit. He and Jack discussed the possible case and they agreed that Ernie would represent himself as an investor under the guise of Eddie Pannoni. Jack would do cover from another table in the coffee shop.

They were off to the coffee shop. Jack went in first and took a table near Bob, whom he knew through Ernie.

Eddie walked in and stood at the door to the coffee shop, looking around, when Bob motioned for Ernie to join him.

"Eddie, meet Willy, I think you guys may have something in common. I can't stay for long, but you two can talk."

Eddie looked in Jack's direction to confirm that he was close enough before Ernie sat down: "I'm not here to fuck around, what have you guys got for me? I went out of my way to come here."

Willy: "What do you know about Egyptian artifacts?"

Eddie: "I know that my New York buyers love that sort of stuff, if and when I can get them."

Willy: "Do you know anything about scarabs?"

Eddie: "Yes, they are very rare and very valuable. Why, all these questions?"

Willy: "I have a couple of scarabs that I am looking to sell. I brought them back from Egypt. I was there last month and came across these while visiting a site in the desert."

Eddie: "Let's see what you have."

Bob: "I have to run guys; Eddie, I'll catch up with you later."

Ernie: "Bob, you're not gonna get a piece of this deal?"

Bob: "No, I am out of it. I'm just making a connection for you guys."

Willy: "OK, Bob, see you later."

Bob left the area.

Willy: "How do you know Bob?"

Eddie: "I don't really know him all that well. I met him through some people a few months ago." This was a story that Ernie and Bob used in the past when Bob brought him in on a situation. This story left room for doubt that Bob knew that Eddie was Detective Ernie Lijoi.

Willy: "Oh, so you guys really don't know each other all that well. That's what Bob said. He said that you had a lot of connections and could handle something like this."

Eddie: "Like what? You still haven't told me anything of interest to me or my people."

Willy: "I want to sell the scarabs for the best price that I can get."

Eddie: "What are you looking for in the way of compensation, how much cash?"

Willy: "I'll take fifty thousand dollars for the both of them, cash."

Eddie: "I'll have to look at them and have them checked out."

Willy: "I can't let them out of my hands."

Eddie: "OK, I'll take a picture of them and get back to you later today or tomorrow morning, is that OK?"

Willy: "Why do you need that?"

Eddie: "I have to check with my people to see who is interested in buying these pieces and what they're willing to pay for them.

Willy: "That should be OK, let's go, my place is just down the street."

Eddie and Willy got up, paid the coffee bill and left the coffee shop with Jack not far behind, watching and covering Eddie.

They went to Willie's apartment, where Eddie took a Polaroid camera out of his briefcase and then took a couple of pictures of the scarab.

Eddie: "Willy, it looks pretty good; I'll be back to you later or in the morning. Got a phone where I can call you?"

Willy gave Eddie his phone number and told Eddie that he would be home after three that afternoon and all morning the next day.

Eddie had enough. Willy's address, his phone number and some pictures which were all he needed to track who Willy really was. He left the apartment with an agreement to telephone back.

After leaving the apartment he got on the bus at the corner and went down a couple of stops where he got off of the bus. Jack was there waiting for him with the car.

"What do you think, Ernie?" asked Jack.

"This guy is a scam artist. He was concerned as soon as I mentioned checking it out. I think that these scarabs are fake. I took a couple of Polaroid's. Maybe we can have someone run this into the museum in Boston and check with an expert for us while we're at the meeting." asked Ernie.

"As soon as we get back to the office, I'll get someone to do that."

"The meeting with the Fed's is in an hour. We still have to make that report so we have everything in front of us," stated Jack.

"I'll do that while you arrange for someone to follow up on this scarab thing," said Ernie.

"Agreed"

Upon returning to the office, Ernie started on the paperwork and Jack contacted a detective in the juvenile division and asked for the favor of running down the scarab information.

"Jack, I'll take care of it for you, no problem," stated Det. Bob Sheldon.

"Bob, there's a little more."

"Whatever you guys need, you've helped us out enough times."

"Thanks; run this guy Willy down. Find out his full name, record, etc. then do a report on what you find out."

Jack gave Bob Willy's address and phone number. Bob would do the leg work.

"How's the report coming, Ernie?"

"Good, I'm almost done. Here, read this, see if you can add anything."

Jack read the information: "No, I think we're all set. You seem to have covered it all, for now anyway."

Just then, Bob Sheldon showed up to pick up the information and the Polaroid pictures of the scarabs.

"These are good shots. I'll stop back here on my way back from the museum," stated Bob.

Scarab (artifact)

"We'll look forward to it, Bob, thanks," replied Jack as Bob left the office.

Bob had just walked out and not five minutes later the door to the office opened and all of the men started showing up for the meeting, one at a time.

They each got themselves a cup of coffee and then sat in the conference room.

"Guys, I'll agree to do this, but I want to be sure that we have coverage and backup as may be needed."

"That's not a problem, Ernie. Jack can work with the team as he has in the past and he'll supervise your cover," stated John Slater.

Agent Paul Saunders of New York asked, "What about my involvement, don't you want a partner while you're in NY?"

"I don't think it will be a good idea in the beginning. I would like to bring you in after I am solidly into the group and only if we see a need for that kind of diversion," stated Ernie.

"OK, if that's what you want, but I can be of help. I know the players."

"Yes, and you know and work in the New York area. These guys are not stupid. They have no reason to look at me, but they may know who you are. They have their ways. I'm only trying to protect us both," stated Ernie.

"Yes but they just killed a bunch of guys because of your case. You don't think they know who you are?"

"No, I don't. It's the Columbians that called for the hit not the New York family as I understand it. They don't care about me; the Columbians may care, but not the family."

"I don't remember telling you that, Ernie. Where did you get the Columbian connection?" asked John Slater of the DEA

"Out of the reports that you gave me to read and it made sense," Ernie replied.

"OK, I was aware of it, but I didn't know that you were on it," stated John Slater.

"I try not to miss anything, John," replied Ernie, "It's my life we're talking about here."

"We know, we're all behind you," stated Paul.

"Now that that's settled, I'll leave the particulars of coverage to Jack and you guys," Ernie said

"That's fine," stated Jack

The meeting went on for about two hours. Questions were asked covering possibilities of who, what and where things could happen. Then the meeting began to break up.

Ernie asked: "John Hageman, Mr. DA, can you handle getting Surelo out and covering it through a bail or by handling the other cases in a way to put him on the street with me?"

Hageman: "We have to advise him of what we want to do, but it is all doable. I may have to put a bail on all of them to make it look good. We'll handle it. You can work with me on that tomorrow," stated the DA.

Ernie: "John, I'm sorry, but I have to close a fraud case tomorrow. I may be tied up all day. How about going to see him on Wednesday morning? I'll call you after I finish up the fraud case."

DA: "It's a date. I'll expect to hear from you tomorrow."

John Slater DEA: "Ernie, make sure that we are all in on your plans."

Ernie: "I will, as soon as I set them up with Surelo. I hope that we can discuss them for flaws before we go forward."

Hageman: "Then we're done here. Does anyone else have anything they want to bring up?"

No answer from anyone.

"Just one thing, guys," stated Ernie, "I'll have to get approval from the chief of police for this operation. Do you see any problem, Captain Richards?"

"I don't see any problem with it, but of course I must check with him. I'll have an answer in an hour or so."

"Thanks, Captain," stated Jack

As soon as everyone left the office; Ernie and Jack turned their attention to the fraud case of the "Scarab Scam."

Chapter 12

Willy

Later that afternoon

Everyone had left the office when Ernie heard a call on the radio.

"January 3 to November 5 or 7."

January was the call sign for the Juvenile division of the Quincy Police.

"This is November 7 standing by," answered Ernie, with Jack paying close attention.

"Are you guys in your office?"

"Yes, we are."

"I will be right there, in a few minutes. I'm picking up the record now and then I'll be right over."

"We'll wait for you," answered Ernie.

A few minutes later, Det. Bob Sheldon walked through the door with the criminal record of one William (Willy) Bonafineli with a picture of him and his prints. Ernie looked at the file and then Jack.

"That's him, a good picture of him. I see he has a record for fraud and has done some time for both larceny and fraud," stated Ernie.

"Yeah, he's another asshole. The scarab that you gave me the picture of is a fake. The expert at the museum, Mrs. Laronse, looked at the pictures of the scarab, then took me down to the gift shop and gave me one. Here it is."

"How much do they sell for?" asked Jack?

"Eighty nine cents," replied Bob with a smile, "Can you guys fill me in on this case?"

Ernie and Jack explained what had happened and the three men planned to do an affidavit for a search warrant and an arrest warrant for Mr. William (Willy) Bonafineli.

"Jack, you do the arrest warrant. I'll do the search warrant and Bob, we'll call you as soon as we have the warrants in hand."

"Good, then there is nothing more that I can do right now?"

"No, just one point, if you don't mind, we'll do the search and arrest tomorrow. Jack, you don't mind if we give Bob the case, do you?"

"No, not at all, we got more shit then we can handle now," answered Jack.

"Thanks, guys," stated Bob.

"Now I have to call Willy and negotiate with him for those pieces of garbage that he's trying to sell," stated Ernie.

Jack laughed: "Don't be too hard on him, Ernie," Ernie laughed.

Ernie picked up the phone and telephoned Willy.

"Hello"

"Hi, Willy, are you ready to do business?"

"Sure, Eddie, any problems finding a buyer?"

"No, I have one guy that's interested, but he'll only pay thirty thousand for all that you have and I get ten percent of that payment."

"Ten percent? That's a lot of cash, man," replied Willy.

"OK, Willy. Nice talking with you."

"Where you going?" asked Willy.

"I'm hanging up. You don't seem interested in my buyer."

"I didn't say that, I was just surprised at the ten percent that you get."

"I'm the broker. Brokers always get paid."

"OK, it's a deal. I need the cash or I wouldn't let them go so cheap."

"Now you're talking. We'll meet at your place tomorrow morning about ten. Is that OK with you?"

"You'll have the cash?"

"I will lay it out to you and my guy will reimburse me when I deliver."

"Great, I'll see you at about ten in the morning."

Ernie hung up the phone and looked at Jack.

"I said not to be so hard on this asshole," stated Jack, laughing.

"I wasn't, but I had to make it a little hard for him. He may have started wondering."

"We're in and we can close it up tomorrow. Ready to go for the day?" asked Jack.

"As ready as I will ever be," replied Ernie.

The two men finished up the affidavits and left the office for the day.

***

Tuesday July 25, 1978

Ernie arrived at the office and sat down at his desk going over all that had happened in the last couple of weeks and trying to make sure that he had not missed anything that could come back and haunt him later.

Jack walked in just an Ernie was finishing up with his reading. "Ernie, do you want to go for some coffee before we wake this guy Willy up?"

"Yeah, I would love some coffee, but we better have it later. Let's go down to the court house, submit our affidavits and see if they get approved. If we have to wait we can go for coffee while they approve or deny the application."

"Sounds like a plan, let's do it," replied Jack.

The two detectives left the office and drove over to the courthouse where they entered through a private back door that they had the key for. This was so that Ernie was not observed by anyone that may be a current or future case. This entrance led directly to the office of the clerk of courts, the man that approves the issuance of any and all warrants in the City of Quincy district.

As they entered, Mr. Robert O'Rourke, the clerk of courts, was sitting behind his desk studying some papers. He looked up and saw the two detectives.

"Hi, boys, I keep forgetting that you guys have a key to that door."

"Sorry if we surprised you, we should have called first," stated Jack.

"That would have been nice, but not necessary. You guys can come here anytime, that's why I gave you the key. What can I do for you?" replied O'Rourke.

Jack handed him the affidavits. O'Rourke took them and started to look them over.

"Give me a half hour, guys, and I'll check these out."

"We'll go and have some coffee, do you want us to bring some back?" asked Ernie.

"No thanks, I'm all set," O'Rourke stated as he lifted the cup in front of him.

Ernie and Jack left the office the same way they came in, and went for coffee.

"Jack, do you want to give Bob a call and tell him that the chicken is in the pot?" asked Ernie, meaning that the affidavits were at the courthouse.

"Yeah, good idea, he may as well be ready when were done."

***

After a half hour they returned to Mr. O'Rourke's' office.

"Here you are men, go and get them." Mr. O'Rourke always said, "Go and get them," as he handed the two detectives the signed papers for the arrest and the search.

"November 5 to January 3," Jack called on the radio as soon as they reached the car.

"Standing by," answered Bob Sheldon.

"All set," stated Jack.

"OK, by the coffee shop," Detective Bob Sheldon was indicating where to meet.

Ernie and Jack drove over to the coffee shop where they met Bob and two other officers with their cruisers.

They discussed strategy, then went to the apartment of William (Willy) Bonafineli where they knocked on the door and announced that they were police officers and wanted to speak with him.

Ernie heard a window slide open.

"Knock it in; he's going out the fire escape. I'll go down and head him off if I can. Jimmy, you come with me."

Patrolman Jimmy Hoffman followed Ernie. They attempted to beat Willy to the bottom of the fire escape."

As they arrived at the fire escape they observed him going over the top and onto the roof. Ernie got on the radio and called Jack.

"Jack, he's going up, not down."

"I'm on it," answered Jack.

"Dispatcher, we need someone in the air searching for this Willy character, he's on the roof of his home. You have the info in the report that we left."

"Yes, I read it. I have Sky-one on the radio. I'll ask him to go to your area and I'll give him a description."

The dispatcher relayed the necessary information to the helicopter and the pilot located the suspect.

The pilot then relayed the location to the cruisers and they surrounded the area. Willy worked his way to the street and was caught after trying to hit one of the cruiser men with a piece of pipe that he found on the ground. The cruiser officer was able to deflect the swing of the pipe with his left arm while drawing his weapon and holding it on Willy.

"Don't shoot, I give up."

The officer had a broken arm from being hit with the pipe. He was lying on the ground and on his side, holding the gun on Willy. He later stated that it took all of his willpower not to shoot that bastard.

Two other officers showed up on the scene, cuffed Willy and called an ambulance for the injured officer, who was taken to the hospital, treated and released.

Willy was taken to the station where he was booked for attempted larceny, fraud misrepresentation of an artifact, assault and battery on a police officer and other charges. Det. Bob Sheldon took the case as the arresting officer.

Back at the apartment they found the scarabs that Willy was trying to sell and they also found two grams of heroin along with paraphernalia used to inject the drug. Everything was taken, bagged, marked and placed into evidence. The illicit narcotics charges were added at the station.

After the search and arrest, they returned to the station.

"Hey, Jack"

"Hey, Ernie," replied Jack.

"I'm ready to head home for the day, we have that meet tomorrow with the DA."

"You're right, I'm with you. Bob, you can handle the rest without us, can't you?"

"Sure, guys go ahead and good luck on that other case, whatever it is."

"Thanks, we'll need it," answered Ernie as he and Jack started out of the police station booking room.

Before leaving the station, Ernie telephoned the DA John Hageman and advised him that the fraud case was completed and that John would have the case in the morning when he went to the courthouse.

"No, I'll have one of the assistants take care of that. I'd rather deal with this Surelo thing and get everything straightened out so that you can move forward as quickly as possible."

"Thanks, John, I appreciate that. Jack and I will pick you up at ten in the morning and then we can go over to the jail and speak with Surelo. Will you advise his attorney?"

"Yes, I'll tell him that we'll be there at around ten thirty in the morning."

"Thanks see you in the morning," Ernie stated as he hung up the phone.

***

Wednesday July 26, 1978

Ernie entered the office and went directly to the file cabinet to pull the reports and notes that were made on Surelo. He wanted to be sure of exactly what Surelo stated about his cousin.

Jack walked into the office and asked if Ernie wanted to go for coffee before they met the DA and go over the points of interest. Ernie agreed.

They went to the coffee shop where they quietly discussed the various options available to them. After coffee, they drove over to pick up John Hageman, the District Attorney.

"John, did you make a final decision or agreement with the court on what we can offer this guy?"

"We'll start by telling him that we can recommend leniency in his case once he has completed his obligation to us."

"What does leniency represent in this case?" asked Jack.

"I can, possibly, recommend ten years instead of thirty plus years in states prison"

"That's our bottom line?" asked Ernie.

"I think that's it, depending on what he does, how well he does and how much he is of help to you," replied John.

"Do you want to go over that aspect or do you want me to do it?" Ernie asked.

"I think we can both speak; you handle the details of what you're planning and I'll speak to the sentencing," stated John.

"OK, then we have an agreement?"

"Yes, I believe so."

Jack kept driving. He soon pulled into the parking lot of the county jail, where the prisoners were being held.

John, Jack and Ernie entered the jail and were directed to the conference room where they could talk with the prisoner Surelo privately.

As they entered the room they observed Surelo was already in the room with his lawyer. Surelo was cuffed to the chair, waiting for the meeting to begin.

"Good morning, Mr. Cohen, Mr. Surelo," initiated Ernie.

"What's so good about it? This fucken place is a rat hole," stated Surelo.

"That's why we're here, Mr. Surelo. In an effort to ease your pain as well as satisfy our curiosity," Ernie answered.

"OK, you wanna get started? I wanna know exactly what you need because I gotta get the fuck out of this shit hole," stated Surelo

"First of all, Mr. Surelo, we will discuss what we can do for you. If you agree, we'll talk. The lawyers do not have to know any of the particulars. It would be better that way for your own protection. Do you agree to that?"

Surelo looked towards his attorney for guidance. Mr. Cohen, his attorney, simply made a gesture with his face, eyebrows and shoulders, indicating that it sounded OK to him.

'I'll agree only on the basis that your offer is acceptable," Surelo replied.

"First of all, let's get something straight; if you and I are going to work together, you do not dictate to me or any of us. We are in charge, we'll listen to your recommendations, but we will make any and all final decisions. Are you in or out?" asked Ernie

"How can I decide if I don't know what you're offering?" replied Surelo

"John, do you want to take that question?" asked Ernie

"Mr. Surelo, I can recommend a reduced sentence, from thirty years to ten years or even less. It all depends on the recommendation of the detectives upon completion of the job, whatever that job may be."

"Ten years, I can't do ten years. I'll be over fifty when I get out. If I get out at all and don't wind up dead."

"That's why I added the recommendations of Det. Lijoi and Wade. Depending on what they say about how you handled yourself and helped them we may be able to do better," stated John.

"I'm more than willing to go along and cooperate, but I just want some indication that I will not have to do time in the end," replied Surelo

John replied: "That's all I can do. I can't tell you what a judge may be thinking in a month or two. All I can say is that if you do your best for us, we will reciprocate in kind. Your lawyer will tell you that we have many options to help you, but you have to put up first."

Surelo looked towards his lawyer: "Let us talk privately for a moment, please," requested Cohen.

The detectives and the DA went out into the hall to give Cohen and Surelo some privacy.

***

In the Room

"Look, Bill, John is correct, they can do a lot, but it seems that you are caught between a rock and a hard wall. It's your decision to help or take your chances. I'm on your side and all I can do right now is, be honest with you. I can fight this thing the way it is, but ultimately we will lose. They found your fingerprints on the money in each of the briefcases. You're on record as saying that you didn't know what was in the brief cases and that's only the start. Remember, the captain was shot. I recommend that you take the deal."

"OK, Joe, I'll go along with them and do whatever I can. I just want to protect my cousin if I can," said Surelo

"Mention it, but don't push it. Wait until you're in for a while and see if you can convince them to give him a break. After all, you're out to protect yourself at this point. You're the one with the thirty years hanging over you, no one else."

"Yes, I guess you're right; call them in will you?"

Cohen called the men back into the room.

"OK, I'll go along. I only ask that if at all possible, you give my cousin a break, along with our deal, of course," stated Surelo.

"No guarantees on your cousin, but if we see an opportunity we will consider it," said Jack.

Surelo replied, "Then, in my opinion, we have an agreement."

Ernie looked around the room and replied: "OK, then you two lawyers can leave. Between the two of you, you can put down in writing everything that has been agreed to so that he can sign it, am I correct?" asked Ernie.

"Yes, we can take care of that within an hour," replied Cohen.

"Thanks, we have a bunch of things to go over. John, before you leave, how soon can you have him out of here?"

"I would think that as long as you men come to an agreement on what, where, how and when to proceed, I can have him on the street within twenty-four hours. That's after you let me know that all is good, Ernie."

"Great, thanks, John."

John Hageman and Joshua Cohen left the room. Ernie, Jack and Surelo began their discussions.

"Surelo, if we are going to be working together on this case, we better get used to calling each other by our first names. I'm Eddie and this is Jack. Jack will be in the background, with the backup team, working and covering both of us."

"You're right. You should call me by my street name of Scar, everybody knows me as Scar. I got that name when I was a kid. I got hit in the face with a milk bottle during a gang war. It took over seventy stitches to close me up. Since then everybody called me Scar."

"OK, from now on, I'm Eddie, you're Scar and of course Jack."

"What do we do first, Eddie?" asked Surelo.

Ernie didn't want to speak of the murders at the card game so he went in another direction.

"Our goal is to apprehend the dealers that supplied you with the shipload of drugs," replied Ernie.

"I got that through my cousin and I want to protect him if we can," stated Surelo.

"We'll do the best we can. What is his position with the New York family?"

"As I understand it, he's very close to the consulate (counselor) of the Joey (Bats) Borgazino organization or family, whichever you prefer and his dad was close to the same men before he died."

"That's good. Then I want you to take me to meet him. After we meet, you convince him to get me a job working with him. The reason for that request will be that I can't come back to Boston for a year or two, due to a scrape with the local police."

"That sounds doable, but then what?"

"You'll hang with me. After a while, once I'm settled in, you can leave and come back to Boston. In reality, you will stay there and assist Jack in the background helping to form strategy and make decisions if necessary," indicated Ernie.

"That's not too bad. I'll be out of the way long before you do any arrests."

"We're in hopes that we will never do an arrest. That will all be done by the New York Police, freeing you and me from suspicion. That is, if we work it correctly." said Ernie.

"Now that will be some trick," replied Surelo.

"None of this work is ever set in stone. We have to play most of it by ear, but that's the basic plan," stated Jack.

"There is only one thing that bothers me," stated Surelo.

"What's that, Scar?" asked Jack.

"These men are not stupid. They have their ways of checking people out and they will find out who you really are."

"Just remember this, my name is Eddie Pannoni, I am from Boston and I have been dealing guns and drugs for years. Jack and I will worry about the rest, but to ease your worry, Eddie Pannoni is a gun and drug dealer and has a criminal record that will be considered outstanding to your friends in New York."

"You can do that?" asked Scar.

"I have been using that alternate life for years, so it's all in place for us. Even my prints come back to Eddie Pannoni."

"OK, I guess you know what you're doing. When do we start?"

Ernie replied, "Someone will be here later with the papers for you to sign and as soon as the DA can get in front of a judge, probably tomorrow, you'll be out on the street. We'll give you a day or so before we start. As soon as you are out, telephone us at this phone number. Later we'll give you more information once we see how things go."

"Agreed," replied Scar.

***

After the meeting, Ernie and Jack decided that they must speak with John Slater of the DEA and then confirm that they have the approval of the chief. They must set and prepare for this New York operation.

Jack contacted the DA John Hageman and advised him that they were all set with Surelo.

John stated that he will take care of it. He'll have the paperwork signed by Surelo and he will appear before the court in the morning. He did not see any problems with the intended outcome.

Ernie contacted the DEA and arranged for a meeting the following morning at ten.

Chapter 13

Preparation

Thursday July 27, 1978

Ernie had breakfast with his wife on the porch over-looking Webster Lake. The air was warm. The sky was light blue reflecting off of the calm lake. Every so often Teresa would say, "Look, over there" and she would point towards a splashing in the water. Little bait fish jumping out of the water and into the air, to escape the school of bass coming to the top of the water to feed on them.

The small animals, like the squirrels and the chipmunks, were going on with their business of searching the grounds for their morning breakfast of worms, bugs and even smaller tasty tidbits.

"Ernie, when do you think this new case will start?"

"I'm not sure, but I think that we'll probably start next Monday as long as we can get everything set up by then."

"If you are going to have to live in New York for a long period of time, can I come down and visit with you once and a while?"

"Teresa, I don't know yet, but every chance I get I'll be coming back home to see you. You know I can't go very long without you."

"It would be nice if you could arrange for me to come to New York with you," stated Teresa.

"Maybe you should move in with your sister for a few weeks, she won't mind. I'm not going to a party, you know. I can't be worrying about you while I'm trying to do my job. You're better off here," replied Ernie.

"No, it's just the thought of you not being here that bothers me, I'll be OK."

"We'll talk when I get home from work. I have to get into the office. Jack will be looking for me in a little while."

"OK, I'll see you tonight."

Ernie left the house and walked out to the car. His friend the mockingbird called to Ernie as soon as he stepped out of the door. He answered and the symphony went on for about four minutes, the bird and Ernie whistling back and forth before he left for work.

***

Jack and Ernie met at the office. Jack contacted the captain to confirm that the chief was not opposed to the men working with the New York police for a couple of months. They received approval.

Ernie telephoned the DEA to confirm their ten o'clock meeting.

"We're all set, let's get a cup and take off."

***

Back at the Jail

The time was ten in the morning when Surelo was rousted out of his bunk by the guards and taken to the meeting room.

John Hageman, the DA and Joshua Cohen, his attorney was waiting for him.

"Hi, Joshua, did you guys work out the kinks in this case?"

"We did and here it is; sign it and you'll be out of here this afternoon."

"This afternoon? Why not now?"

"The DA has to take this before the judge and work out your release without your co- defendants being made aware of what's being done. We'll worry about getting that done. You only have to sign here," stated Joshua as he pointed to the location for Surilo to place his signature.

"Joshua, you're sure of this, this is the best way out?" asked Surelo.

"This is your only way out, my friend," replied Joshua.

Surelo signed the paper. He handed it to his lawyers who informed him that as soon as he was released, he is to contact the detectives that he met.

He agreed; the lawyers took the paperwork and made the needed arrangements. Surelo would be on the street that afternoon.

***

The Federal Offices of the DEA

Jack and Ernie drove to Boston after coffee and entered the federal building where they met with John Slater and Paul Saunders of the DEA. Also present was Peter Starling of the ATF and a group of men that would be on the team for this case. Their job was to do whatever is necessary, to bring this case to a safe and satisfactory completion.

"Ernie, as I understand it we are all set to go on this case?" asked John Slater.

"Yes, but all Surelo knows is that I'm after the drug dealers, he knows nothing about our goal to apprehend the people behind the card game massacre," replied Ernie.

"Good, that means that all we have to do is set you up with a place to stay, some cash, a background. Once that's completed, the backup team and you will be ready to go," replied John.

Paul jumped in, "My team in New York can handle the backup. Jack can work with us. I'll be available in the event that Ernie should need some help or someone to lay things off on. He can always bring me in, if he deems it necessary."

"Good, then that's covered," stated Jack.

"Paul, do you guys have an apartment in the area controlled by the Borgazino family?" asked Jack.

"Yes, we have just the place. I'll deliver Ernie there. The apartment is all set up with cameras and voice recorders," answered Paul.

"Then all we need is the criminal record. Ernie, is the one we have used in the past good enough for Eddie Pannoni, in this case?" asked John.

"I think so, but we need an updated picture. Ernie changes so much that we want them to recognize him as Eddie," replied Jack.

John Slater picked up the telephone to call the photographer to come in and take Ernie down to update the pictures.

"I think we covered everything for now except cash. This is five thousand cash and here is a credit card good for another fifty thousand dollars in the name of Eddie Pannoni and you have plenty of identification under that name. Please, be very frugal," asked John Slater.

"I'll take care of it, John. Who wants to go to lunch? It's on me or my uncle, depending on how you look at it." stated Ernie as he joked in reference to the credit card.

Everyone laughed, knowing he was joking, except John who just looked at Ernie and shook his head.

"Ernie, all kidding aside, when you work your way in, you will be getting your end of the income for your work with the family. That money will all be turned in here and you will take your expenses from those payments. Keep good records so that we don't run into a problem down the line in our cases against these people," stated John Slater.

"John, I don't mean to be rude, but we have done this before and we have never had a problem. Between Ernie and me, we have always kept good expense and income records," stated Jack.

"Yes, I know, Jack, but I have to make sure that it is said. You know that," replied John.

Jack simply smiled back.

It appeared that they had all their bases covered. It was time to get started.

"Paul, I'll telephone you when I'm on my way down to New York and we can meet up somewhere. I'll call you Monday as long as everything is still a go at that time," Ernie stated.

Paul replied, "That's fine, you have my numbers. I'll head back to New York today and be ready for you, Jack and Surelo when you get in. I'll be expecting your call."

The meeting went on for a few more subjects and then broke up. Everyone knew what they had to do.

It was about three in the afternoon when Ernie and Jack were back in the office discussing the upcoming case. The phone rang.

"Hello"

"Eddie?"

"Yeah?"

"It's me, Scar Surelo, I'm out and about."

"OK, are you going home to your house?"

"Yes, I would like to," said Scar.

"OK, have a good weekend. We'll pick you up Monday morning at about seven and start out on our trek."

"You're OK, Eddie, thanks. I could use some relaxation after that shit hole I was in."

"Listen to me. Do not get into any trouble or the entire deal is off. Have a good time, but be smart about it," instructed Ernie.

"Don't worry, I won't screw this up."

"OK, we'll see you Monday morning about seven. Pack for at least a week's stay."

"See you Monday. I'll grease the operation by calling Ronny over the weekend and getting him ready for us."

"Sounds good, but don't tell him what we're doing," replied Ernie.

"I will say nothing except that we are coming and you need to get away from Boston for a while like we discussed."

"That's good. This should work out well for all concerned."

They hung up. Ernie told Jack exactly what was just said on the phone so that he was aware of everything going on.

Ernie and Jack later left the office for the weekend.

***

Brooklyn
July 31, 1978:

Early Monday morning Jack, Ernie and Surelo took off for Brooklyn, New York. When they reached the halfway point they stopped for some coffee and to make some telephone calls. Ernie telephoned Paul Saunders to confirm a meeting location.

"Scar, you better call your cousin and tell him that we'll see him in the morning," directed Ernie.

Scar telephoned his cousin Ronny Surelo and told him they would be in late: "We'll meet in the morning."

There was a quiet moment by Scar and then he hung up the phone.

"Ernie, Jack, he wants us to meet him at the club tomorrow morning at ten unless we get in earlier than expected. He'll be at the Old Mark Lounge tonight after six," stated Scar.

"You mean at the Calabria's Social Club, the one owned and operated by the Borgazino Family?" asked Jack.

"That's the one," replied Scar with a smile.

They finally arrived at the location where they met with Agent Paul Saunders at eleven in the morning.

Paul took them to an apartment located in an apartment house at the corner of Grand Avenue and Clawson Avenue in Brooklyn, just down the street from the Old Mark lounge and the Calabria's Society Social Club. The agency had rented the apartment for this operation and placed it in the name of Eddie Pannoni.

The men moved their belongings in and went to lunch at a luncheonette at the corner of Grand and St. Marks Avenue. This luncheonette was owned and operated by Tony (Two Scoops) Linardo.

Tony (Two Scoops) Linardo was a tall man, about 6 foot, 280 pounds, grayish black hair, brown eyes and around seventy years old. Tony was a very easy person to speak with. He tried to get along with everyone by using his jovial personality. Two Scoops was so used to dealing with the public at his business that he had learned the graces of turning an argument or disagreement into a joke that made everyone involved laugh.

The luncheonette had a counter running down the left side of the room as you entered. He served ice cream along with other items. His nickname "Two Scoops" came from that fact that he always served ice cream with two scoops, especially to the kids. He enjoyed watching the kids being happy, eating his ice cream. That was the story that Two Scoops told everyone, it wasn't a fact as Eddie would find out later.

Scar indicated that Two Scoops was well connected in the neighborhood and had an organization set up in one corner of the basement of the luncheonette. This set up contained four telephones that were manned day and night to take bets on numbers and horses. Two Scoops made about thirty thousand dollars a year after all costs, from this gaming operation alone. Then he had the restaurant and some minor jobs that he did for the family.

The Borgazino Family made an additional twenty thousand a year from this gaming operation and this was only one of several rooms that they had located all over their territory. At one time, Tony (Two Scoops) Linardo was a big man in the family and highly respected for his expertise.

Paul, Eddie and Scar entered the luncheonette.

"Hey, Scar, Ronny didn't say that you were coming in."

"Hi, Scoops. No, he wouldn't have. You know him, closed mouth. How's it going?" asked Scar.

"Making a buck, you know," as he looked at Eddie and Paul. It was obvious that he didn't want to talk in front of them. He didn't know them.

"Oh, this is a good friend, Eddie 'P' and his buddy Paul."

"A good friend, you say?" asked Tony Two Scoops.

"Yes, a good friend" this statement was an indication that Two Scoops could talk freely in the company of Eddie, but that Scar was not sure of Paul.

"OK, sit down and I'll have the wife cook you up some lunch. Wait a minute," said Tony Two Scoops, "did you hear about that new decision that came down from Rome?"

"No," said Scar.

"Hell is the only place where they have TV's on every corner and in every room in the men's section.

Yeah, replied Scar waiting for the punch line.

"Yeah, the problem is, they have no remotes. Can you imagine that?"

The men all laughed and walked over to the table. They sat down and the first question from Eddie was:

"Why did you OK me and not Paul in that little conversation you had with Two Scoops?"

Scar: "If I OK both of you at once, they will be looking for him and he isn't gonna hang around, as I understand it."

Eddie: "Right, we may bring him in later if we need him."

Scar: "Then I did the right thing?"

Paul: "Yes, you did; thanks."

They had lunch, went back to the apartment. Paul showed Eddie all of the cameras and microphones that were set up. He left the apartment stating that he would meet with Jack and they would be around at all times if needed. He gave Eddie some phone numbers to call if he needed anything.

"One more thing, follow me," said Paul.

Eddie followed Paul outside. Paul opened the door of a 1976 black Cadillac Eldorado, convertible. "This is your car. It's registered to you for the investigation. All of the papers are in the glove box. This car has a tracking beacon that'll make it easier to find you in the event that we need to. I'll take off now. We will be in the background if you need us for anything. Give me the keys to your car and I will store it in the garage, at our headquarters for you. I'll come back to get it with another agent later."

"Thanks Paul, I guess we're as ready as we can be," stated Ernie.

***

That evening at seven, Eddie and Scar went over to the Old Mark Lounge to show their faces and meet with Ronny Surelo, Scars cousin, if he was around.

They could hear voices and common noises coming from the lounge as they approached. As they entered the lounge, the entire place got quiet. They observed six men sitting in one corner at a large table. Others were scattered throughout the lounge. Suddenly, they heard a voice come out of the smoke filled room.

"Scar," yelled one of the men from the large table, as the noise started up again. The men at the door seemed to be known by the right people.

"Ronny, great to see you!"

"Come on over, have a drink," stated Ronny.

Eddie and Scar walked over to the large table where everyone was dressed in suit jackets, some with ties. They could all be businessmen relaxing after a long day at work.

"Ronny, this is a good friend, Eddie 'P' out of Boston. He went to college in Boston, Massachusetts and is well known there," stated Scar.

"He's a friend you say?" asked Wheeze, who was sitting at the table.

"Yes, a good friend," replied Scar.

"Ronny tells me that he needs some time away from that area," stated Wheeze

"Yeah, he's had a little run in, he left some remains where they could be found and doesn't want to be around for the cleanup," stated Scar talking about Eddie. Scar was telling Wheeze that Eddie left a dead body in Boston and didn't want to be around to answer questions to the police for a while.

"Hey, Scar, that's enough. No reason to tell my life story," stated Eddie.

"Eddie, nice to meet you, I'm sure that you understand that we have to check you out before we can place you with us," said Wheeze.

"Yeah, no problem, I understand," replied Eddie.

"Have a drink, enjoy the party. You come highly recommended when Scar and Ronny are standing for you. Are you and Scar staying with Ronny?" asked Wheeze.

"They're welcome to stay with me, Scar knows that," yelled Ronny.

"Thanks, Ronny, since I may be here for a year or two and who knows maybe permanently. I arranged for an apartment, one of the ones in that apartment house over on Clawson and Grand Avenue. Stop by anytime," stated Eddie.

"Good, you're just down the street. Stop by the office tomorrow sometime and we'll see what can be done," stated Wheeze.

"Thanks, I appreciate anything right now. Waitress, set this table up for me, please," stated Eddie.

"Thanks, Eddie, but don't put no money up. We don't pay for drinks around here," said Ronny.

Suddenly Wheeze was grabbing his chest. His face went white as a ghost and his breathing was shallow, he was having a hard time.

Eddie walked over to him, placed his hand on his neck and felt that his pulse was racing very fast.

"Wheeze, are you on any meds?" asked Eddie.

"My nitro, I left it home and I feel like shit," replied Wheeze.

"Ronny, go into the kitchen and get some aspirins. Scar call for an ambulance," directed Eddie,

Ronny returned with the aspirins and Eddie gave Wheeze two of them and told him to chew them. He did.

The ambulance showed up and Wheeze was beginning to feel better from the aspirins.

They took him to the hospital where he was treated and released.

Eddie and Scar joined the party along with a few women that the men had invited.

***

An hour later, Wheeze returned to the party.

"I'm going home, I just wanted to stop and thank you, Eddie. The doctor said that the aspirins helped. How did you know enough to do that, give me aspirin?"

"I learned that from my father's doctor. My dad had a heart problem and the doctor told me to carry two aspirin. If he had a problem, I was to give him the two of them and call for an ambulance"

"How is your dad now?" asked Wheeze.

"I'm sorry to say that he has passed on."

"Thanks, Eddie, I think you saved my ass and I will not forget it."

"My pleasure, Wheeze," stated Eddie.

"I owe you, my friend, I owe you big time," stated Wheeze.

The night ended around three in the morning.

***

Tuesday August 1, 1978

At about ten in the morning Scar and Eddie entered the Old Mark Lounge. They walked straight through the entire lounge to a door in the back. This door was a private entrance into the Calabria Social Club.

Scar opened the door and held it for Eddie. As he walked in the entire room went quiet for a moment, then Scar walked in.

"Scar, who's your friend?" asked Spitball.

"Spitball, meet our friend Eddie out of Boston."

"Oh yeah, we heard about him. I think Wheeze is waiting to speak with him now," said Spitball.

Eddie and Scar entered Wheeze's office.

"Eddie, Scar, good to see you guys. Eddie, you're all clear, just one question; what the fuck is Cedar Junction, a fucken club house?"

Ernie laughed, "No, that's the Walpole State Prison. The people there had the name changed. I guess they'd rather fool themselves into thinking it's a clubhouse."

"The name definitely sounded quite different," said Wheeze.

"Yeah, it is," replied Eddie.

"Scar, you go out to the main room and wait for us. Eddie, follow me, I want you to meet the boss," stated Wheeze.

They left Wheeze's office and went into the next office down the hallway.

"Joey, meet Eddie Pannoni. He's out of Boston and has plenty of qualifications," stated Wheeze.

"Did you check with our connections?" asked Joey Bats.

"Done," Wheeze replied.

"Eddie, wait outside for a moment," requested Joey.

Eddie left the office, but could hear the conversation from the hallway as he waited to be called back in.

"Wheeze, he's ok, you say?" asked Joey Bats.

"Yeah, he did a stretch in Walpole, was recommended by Scar, Ronny's cousin and has a few convictions, mostly drugs," replied Wheeze.

"OK, we'll try him out. Two Scoops needs someone for a couple of days to keep the records for the phone men. Give him that to do and then maybe we can team him with Ronny on the warehouse. Yes that'll be a good test for him," stated Joey Bats.

"OK, Boss. I have a funny feeling that this guy will work out fine," stated Wheeze as he called to Eddie to join them.

"We know it's not your specialty, but we need someone for a couple of days to work with a guy named Tony Two Scoops. It's an easy job, you'll keep the records of the bets for a couple of days," stated Wheeze.

"That's fine with me, whatever you guys need. I met Two Scoops, nice guy," stated Eddie.

"Good, then we'll count on you for that and in a few days we can talk again about something that may be more along your line of interest," said Wheeze.

Eddie was given the particulars and left to see Two Scoops where he was shown the operation and what he had to do. He was set for the next two days. This would give him time to meet everyone and more importantly to become familiar to all the men involved with the family.

Scar was released to work with Jack Wade and the cover team. He thanked Ronny for helping Eddie and told him that he would have to return to Boston, but would stop back in a few weeks.

Ronny, told Scar not to worry about, Eddie. He would cover Eddie and watch out for him.

Scar would hook up with the cover team and with Jack the next day, leaving Eddie to follow up on the case. He would be available if he was needed.

***

For the next two days, Eddie worked with Two Scoops and did a great job. Two Scoops told Wheeze that Eddie came up with a better way of keeping the records which would be followed in the future by whoever did the job. He was happy with Eddie's work and made it known.

Chapter 14

Warehouse

Thursday night
August 3, 1978

Eddie finished his day's work. He had met with many of the crew over the last two days and felt that he was being accepted amongst the family members.

That night at the lounge, Wheeze told Eddie that he would be assigned to Ronny's crew and that they had a thing this weekend.

"Sounds good to me," stated Eddie.

Ronny was sitting at the table and said, "Meet me at the club tomorrow around noon and we'll talk."

"I'll be there," Eddie replied.

The next day Eddie had breakfast at Tony Two Scoops'. Tony was happy to see him and didn't charge Eddie for breakfast. Instead, he handed Eddie an envelope with two hundred dollars cash in it, with the statement, "Thanks for the help, Eddie."

Eddie took the envelope. He thanked Tony after he looked into the envelope. Eddie understood that this was payment for his two day's work.

After he left the luncheonette, he walked over to the Calabria's Social Club. He entered and walked back to the office, greeting some of the men as he walked by. He arrived at the door to Wheeze's office and observed Ronny and Wheeze talking.

Wheeze looked up. "Come on in, Eddie, we were just talking about you."

"Not bad, I hope?" asked Eddie in a joking manner.

"No, why don't you wait in the card room with everyone else. I'll be right in," stated Ronny.

Eddie went to the card room to speak with a few of the men.

In the office Wheeze was instructing Ronny on how to use Eddie for this first job.

A few minutes later, Ronny entered the card room and sat alone at a table near the office.

"Eddie, join me please."

Eddie went over and sat with Ronny.

"Eddie, this will be your first job with us. This job will give you an idea of how we work and give us an idea of how you work"

Eddie: "As I said, whatever you guys need, I appreciate the chance to get away from Boston for a while."

Ronny: "Wow, you really have a big Boston accent. That may come in handy someday."

Eddie: "Can't be helped. That's where I've lived."

Ronny: "No problem, we actually admire it. The guys were just talking about your accent this morning. Now, down to business; we have a warehouse to do. Your job will be the security guard. Meet me here tonight at midnight and we'll take off. Spitball and Cheech will be with us, Wimp will drive the truck"

Eddie: "Midnight, I'll be here."

Eddie left the club, got into his car and drove off. He drove quite a ways to a telephone booth until he was sure that no one was following. He telephoned Jack and Paul to advise them of what was going on. They said that they would be watching. They made an agreement that Eddie would call in nightly to whoever was on the dispatch. The code word would be "Chico".

Jack told Ernie that whoever answers the phone will say that this is "The Pizza House" and ask for the order. His reply would be "Chico". That would clear the line to talk. Eddie was further advised that there would usually be someone nearby watching his moves in the event that he needed help in a hurry.

Things were starting to pull together. Eddie was becoming a part of the Family and being accepted. The most important part of the operation was that he was respected by the other Family members, thanks to Tony Two Scoops.

Tony spoke of Eddie's plan and loved it. It was set up to protect the income by simply labeling everything as stock items with a code that represented the bets, yet appeared to be simple stock orders.

Tony, being the head of the gaming operations for the Family, ordered all of the offices to use this new code program that Eddie had set up.

The advantage to Eddie and his team was that Eddie, being the creator of the code, knew the code and how to break it. This would become a future advantage to the agencies working the case.

That night at midnight, Eddie showed up at the Calabria's Club to meet with the men for his first job.

Ronny was sitting at his table with the other men when Eddie entered the room.

Ronny: "Eddie, come on over, have a seat. Guys, Eddie will be taking care of the security guard."

Eddie: "I would like an opportunity to look over the situation before I make a decision as to how to handle the guard, is that acceptable?"

Ronny: "It's your baby; just take care of him so that we can get the stock emptied out. You'll have about fifteen minutes."

Eddie: "That should be plenty of time."

Ronny: "Ah, here's the Wimp. Hey, Wimp, you're driving."

Wimp: "No problem, Ronny."

Ronny: "Everyone else will be loading the truck with me. Once we're loaded we can get Eddie and take off to 2659 Knapp St., Brooklyn, our warehouse in Sheepshead Bay, where we'll unload. Everyone understand?"

The men all responded that they understood.

"I know you guys are packing, but, Eddie, do you have a gun?"

"Yeah, I have my own, a Glock- G17, 9 millimeters, thanks."

They all took off for the warehouse job.

About an hour later they arrived at the warehouse where Eddie looked over his part of the job. He observed the security guard walking the perimeter of the property and clocking in at the corners of the building.

"Ronny, how often does he do that, walk around the building?" asked Eddie

"Every hour" replied Ronny

"OK, I'll take care of him right now. No use in waiting another hour for him to make another run," stated Eddie.

Eddie snuck up to the fence, cut the chain link and crawled into the yard out of sight of the guard. As he got closer, he noticed that the guard was an older man about 65 years old. Eddie didn't want to take a chance of harming him. He called to him.

"Sir, can you help me?"

The old man heard the voice and looked over in Eddie's direction: "What are you doing here, boy. Don't you know this is private property? You'll have to leave."

"Yes, I understand." Eddie pulled his weapon and held the man at bay while he tied his hands behind his back. He then gave the OK to the rest of the organized crime family to go ahead with the job.

He turned to the old man: "Look, you stay here and nothing will happen to you. When the police arrive they will call federal agents, because this involves federal stamps. When they interview you, say that you heard the name 'Chico' and say no more until they explain."

"I'll do as you say, young man. Please, this is just a job for cheap pay to keep me busy in my retirement years. I'm not looking for any trouble."

"Good, just stay here until we're gone and remember 'Chico'.

Eddie joined the rest of the men in loading the truck with over four thousand cartons of cigarettes and then they left the area.

These cigarettes would sell in the stores for ten to twelve dollars a carton. The Family would sell them for five to eight dollars a carton. This was considered a good income for the Borgazino Family. This work, kept the soldiers busy selling the stock.

They drove to the warehouse in Sheepshead Bay and unloaded the cigarettes after which everyone left for the night agreeing that they would all meet at the club around noon on Saturday.

Eddie left the group and drove to a secluded phone booth. He telephoned Jack and Paul then reported everything that happened.

They arranged for the guard to be taken from the scene and filed the appropriate reports.

It was decided that Eddie would take a couple of hundred cartons to sell. The government would buy them to give him cover. This would make him look good within the Family.

***

Saturday August 5, 1978

At noon, Ronny walked into the Calabria's Club and joined Wheeze at his table.

"I assume it all went OK, Ronny?"

"Eddie did a good job. We went in, bada bing, bada bang and we left, Fugheddaboudit," stated Ronny.

"The product?" asked Wheeze.

"At the warehouse, where else?"

"The warehouse, what the fuck is it doing there? You have to move that shit and get rid of it. Get all the men together and load up their cars. Let me know how much each man takes and make sure they know that we get fifty percent of the take."

"Hey, Wheeze, what's going on? You don't usually get upset about the small shit like this. The cigarettes will be taken care of. What's wrong?"

"Ronny, I'll tell you, but for now we have to keep it quiet," replied Wheeze.

"OK, tell me maybe I can help."

"No, you can't. I think we have a rat. The info about the cigarettes was moving on the street as fast as you did the job. Someone is talking and I'll find out who it is. For now keep it quiet. We can trust Eddie as far as I'm concerned. He's new, from out of state; he came in highly recommended and has a good record, besides he doesn't know anyone but us here in New York."

"That's true and my cousin, Scar, is highly trustworthy. We can count him out, besides he's out of state and knows nothing about the cigarettes."

"We'll get to the bottom of this, give me some time," stated Wheeze.

"Wheeze, if we can trust Eddie, why don't we move him into a position where he can be used better?" asked Ronny.

"You're right, you can use him on your next trip to Florida and he'll be your assistant. You need someone with you. Right now, he's the only one I would trust."

"Great, I like the guy so it will be easy to work with him. He took care of that guard without firing a shot or even fighting with him; it was very interesting how he psyched the guard out."

"Yes, I heard from Spitball, he turned it into a funny story."

They spoke for a few minutes and Ronny saw Eddie walk into the club.

"Eddie, over here," yelled Ronny.

As Eddie walked past one of the tables, some of the men were playing the card game, Texas Hold-em. Spitball spoke to him and the other men: "Oh, there goes the doctor, the psychiatrist. You did some job psyching that guard, much better then burying him."

"Thanks, Spitball" replied Eddie as he joined Ronny.

"Hi, Ronny, how's it going?" asked Eddie.

"Fugheddaboudit," was the reply. "We'll do about ten grand for the family and ten grand that we'll split up, not bad."

"Not bad at all."

"Look, Eddie, we have a small problem."

Eddie looked up at Ronny: "What's the problem, maybe I can help?"

"I really can't say right now, but we're gonna use you in a higher position since we know that we can trust you. I want you to start off by running the cards games tonight and tomorrow night. It's an easy job; all you do is make decisions on any game question and collect the cash from the dealers."

"Where do I put the cash?"

"In the safe, I'll give you the combination before the day is out."

"No problem, Ronny, anything else that I can do?"

"Yes, you will be my right hand man for a while. We'll be going to Florida at the end of the month. You'll be working with me. This is to be kept between you and me."

"No problem, anything else?"

"Yeah, I'm gonna have some jobs come up that I may ask you to handle."

"Ronny, I don't mind at all, but what about the other guys? They have seniority over me and may take offense."

"Don't worry about them, I'll cover any problems. We need to do some looking into these guys and see who is talking to who. I've said enough for now. Keep that under your hat. I never told you that."

"What is it you New Yorkers say? Fugheddaboudit," Eddie smiled.

"Good," replied Ronny.

"Hey, I might be getting to be one of you guys. I used that word right I think?"

"Yeah, you used it right. You may become one of us more than you know right now."

"OK, Ronny, I'll cover the games this weekend."

"Good, see you Monday afternoon unless I decide to stop by and play for a while," stated Ronny.

"I'll take off and get ready for tonight," said Eddie

Ronny showed Eddie the safe and the combination so that he could store the cash. Eddie then left the club and drove off in his Cadillac.

He went directly to a remote phone and called for a meet with Jack, Paul and the team. Eddie was advised that the best location would be at Cross Bay Blvd. in Rockaway Beach, the parking lot of the Jamaica Bay Wildlife Refuge building, a remote area picked by Agent Paul Saunders. The meet was set for one hour later.

Eddie arrived at the location of the meeting and there were three other vehicles there with Jack and Paul in one vehicle. The other two had the cover teams in them.

Eddie joined Jack and Paul in their car while the other teams kept watch for anything and anyone that may be suspicious.

Ernie: "We may have a problem, guys."

Jack: "What happened?"

Ernie: "These guys have someone somewhere that's advising them about what you people know."

Paul: "What, are you kidding? Not any of my men."

Ernie: "I'm reading between the lines, but Ronny said that they trust me. They want to move me up and have to look into their own men and see who is talking to whom?"

Paul: "Who knows what they may have heard and misinterpreted."

Ernie: "The best part is that they trust me and I'm going to Florida as Ronny's partner at the end of the month."

Jack: "Sounds like someone may be talking to the wrong people. They may not even know it. We'll do some checking and maybe put out a story and see if it comes back."

Ernie: "If you do that, let's coordinate it so I know what to look or listen for."

Paul: "We'll do that and I have something for you. One of your Family members has already turned you in. He must be jealous. This report came in just yesterday."

Ernie: "Who is it?"

Jack: "I have the report right here. Spitball is his street name. His real name is Settimio (Spitball) Adamino a real piece of shit in my book."

Ernie: "Thanks for that, guys. I'll watch out for him. You look into who he's talking with. There may be some connection."

Jack: "Ernie, you know that I will never let that kind of a rock go unturned."

Ernie: "I know. I'll be working the card games this weekend. Do you guys have anything else, guys?"

Paul: "No, be safe, that's all."

Ernie left the car and took off in his Cadillac. The other men returned to their duties.

Chapter 15

Games

Saturday Night
August 5, 1978:

On his way to the card game, Ernie stopped to telephone Teresa, his wife. She was happy to hear from him
and he was even happier to hear her voice. Ernie told her
that he was going to try and get away sometime this week
and come home for a couple of days.

"Jack and I both want to get back home for a couple
of days."

"Just let me know when you're coming."

"I will. Is everything OK there?"

"Yeah, don't worry about me, I'm fine and everything is OK here."

"You have the number that I gave you and you know
the code; if you need me just let Jack or Paul know."

"I will, I don't know Paul, but I will ask for him if
Jack's not there."

"I'll have to introduce him to you, one day. He's a
nice guy. You can trust him."

"Ernie, please be careful."

"I will, I miss you. See you soon."

"I miss you also, bye."

They hung up the phones. Ernie promised himself
that this would be the last time that he would accept a
case so far away from home.

Eddie received instructions to be at the card game before seven in the evening so that he could set up. He was
there at 6:30 that night. Ronny showed him what was required and then left the club.

The night went quietly and the last game broke up at
four in the morning. Eddie put the money away in the
safe, locked up the club and went back to his lonely
apartment.

***

Sunday

As he left the apartment, that calm and quiet Sunday
morning, he stopped at the top of the steps. He looked
around; no mockingbird to hold a whistling symphony
with. He missed that bird. He missed his wife. He missed
home. He was getting lonely. He thought to himself that
he was going to have to find a way to clean this case up as
quickly as possible. He may have to be bolder then he
originally thought.

Eddie went over to see Tony Two Scoops' for breakfast. They spoke for a while as Eddie finished his meal.
Tony told Eddie that he had heard of the problem and was
advised that Eddie was the only one to be trusted at that
point.

"Why is that, why would they trust me? I would think
that they would suspect me since I'm the new guy."

"Normally, you would be right, but someone told the
feds about our recent delivery and about Ronny getting
shot. You weren't anywhere around during those things
so that clears you."

"I see. What happened to Ronny?"

"They had a thing that the Columbians requested and
paid top dollar to have completed. The New York Family
brought in a shooter from California. Ronny was cover

and took an ounce, he got scratched," stated Tony Two Scoops.

"Oh, I see he was in on a hit and got shot himself. We're not supposed to do that," stated Eddie.

"No, the asshole let the money sitting on the table distract him or so he says," stated Tony.

"That can happen to a beginner. It sounds like that card game thing that I read about in the newspapers last month," replied Eddie

"I've said enough in public, I have customers with big ears, but you hit the nail on the head. I heard it was an easy job. In my day, no one would have been hit. These young kids get distracted easily."

"Well, Tony, I'm happy to hear that I'm not suspected of anything. This is slowly becoming my home, I like it here," stated Eddie.

"We like having you here. I hear good things about you, Eddie."

As they spoke, a white male about 5'9" tall, 180 pounds, brown hair and brown eyes with a pair of eyeglasses balanced on his long nose, walked into Tony's shop. Eddie could only think of a TV personality from his younger years call Jimmy Durante and what he use to say when he ended his show: "Good night, Mrs. Calabash, wherever you are."

"Hey Nose, how are you? When did you get out?" asked Tony.

"Yesterday, Tony; how about some breakfast?"

"Sure. Come over here, sit down and meet our friend Eddie. Eddie, this is Eddie, The Nose. I'll get your breakfast," said Tony.

Eddie couldn't help it. Nose was younger and probably didn't know about Jimmy so he asked him.

"Nose, do you know who Mrs. Calabash is?" asked Eddie.

"Yeah, Yeah, I've heard all the jokes. He's a funny guy, Tony," said Nose.

"Nice to meet your nose; sorry, I couldn't resist a little ribbing," said Eddie as he laughed out loud.

"No problem. I'm used to it. She was his wife, wasn't she?" Nose and Tony joined him in the laughter.

"I always thought that Mrs. Calabash was his mother, but I could be wrong. Nice to meet you, Nose," replied Eddie.

"Same here," said Nose.

Tony suggested that she was Jimmy Durante's wife who had passed away and it was his way of honoring her.

"So you just got out? What did you do your stretch for and how long? That is if you don't mind telling me?" asked Eddie.

"No not at all. I did a drugstore – not for the drugs, although I did take a bunch. We did it for the safe and to help out a friend of mine. I got caught a block away with the drugs, stupid move for a guy with my experience."

"How long did you have to do?"

"I got a nickel, reduced to three and did one less good time of three months. Normal shit," stated Nose.

"So, you did nine months total. Well, nice to have you out. I gotta run. I'll see you later at the club," stated Eddie.

"See you then," replied Nose.

Because of the information that he just received, Eddie telephoned Jack and advised him of what he had learned.

Jack and Paul were happy about this discussion with Tony and made sure that a typist made a permanent record of the entire story.

After talking with the typist, Eddie decided that he should stop by the club.

Paul: "Ernie, I have some mini-microphones for you to place in the club and the lounge as you run around there tonight working the card game."

Ernie: "Good idea, I'll need four of them."

Paul: "Meet us at the same place and I'll give them to you. I'll also bring along the reports for you to sign"

That afternoon, Eddie drove over to the meeting place where he was given the micro pickups to be placed around the club and the lounge.

Paul: "Ernie, this guy Eddie the Nose is Edward Haronetti, aka Eddie the Nose. Everything he told you is correct, but there is a note in his file that he is a highly volatile person, be careful of him."

Ernie: "I will thanks."

That evening, Eddie went to the club where he saw Eddie the Nose sitting at one of the tables and waved to him.

Ronny: "Hey, Eddie, you know The Nose?"

Eddie: "No, not really, I was introduced this morning by Tony Two Scoops."

Ronny: "That's good. Nose is a good guy to have on your side. He can be trusted."

Eddie: "Good to know, thanks."

To Eddie, a statement like that, coming from Ronny, meant that Nose was a vicious person that would kill at any time, a common representation in the world of organized crime.

The night went well until about three in the morning.

Eddie had one table of players left and told them that at four he was closing down the room.

One of the men, a black male about 6 feet tall, well dressed with two gold teeth in the front of his mouth and a diamond earring, had been losing quite heavily. This male known only as George stood up from his seat. He didn't say a word. He simply threw his cards on the table, looked at Eddie and walked out of the club.

"He's pissed. He must have dropped two grand here, Eddie," said Spitball who was playing at the same table with George.

"He'll get over it," stated Eddie. They all laughed and joked for a moment when the door opened again.

Standing in the doorway was George with a pistol in his hand. He was pointing it at Eddie.

"George, what the fuck is wrong with you?"

"Nothing, but I don't want you to close at four. I need several hours to get my money back."

"You want your money back? I'm not here to kiss your ass; I have to get some rest. I've been going all day. You can play another night."

"No, I'm playen tonight. I'm getten my money back."

"What about the other guys? They wanna take a break, too. Tomorrow's another day and put that gun away before someone takes you serious."

The black man fired a shot and hit the floor right between Eddie's legs. "Is that serious enough for you, asshole," stated George.

Eddie looked at George and then at the other men who were remaining quiet, "What is it you guys say? George, don't get my Brooklyn up! Put the fucken gun down, right now."

"Or what will you do? I'm not done playen yet," replied George.

Eddie had been inching closer and closer to George as he and George spoke. He was now within reaching distance. George had a crazy type of glare in his eyes which indicated to Eddie that he was high on some drug, probably heroin. Eddie figured he could talk him out of the gun; if not he would be forced to take a chance.

"Now, George, you're a nice guy, everyone likes you. Why do you wanna destroy that friendship?" asked Eddie, trying to distract him to get into a better position to grab the gun.

"I don't give a fuck about anybody, I need that money. That money represents many more thousands to me," stated George.

Eddie could tell that Georges' mind was on one track, the money. He probably needed to buy more drugs. He needed to cut them and distribute them to others thereby making money as he served his own needs. George was a typical drug user.

Eddie was close enough, he started to speak to George in a clear, soft voice and then as he spoke he grabbed the .38 caliber handgun around the gun barrel stopping the barrel from turning and George from being able to fire the weapon.

He twisted the gun and a shot went off which forced George to let go of the gun. Eddie now had control of the weapon.

The men were watching to see what Eddie would do.

Eddie moved so fast that that all the viewers could see was a blur. He grabbed the gun and slapped George across the head with it, then punched George in the face a couple of times. A few body shots and George went down hard.

Eddie figured that he had put on enough of a show for the men in the room.

"Take this piece of shit out and throw him in the alley," Eddie directed the instructions to Spitball.

"Hey Eddie, he's gonna be pissed in the morning. You sure you don't want me to take him apart and drop him in the bay or the junk yard?" asked Spitball.

"No, he's a good customer, he'll be OK. We can always do that if needed," replied Eddie.

"Hey, Cheech, help me out here." Cheech and Spitball moved George into the alley and threw him into a puddle of dirty water that was leaking from the sewer pipe coming out of the building.

"He deserves that shit after doing something like that," stated Cheech as he laughed at George laying there with his clothes all covered with brown, dirty water.

"I hope the fuck he drowns," said Spitball as they both returned to the club.

"I guess the night is over?" said Spitball.

"You bet your ass it is. I'll hold this gun until he comes back and begs for it," stated Eddie

Eddie cleaned up, put the cash away and placed the mini microphones in various areas, after everyone left the building. He then locked up and went home for the night.

When he arrived at the apartment, he telephoned Teresa.

"Is everything OK, Ernie?" asked Teresa.

"Yeah, all is well. I had a small incident that shook me up a little. I wanted to speak with you because you're the only one that has the voice that can calm me down. Your voice relaxes me. I know it's late, but I had to speak with you."

"That's OK, I don't mind. I'm happy to hear from you."

Ernie spoke with his wife for a while before he hung up the phone. He felt better after he spoke with her. He always did. His wife Teresa was his rock.

***

Monday August 7, 1978:

Eddie stopped in at Tony Two Scoops' around noon for coffee and toast, where he met with Nose and Spitball.

"Hey Eddie, we were just talking about you. Let's go in the back so that we can talk without anyone hearing us," stated Spitball.

They all walked into the back room where Tony had a table that the Family men used.

"Eddie, we have a deal going at the airport. Nose has a guy inside that handles all of the lost merchandise. He turns over to us all that he gets every month or so and does the paperwork with names from the phone book."

"Sweet deal, but how much do you get in cash?" asked Eddie.

"We take them down to Sheepshead Bay. We have a boat there, we go through them and get all kinds of good stuff; jewelry, cash, gold and precious jewels as well as once in a while we find some antiques, then we deep six the junk" stated Nose.

"So why do you want me?" asked Eddie.

"Let's face it, Eddie. Joey Bats and Wheeze like you. They're always talking about how much of a good soldier you are. The closer you get to them the better off your friends are. We want to be your friends. That's why we're making this offer for you to come in with us on this," stated Nose.

"What do I have to do?" asked Eddie.

"The same thing you did at the cigarette warehouse, distract the guard" said Spitball

"OK, I'm in," replied Eddie.

"Good, we'll leave from here right after breakfast," stated Nose.

***

They went to the airport. Spitball had a special pass to get in through the service entrance. He said that he obtained the pass from his connection who worked at the air port. They drove through the gate and up to the back of one of the baggage doors.

Nose: "Eddie, do you see that guy standing over by the door, the grey-haired guy?"

Eddie: "Yeah, I see him."

Nose: "He's the security. Go and take his mind off of what we're doing while we load this stuff."

Eddie: "You got it."

Eddie exited the vehicle and walked over to the security guard and asked him if he saw a clipboard with the name Chico on it. This guy will make a good witness at a later date as long as he remembers that he was asked about the clipboard and the name Chico.

Eddie went into this long discussion about how he was taking the numbers off of the runways and needed that clipboard to keep track of what he was doing. The security guard walked around with him, looking for the mystery clipboard.

After a while, Eddie saw that Spitball and Nose were in the truck. They were ready to leave. He thanked the guard for his help and told him that he would have to start his work all over in a week or so. Eddie left the area of the guard. He joined Nose and Spitball as they drove off.

They drove to Sheepshead Bay, the back section that is mostly all marsh and a couple of boat slips.

"We'll unload the baggage into that 22 foot Larson," stated Nose, as he pointed to the boat.

"What the fuck do we need a boat for?" asked Eddie.

"We take the boat out a mile or so and as we go through the baggage and finish with it, we throw the remaining junk overboard," stated Nose.

"Who the fuck ever thought this one up?" asked Eddie.

"I did," replied Nose, "You like it?"

"I love it. This is beautiful," replied Eddie.

As they were loading the boat, Eddie noticed that this boat was an obvious fishing boat, with fishing rods in the holders and all the gear needed to go fishing, a perfect cover.

They found jewelry, gold, silver and two thousand in cash with some small items that could be sold to a hock shop.

They returned to the boat slip and Eddie left the area while Nose and Spitball took the items found to a fence.

"Eddie, is a grand enough for now? We'll give you the rest of your end after we sell everything," asked Spitball.

Eddie: "Sure, that's fine with me. I'll see you guys at the club."

Eddie left and telephoned Jack to let him know what had happened.

"Man, am I glad to hear from you. We lost you and didn't know where the hell you were. I was worried."

"Wait until you hear this one," stated Ernie as he began to tell Jack what happened.

Jack put another typist on the line with Ernie to get the report down in writing.

When they were finished, Eddie told Jack that he would be meeting with Ronny and that he (Jack) should start getting all of the reports and criminal records together with the New York Police and start doing affidavits.

"Look into everything and get together with the district attorney. Find out what he needs, or what questions he may have. You know what to have him check for," Ernie told Jack.

"We'll take care of it, Ernie," stated Jack.

"Can we meet somewhere for a quick moment? I want to give you this gun that I took away from George."

"OK I'll meet you on Grand Ave by your apartment and just take the gun." stated Jack.

"In ten minutes," stated Ernie.

They met and spoke for a few more minutes, making plans to go home for the weekend. After Jack left the area, Eddie headed for the club.

Later, Eddie walked into the club. Sitting with Spitball and Cheech was George. He immediately rose from his seat upon seeing Eddie walk in. He walked towards Eddie with his arm out to shake: "Eddie, I'm very sorry. I must have been high as a kite and went a little crazy. Thank God you stopped me."

"That's OK, George, but I didn't expect to see you. How do you feel?"

"As long as there are no hard feelings, I'm fine. I would like to ask you if you have my gun for me?" asked George.

"You're gonna have to swim for it, George," replied Eddie.

"What are you saying, Eddie. I don't understand?"

"George, after I closed the club, I went down to the Kent Street ship yard last night. I went to one of the docks and dropped the gun over the side. It's in thirty feet of salt water now. I didn't want to carry it with me. Who knows what the fuck you did with that gun," stated Eddie.

"Ah, shit. That's OK, I was gonna get rid of that piece anyway. I've used it too many times already. You did me a favor. Look, there are no hard feelings are there? I want us to be friends," stated George.

"No hard feelings, George, but just do me a favor and leave the guns home in the future."

"I will, Eddie, I promise," stated George.

"Yeah, I've heard that one before," Spitball said, laughing with Cheech.

"Hey, Eddie, come on in here," called Ronny, from across the room, signaling for Eddie to come into the office.

Eddie entered the office where Wheeze and Ronny were talking: "How's everything going, guys?"

"Eddie, have a seat. We're just trying to figure out how many guys named Eddie come in here to play cards and hang out. We have four that play cards, you and Eddie The nose. That makes a total of six men. Can you think of anyone else?"

Eddies mind started spinning with thoughts that someone tipped them off about the investigation. Eddie would have to be cool and stupid. He may be making his last statement:

"No, that's all that I know about, but you know this place better then I. What happened?" asked Eddie.

"We're getting info on a guy named Eddie. We don't know much. Our guy in the FBI is trying to get more, but he's having a hard time. There's something about a ship full of drugs, also. Does that mean anything to you?" asked Wheeze.

Eddie looked at Wheeze shaking his head negative: "No, I don't know anything about any ships of drugs."

"I didn't think you did, I'm just bouncing some thoughts off of you. You seem to have a good mind and I'm trying to take advantage of it," stated Wheeze.

"Sorry, Wheeze, obviously if I was a cop or something like that, I wouldn't make any statements anyway. I can assure you that you have no worries with me. Keep one thing in mind; those feds use code names for everything. If anyone is talking, you can bet your ass that he has a code name which makes the name Eddie a code name," stated Eddie.

"You see, Ronny, I told you he has a good mind, I never thought of that point. Besides, I trust him. He saved my ass that night, remember?" asked Wheeze.

"Yes, I do. I forgot about that," replied Ronny.

"The only ship that was taken, that I know of, was in Boston somewhere, but I understand that they caught the guys involved. Our guy in the FBI didn't look into that one because it was so far away and no connection to us that he knew of," stated Wheeze.

"I'm from that area," stated Eddie. I know a lot of people up there."

"Eddie, why don't you go up there next week? Wait a minute." Wheeze turned to Ronny, "When is that meet on the delivery, Ronny?" asked Wheeze.

196 -   Ernie Lijoi, Sr.

"We meet at the house on August twenty-fourth at about ten in the morning," replied Ronny.

"Good, Eddie, do you think you could find anything out if you went up there?"

"Who knows? All I can do is give it a shot."

"OK, take your time, nose around a bit for us. Here's two grand, your end of the cigarettes deal. Go up there and look around ask questions and see what you can find out. Take a few days," directed Wheeze.

"I'll do that, no problem. I can stop by and see some of my ladies as well," added Eddie.

Eddie left the office and went out into the main card room where Cheech, Spitball, Nose and Wimp were playing some cards and talking about the recent jobs that they did. They were figuring out how much cash they all had coming.

"You guys are always talking business. Take a break, I am. I'm going on a little trip to relax and recuperate," stated Eddie.

"Recuperate? Did George scare you that much?" stated Cheech as he laughed.

"Very funny Cheech, ha, ha, ha, no, I have a small job to do for Wheeze."

"Oh, what's up?" asked Nose.

"Nose, you certainly have the correct name. You'll have to ask Wheeze. I can't talk about it. You guys know that," answered Eddie.

They went back to talking and playing cards. Eddie walked out of the club. He was happy that he was walking out instead of being carried out of the building through the back door alleyway.

"Hey, Eddie, hold up a minute," yelled Ronny.

Ronny joined Eddie and they went into the Lounge. Ronny asked Eddie to join him for a cup of coffee so that they could make plans for the trip to Florida.

They discussed the trip and agreed to leave on the twenty=third of the month. Leaving on that date would place them in the Florida home a day early.

"Ronny, what do we have to do in Florida? No one mentioned anything."

"We meet the Columbian connection. Wheeze has a lot of confidence in you. He wants you with me because he believes that between the two of us, we can handle any situation that may arise."

"I see. Thanks for the opportunity."

"Hey it's Wheeze's decision, not mine. I would take Spitball or one of the guys that have been here for a while, but he's the boss under Joey Bats. I don't mind taking you, but you're new and they deserve a break. You still have a lot to learn," stated Ronny.

"I understand, Ronny."

After they talked, Eddie left the area and immediately telephoned Jack.

"Jack, we have a problem. They suspect some guy named Eddie, but they don't know exactly who Eddie is. Their connection is an FBI agent, or so they say, he is the man supplying Joey and Wheeze with the information. The question is, amongst others, is the rat, a rat knowingly or not and that is unknown at this time."

"That's strange because the report that we had the other day was from the FBI. That report went through the hands of three different civilian assistants, all of whom initialed the information as they handled it. That's the procedure used for evidence that may be submitted to the court one day."

"Yes, I understand and I believe that you should ask Paul to pull the telephone records of those three people and check them against the telephone records of Wheeze as well as Joey Bats." Ernie said.

"We already have Joey's and Wheeze's phone records. We will get the others and compare them," stated Jack.

"No, not you, we're going home for a few days. Ask Paul to do it. Wheeze wants me to check into what's going on up there. That will give you, Scar and me a chance to get back for a few days," stated Ernie.

"Ernie, that's great, but they may be setting you up in some way. I think that this case may be getting too dangerous for you. They're bound to put two and two together sooner or later," stated Jack.

"We'll discuss it as we drive home. We'll figure something out," replied Ernie.

"Wait a minute. They just put the analysis from the test firing on George's gun, the one that you gave me, on my desk. Let me look it over real quick," said Jack.

"Ernie, you just solved two murders. That asshole shot two different people. We have two bodies with holes in them. One was about a year ago and one three months ago. They're both dead, the gun that you turned in is the murder weapon."

"Wow, bring a copy of that report with you. Maybe you should bring everything that you can so that I can read them during the next couple of days. Give someone the job of placing George at the scene of those murders or in the cities anyway. Wait, maybe we should have the DA review it first"

"I will, where do you want to meet?"

"OK, meet me at that same meeting area where we met before, in one hour and we'll take off with the Cadillac."

"Agreed"

Chapter 16

Home

That Afternoon

They were on the road home. Eddie was excited about seeing Teresa again and Jack about seeing his family. Scar was happy to be out of jail.

"Scar, you've been with Jack. I assume that you're aware of our predicament?" asked Ernie.

"Which ones; the family that now thinks they know who you are? The questions about the ship full of drugs in Boston? The dead bodies, which were killed with George's gun? Or the Florida trip? You guys seem to get yourself into more shit then we do."

"Yeah, you're right, but we do it for a better reason," stated Ernie.

"I guess cash isn't enough for your type," said Scar.

"Scar, any suggestions?" asked Ernie.

"Fuck them, don't tell them nothing," replied Scar.

"No, Scar, you know I can't do that. The first thing that would happen is they will start looking deeper, without me as a buffer. Eventually they'll find you and your cousin. What do you think they will do to the two of you?" asked Ernie.

"Yes, I guess you're right, but I don't know what to say," stated Scar.

"Let's think on it for a while, guys, and we'll meet and talk about it again on Monday morning. I'll call you both then and we'll get together to start back to New York," stated Ernie.

Jack and Scar agreed

"Jack, did you bring that file on George?" asked Ernie,

"Yes, I have it here." As he offered it to Ernie.

Ernie took the file and read that George was actually George Studs, a black male about 6 feet tall, well dressed with two gold teeth in the front of his mouth, a diamond earring stud, black hair and brown eyes.

"He's one guy that will not be selling any more poison to anybody," stated Jack.

"Nor will he be placing any unneeded holes in anyone, once we're finished with him," replied Ernie.

Scar jumped into the conversation. "I knew him when we were kids and he was an angry guy then. This doesn't surprise me about him. You must remember it was probably business hits that he did. Strictly business, that's all."

"That's good to know, Scar," stated Jack.

The ride home seemed to take a long time. They finally arrived and dropped Scar off at his car. Then Jack and Ernie went home.

***

Ernie and his wife went to the camp for the weekend. They had a great time relaxing, eating at the camp, going out for dinner and enjoying each other's company.

"How long will you be able to stay at home, Ernie?"

"I will be here for a few days and then I must go back."

"How much longer will this case take?"

"I'm hoping that we will be able to close down the operation within a month."

"That's good. It gets lonely at home. Thank God I have my sisters and friends."

"I know, Teresa, I'll do the best I can to finish this up and get back home permanently."

The weekend was quiet and peaceful. Ernie fished, Teresa cooked some of the fish and on Sunday afternoon they returned to their home in Massachusetts.

***

Monday morning, as Ernie left the house, he heard his old friend the mockingbird. He smiled and returned the music. He had missed that bird and spent a few minutes with him whistling back and forth.

Ernie drove off to pick up Jack. Together they picked up Scar and began the three-hour drive to Brooklyn, New York.

"So, did you guys think about what we can say when we get back and I talk to Joey Bats?" asked Ernie.

Scar: "I have no idea. Just keep me the fuck out of it."

Jack: "Ernie, don't tell me that you didn't come up with two or three different scenarios?"

Ernie: "Yes, I have a few ideas, but they all start with nothing."

Jack: "I understand; you want to say you learned nothing and go with their responses?"

Ernie: "Yeah, that seems to feel like the best way to go right now."

Scar: "You're a sneaky guy, Ernie. I like it."

Ernie: "I hope it works. We'll see, I'm sure of that."

That afternoon they arrived in Brooklyn, where they had a meeting with Agent Paul Saunders and his team.

They were directed to a large conference room where they all had some coffee and sat around discussing the case.

Jack: "What happened over the weekend, Paul?"

Paul: "I was just about to tell you guys that there has been some unpleasant information coming in."

Ernie: "What happened?"

Paul:" We traced the telephone calls from Joey Bats to a pay phone in New York City near the Federal Building, which wasn't any real help in and of itself."

Ernie: "Did you follow up on that information?"

Paul: "Yes, we decided to sit on the phone and we took pictures of everyone that used the phone booth."

Jack: "Were you able to identify anyone?"

Paul: "You're gonna like this. Only one guy that used the phone to make calls was present when the phone rang. He answered the phone. He's a civilian assistant that does statistics for the department. He sees all of the reports that are generated. We're gonna have to fix this problem. Effective today we're moving him into a different job until this case is over."

Ernie: "Why?"

Paul: "Why? Are you kidding?"

Ernie: "No, let's leave him there and feed him info that we want them to know. We move him and they will get suspicious."

Paul: "Yes, you have a point there. I can place someone before him as a buffer to screen out the true shit and feed him what we want."

Jack: "That's the best way to go. We saw this happen once before and they took the guy out immediately. That made things worse. This is the best way."

Paul: "I agree and that's what we'll do. I'll speak with my boss and we'll do what is necessary to make this plan work"

Jack: "Did you get anything from the bugs that Ernie placed?"

Paul: "That's the other thing I wanted to discuss. I think they may believe that Eddie is Ernie or that he is a rat. We're not getting all of the conversations so it's a little hard to be certain of everything."

Ernie: "What makes you think that they know who I am?"

Paul: "We heard some conversation about the ship you grabbed in Boston and the people that were connected to it."

Jack: "They know about Scar?"

Paul: "They seem to know that he was connected to it and was arrested, but they can't tie Eddie in directly, not yet anyway. They know that Eddie was brought in by Scar."

Ernie: "Scar, did you hear that?"

Scar: "Yeah I heard that. Fuck them. They ain't gonna fuck with me. They'll start a fucken war and they don't need that kind of heat."

Ernie: "I have an idea, but I don't want to do anything to jeopardize Scar's life."

Scar: "What do you have in mind?"

Paul: "Yeah, what's on that mind of yours? I've heard that you come up with some great ideas."

Ernie: "I think that I should tell them, in a way that shows how amazed I am, that Scar was one of the people that were picking up the drugs when the ship was busted."

Paul: "Yeah and what will that do?"

Ernie: "I'll claim no knowledge. Paul, you said that they haven't tied me to the ship. I'll be innocently giving them Scar as a suspect. He's been away all this time so they'll discount him. They should place some trust in me because I'm being honest with them and they'll know it. Joey Bats and his crew will have to look somewhere else. It should work."

Jack: "You know, Ernie, we've been working together a long time. You never cease to amaze me with these scenarios that always seem to work out in our favor. Guys, I believe him and I believe it will work."

Paul: "We'll take care of Scar and give him a new identity if necessary."

Scar: "What are you guys worried about? They will all be in jail and nobody is gonna fuck with me, don't worry about me."

Paul: "Scar, you would be better off in protective custody with a new ID, but it's up to you to decide and we will honor your decision. You can decide at any time to go into a program and we'll get you into a good one."

Scar: "I appreciate that, but I'm not worried about these guys. I'll be in Massachusetts three states away. They won't bother me."

Paul: "OK, just remember that you have the option."

Scar:" I appreciate that. I appreciate what you guys are doing for me right now. Just keep me out of jail and I'll be safe. Don't worry, I can protect myself."

Jack: "We'll do the best we can for you, Scar. Don't worry."

Ernie: "Yes, I agree, Scar. We can't make any guarantees. Your attorney explained that, but we will do all we can and thank you for understanding our position on this."

Scar: "Look, I can give a fuck less about your position here. I just want to stay out of jail."

Ernie:" We appreciate the fact that you are, in reality, placing your life on the line for this case by not opposing what we want to do. You have the right to oppose this aspect of the operation. I want to be sure that you understand that."

Scar: "I ain't fucken stupid. I understand and I don't care. Believe me, they won't touch me."

Jack: "OK, Scar, but we're going to draw up a short document containing the important points and have you sign it so that we have it on record. This is for everyone's protection."

It was agreed. Paul had the document drawn up by one of the men in the legal department and Scar signed, with Ernie, Jack and Paul as witnesses.

Paul: "Just remember you can always go into protection."

Scar: "Yeah, yeah, I understand."

The meeting broke up and Eddie (Ernie) went back to his apartment in Brooklyn. The next day Eddie would go to the Calabria's Social Club to speak with Joey Bats and Wheeze.

***

Tuesday August 8, 1978

Eddie went to breakfast at the luncheonette belonging to Tony Two Scoops. Eddie went there for more than just breakfast. He wanted to see how Tony reacted to his presence. His reaction would give Eddie an idea of what to expect from the men at the club.

"Hi, Tony, what's new with you?"

"Oh, hi Eddie, nothing, all is OK," Tony replied coldly, instead of in his friendly talkative way.

Eddie felt that he was getting a cold shoulder. He knew that Tony would normally be friendlier. This was not good. He had breakfast and went over to the club.

As he walked in, he saw a couple of men sitting at a table. He said hi to them and they simply replied with a hi.

Eddie walked into Wheeze's office and stood just inside the doorway as Wheeze finished up on the telephone. Wheeze signaled for him to come in closer and take a seat.

Wheeze: "We've been waiting for you to get back."

Eddie: "Joey didn't seem to be worried about how long I took."

Wheeze: "Yeah, that's right, but he wants to talk with you. No matter what happens, remember that you and I are friends, but business is business."

Eddie: "What the fuck happened? Did I fuck up somehow?"

Wheeze: "I'll let Joey answer that, after we all talk. Follow me."

Eddie followed Wheeze into the office of Joey Bats.

Joey: "Eddie, I'm glad that you're back. I wanted to speak with you."

Eddie: "I'm here. Speak with me. I don't understand Wheeze's attitude. I get the impression that I fucked up somewhere."

Joey: "Maybe not. What did you learn in Massachusetts?"

Eddie: "I have some bad news. I'm sorry to have to tell you this, but Scar was arrested. I didn't know anything about it. I guess he had a delivery of a shipload of drugs and got busted by the Fed's and local cops. He was one of the recipients of the load."

Joey: "You didn't know anything about this?"

Eddie: "No, he never said anything. Why should he, it's not my business. I was too involved with my own problems to notice anything in the papers. He never said a word."

Joey looked at Wheeze: "Maybe we should be looking at Scar?"

Wheeze: "He wasn't here for anything and he knew nothing about what was going on. He may be an error and we don't want to start a war by killing the wrong guy. I need more proof."

Eddie: "Guy's, I don't know exactly what you're talking about, but if you think Scar is a rat, I think you're all wrong. Why wouldn't he have turned me in, instead of helping me to get established here?"

Joey: "Good point. Don't worry, Eddie. You brought back the right answers. You're in the clear for now."

Eddie:" Thanks, Joey. Do you guys need me to do anything?"

Wheeze: "Get together with Ronny. You two are going on that trip we discussed."

Joey: "Wheeze, I told you, I don't want you discussing that shit in front of me, with anyone. Direct these guys when you're away from me."

Wheeze: "Sorry, Joey. Eddie, we'll talk outside."

Wheeze and Eddie walked out of the room and Eddie was told to meet up with Ronny and get set for the trip to Florida.

Eddie left the club telling Wheeze that he was heading home and would be by the club that night to play some cards.

***

That night at about eight o'clock, Eddie walked into the Old Mark Lounge and stood at the bar with Spitball and Cheech. A few minutes later Nose walked in and they all sat together. A few girls came over to the table. One of the girls was with another man until Nose walked in. Her name was Jeanie Reva, a while female, 5'5" tall, very well built with red hair, blue eyes and skin that was as light as snow, all of this added up to a beautiful woman of twenty seven years of age. She saw Nose walk in and she walked away from the guy buying her drinks and joined Nose by sitting on his lap.

Sitting at the table was Nose, his girl Jeanie, Spitball and a girl friend, Cheech and Eddie with several girls hanging around the table, listening to the conversation and kidding around.

These extra girls were always there looking to join the big men in the Brooklyn area most of whom were sitting at that table.

The man that was with Jeanie didn't care for the fact that she just walked off without saying anything and was now sitting on Nose's lap.

He walked over to her and tried to speak with her.

"Jeanie, if you wanted to be with this guy, why didn't you say something? I've been buying you drinks all afternoon. I thought that we had something going."

Nose stopped her as she was starting to tell the guy to go fuck himself. "Don't say that, Jeanie. That doesn't sound nice coming from a lady. Hey buddy, go fuck yourself and get the fuck outta here."

The guy's face turned red. He grabbed Nose by the shoulder and tried to lift him to swing at him.

Nose pulled out his gun and fired a shot into the guy. The gun went off and he went down. Spitball and Cheech stood up, from the table, and began kicking the guy because he was still moving. Eddie sat there and yelled at them in an attempt to save the guys life.

The entire place went quiet. People got up from their tables and walk away others walked out from the bar area to look and then walked out of the door. Some people were just standing there watching the men kick the guy on the ground.

Eddie could hear one patron comment, "This is getting crazy. These guys do whatever the hell they want."

Another answered him, "You gonna stop them?"

The first man never replied, he simply walked out of the lounge.

There were two girls standing there watching and they seemed to enjoy seeing Spitball, Cheech and Nose kicking the guy.

Eddie yelled, "He's had enough. I think you killed the asshole."

"Yeah, Eddie, I think you're right," stated Spitball, laughing as he spoke.

"Eddie grab your car and meet us in the alley," instructed Nose.

Eddie went and got his car. He pulled into the alley and they loaded the body into the trunk.

"Head down towards the shipyard, there's a junkyard in the back. We'll bury him there," stated Nose.

"Hey, Nose, now we have to bury this fuck. You cause more work for us than anything else. This is the third time with that same broad," commented Spitball.

Eddie looked in the rear view mirror at Spitball, who was sitting in the back seat with Cheech. "Yeah, Spitball, but you were kicking the shit out of the guy, just like everyone else."

"I didn't say I didn't have fun. It's the work that I don't like. All that digging," replied Spitball.

They came upon a fence and Nose got out of the car to unlock the gate. They entered the junkyard.

Nose directed Eddie to the far back side of the yard. As they drove, Eddie noticed that all of the cars and pieces of steel were piled up to look like small hills. They came to an area where there were about 100 cars, all small Volkswagens and small cars with no wheels; they were all rusted out. Some of them sat on the ground in what appeared to be a ditch. In most cases, the bottoms of the cars were below ground level. The cars were not piled up. They were set up in a parked position next to each other with about fifteen feet on each side of each car in long rows.

"Here we are. Drive over to that small red rusty Volkswagen and back up to the front of it," directed Nose.

Eddie did as directed and backed the car up to the red rusty Volkswagen. The men exited the vehicle and Nose directed everyone to lift the Volkswagen and place it on its side.

Eddie: "That car's too heavy to roll over."

Nose: "No it's not; the engine is out of it. They take the engines apart and sell the parts. I used to work here."

The men all got on one side and rolled the Volkswagen easily, so that it only went onto its side.

Two of the men grabbed pieces of steel and began digging a shallow grave. They opened Eddie's trunk and took out the body, threw it into the grave and covered it up.

Cheech: "Go over to that Chevy. In the back are a few bags of lime. Grab some and throw it over this guy. That'll take care of him after we put the Volkswagen back in place."

Eddie: "Nice set up, Nose."

Nose: "Yeah, when I started working with the family, I came in here and set these cars up. Everyone uses this area. Anytime you need it, the key to the gate is in the club."

Eddie: "The owner has no objections?"

Nose: "He did at one time. Do you see that rusty blue Volvo over there?"

Eddie: "Yeah, I see it."

Nose: "He's sleeping peacefully. He signed all this over to me before he went to sleep."

Eddie: "Then you own all this?"

Nose: "Of course, I couldn't let it go to waste."

Eddie: "He didn't have a family?"

Nose: "Yes he did. His wife is now my favorite girl. She thinks he left her. She thinks that he took off after selling me this business and property. I take care of her and pay her a specific amount every month in exchange for her running the place."

Eddie: "Do you make any money on this place?"

Nose: "Yeah, I make about three grand a month after she pays everything. You're awful curious, Eddie. Why is that?"

Eddie: "I'm new around here. I want to know what my assets are and understand them."

Spitball: "That's logical. I can understand that."

Cheech: "Me too."

Nose: "I guess."

Eddie: "Fugheddaboudit."

Nose: "Yeah, let's go and have drink. I'm bushed after all this work."

The rest of the night went quietly and there was no trouble; they had been through enough for one night.

Ronny never showed up at the lounge or the club. Eddie would see him the next day.

***

An hour had passed since Eddie and the family planted the body. Eddie left the club as soon as he could and called Jack. He had Jack and the teams meet him at the junkyard gate with some tools to open the gate lock.

They entered the yard, turned over the Volkswagen and pulled out the body. The man was not completely covered with dirt, but a bunch of lime went flying into the air as they pulled him out of the shallow hole. Nose had counted on the vehicle to hide the body. The man was still alive, but in a coma. The doctor at the hospital stated that he would have died within a couple of hours had Eddie not come back with the team.

They checked his wallet and found that the guy was a Walter Wintell of Huntington, Long Island. According to his papers, he had a wife and three kids. Jack went with the New York Police to contact his family and explain that he would have to be kept in protective custody.

"Jack, don't mention the girls unless you actually must do it," requested Ernie.

"No, no I won't mention anything more than is necessary. We may never need his testimony, why destroy his married life," Jack replied

Eddie left the area and went home to clean up.

Chapter 17

Vermin

Wednesday August 9, 1978

Eddie got out of bed around eleven in the morning and went down to Tony Two Scoops' place to have breakfast. He also wanted to see if Tony's reaction had changed. He was hoping that his meeting with Joey and Wheeze the previous day had cleared the air.

Tony: Eddie, how are you? Let me get you some breakfast. I heard that you guys had some fun last night."

Eddie: "Yeah, we took a short trip because Nose got a little embarrassed."

Tony: "Yeah, shit happens, what are you gonna do? How are things going with you?"

Eddie: "I'm doing fine. No problems that I know of."

Tony: 'Good, enjoy your breakfast. I have a customer to take care of."

Eddie looked at the customer. It was Jack, who sat down and ate breakfast at another table. He did not speak with Eddie, but he did give Eddie the eye to meet him later. Eddie nodded back in the affirmative.

Eddie finished his breakfast and left the restaurant. He sat in his car and waited for Jack to come out. Jack took off in his car and Eddie followed him to the area where they usually meet.

"What's up, Jack?"

"Ernie, we may have a problem," replied Jack.

"I just fixed the other problem. Now we have another one? What is it?"

"We're hearing conversation where they say that they're still not one hundred percent convinced that you are the not the man or working for him," stated Jack

"I thought that we got that all straightened out?" replied Ernie.

"We loved what you said. We heard the entire conversation and you did a good job, but that civilian keeps telling them that the guy's name is Eddie."

"Then why don't you feed him the name Eddie with an indication that it's a code name and not the real name?"

"Yeah, we're trying that now, but I wanted to make sure that you were aware of what's going on, in case they don't buy it."

"I appreciate that, Jack, thank you. If you guys set it up right I should be OK, if not, well, I can't live forever."

"Shit, don't say that. I know you're only joking, but how would I do these cases without you?" said Jack with a smile.

"Jack, by the way, no one told me the name of this guy, the civilian that's talking to Joey Bats?"

"Oh, I think we all thought that you read it in the reports. Sorry, his name is Leonardo Paloma; he is a 28 year old Italian male. He's working that desk because he can read and write in Italian and Spanish, in case anything of interest comes through, he would normally translate."

"Thanks, I'll keep my ears open. You never know when someone may slip with the name or a connecting name," replied Ernie

"Yeah, so far we haven't tied him into the family on a blood level, but you never know"

"OK, I'll keep my eyes and ears open."

"Good luck, Ernie."

"Thanks."

Ernie left the area and headed to the club.

As he entered the club, everyone seemed much friendlier then the day before. They were all talking about all kinds of jobs that they were working on. Nose wanted Eddie to join him next week to do the airport again.

Eddie agreed and kept walking back towards the offices of Joey and Wheeze. He saw Ronny standing in Wheeze's office doorway and walked over.

"Hi, Wheeze. Ronny, sorry I missed you last night. We got a little busy in the lounge."

"Yeah, I heard," stated Ronny as he laughed.

"Yeah, I heard about that. This shit is gonna have to stop. We're getting a bad reputation in the area. Ronny, talk to Nose, tell him that we want this shit stopped. We don't need the heat, especially with this load coming up that you two will be setting up," stated Wheeze

"I don't want to be disrespectful, Wheeze, but can you tell me anymore about what we're gonna do in Florida?" asked Eddie

"Ronny can fill you in, but you and I have to talk again, later."

"No problem, just let me know when," replied Eddie.

Ronny and Eddie left the office. They went to Tony Two Scoops' place. Ronny wanted to have a cup of coffee and sit quietly to talk about the upcoming trip to Florida.

As they walked through the Old Mark Lounge which was connected to the Calabria's Social Club, Eddie asked if Ronny would rather stay there and talk.

"No, let's go over to Tony's place."

As they exited the lounge and stepped onto the street, a series of shots began to ring out. The wall, door and window of the lounge were shot out and covered with bullet holes. Eddie hit the ground and Ronny stood there frozen.

Eddie grabbed Ronny's arm and pulled him down. They crawled to the parked cars on the street to use them as cover. The area became silent, as quiet as a mouse.

Men started coming out of the lounge from the club. No one understood what was going on.

Joey Bats came out, looked around and then looked at Wheeze.

"Wheeze, anything happen lately, anything different any arguments or fights?"

"Just that guy the other night, Nose had a run in with a guy who's in the junkyard right now, but that's over and should be settled."

"Yeah, you told me about that one," stated Joey as he stood there deep in thought: "Maybe this is some retaliation?"

"Let's go inside. Spitball, get someone to clean this shit up before the cops get here."

"OK, Boss."

Wheeze, Ronny, Eddie and Joey Bats went into Joey's office.

"Look, I told you that I didn't want any more rough play in the club or the lounge," Joey stated to Wheeze.

Wheeze: "I've told the guys. I think they understand that we don't want the heat."

Joey: "Stop me if I'm wrong. We're clean with the other families. Our dealers are happy. The suppliers are happy, we owe no money. I can't see any other problem, except that thing with Nose."

Wheeze: "I'll find out. I'll put Eddie and Ronny on it right away."

Joey: "You know, Wheeze, that guy Nose is a fucken thorn in our side. This is not the first time he's fucked up against our orders or wishes."

Wheeze: "Yeah, you're right."

Joey: "OK, take care of this, find out who did it and why."

Eddie: "We will, Joey."

Ronny: "You can count on us."

Eddie: "One question. Once we find out who and why, what do you want us to do?"

Joey: "Just let Wheeze know, that's all for now. We'll decide what to do after we're sure of who it is."

Eddie; "OK, you're the boss."

Ronny and Eddie left the office while Wheeze stayed behind with Joey Bats.

As they walked into the main room Ronny asked: "Eddie, any ideas? How do we find out who that guy was?"

Eddie: "The body must have a wallet with his driver's license in it. The girl that was with him may know his name and more. The Bartender may know who he was and if he was with anyone."

Ronny: "Good ideas, let's start with the girl and the bartender. I don't want to dig up that body unless we're forced to."

They checked with the bartender who indicated that he was in the lounge quite a bit with a guy named Peter and that Peter was there almost every night.

They agreed to go by the lounge that evening and speak with Peter if he showed up and also talk to the girl, Jeanie Reva, who was around all the time. Ronny stated that he knew her very well.

"OK, Ronny, then I'll meet you back here at seven. Is that Ok with you?"

"Yeah, that's OK. I'll see you then."

The two men parted for the day.

Later that day, Eddie met with Jack, who informed him that Walter Wintell, the guy that was shot and placed in the Volkswagen grave, would be OK. Jack and Paul were waiting to hear from the doctor that the victim could be interviewed.

"I'm glad to hear that he'll be OK. He could turn out to be a big asset," Ernie said.

They two men separated and Ernie went home to rest for a while before that evening.

***

That Evening

Eddie got to the club before Ronny and spoke with the bartender, Jimmy (Apples) Appilotino.

Jimmy stated that he knew Walter's friend Peter better then he knew Walter. Eddie got the information about where Peter lived. The bartender stated that his last name was Shovello and he lived just a few blocks away from the club on Washington Avenue in Brooklyn. The bartender stated that Peter lives right next door or in the same building as Fuggies Pool room. Fuggies was a local hang out where the guys played billiards.

Eddie asked what Peter looked like and Jimmy said that he was an older man about 45, grey and black hair, brown eyes and about 5'7" tall.

Eddie thanked Jimmy Apples for his help and left the bar area.

Ronny walked in and over to Eddie: "Hi, Eddie, let's talk to the bartender."

"I already did. I got all that we need. Let's go."

"Where we going?" asked Ronny.

"Do you know a place called Fuggies?" asked Eddie.

"Yeah, that's the pool room on Washington Avenue. Fuggy is the guy with Tourette's syndrome, he curses and spits uncontrollably, but he's a good guy and easy to get along with. Why do you ask about him?"

"The guy that we're looking for lives right next door to the pool room. His name is Peter Shovello."

"Let's go and see if we can find him. He'll be worth talking to," directed Ronny.

The two men left the lounge and drove over to Fuggies Pool Room.

As they entered the pool room everyone looked and recognized Ronny, who grew up in the area.

"Any of you guys know a guy named Pete Shovello? This is Eddie, he's OK and he's my partner," Ronny stated loudly.

"Yeah Ronny, he lives upstairs and works at the shipyard. Why do you need him?" stated a voice from the back that Ronny recognized.

"You know, Stew; you make me think you're writing a book sometimes. Which apartment does he live in?"

"Sorry, Ronny, he lives in apartment three, second floor."

"Thanks."

Ronny and Eddie walked into the building and up to apartment number three. They knocked on the door.

"Who is it?"

"Peter, it's Ronny from the Old Mark."

The door opened and standing there was Peter Shovello who looked exactly as he was described by the bartender, Jimmy.

"Ronny, what can I do for you?"

"Did you hear about the shooting at the lounge earlier today?" asked Ronny.

"No, but I saw the shooting at the lounge last night. You were there," as he pointed and directed his comment towards Eddie.

"Yeah, I was there."

"Well, what do you expect? The guy had a family that cared and wanted to retaliate"

"Then you know who did the shooting?" asked Eddie.

"I know that the guy you call Nose, he shot my buddy. I know that," stated Peter.

"Who shot up the Old Mark lounge today?" asked Ronny.

"It had to be his kid, Walter (Wally Junior) Wintell," stated Peter.

"Do you know that for sure?" asked Eddie.

"Can you call him and have him come over here?" asked Eddie.

"Why should I do that? You'll only kill the fucken kid," stated Peter.

"I give you my promise that we will not harm him," stated Eddie.

"I'm supposed to believe that?" replied Peter.

"Yeah, I said it and that's the way it will be, you calling me a fucken liar?" Eddie sternly replied.

"No, no, OK, I'll call him, but let's meet in a public location."

"OK, meet us at the bar at three tomorrow afternoon. By the way how old is he?"

"He's thirty years old. We'll be there. Eddie, I'm taking you at your word, He will not be harmed. His mother couldn't take losing his dad and then him as well."

"I gave you my word. Don't worry."

Eddie and Ronny left the apartment: "You gotta be kidding me with this promise not to harm the kid," stated Ronny.

"No, I wasn't kidding. If he shows up he'll walk out safely, we have plenty of time to handle him after we meet," replied Eddie who had organized a plan as they spoke.

"Look Ronny, I'm tired, I'll see you tomorrow at the club."

"OK, I'll see you then," stated Ronny as each man went his own way.

Eddie drove off to a phone booth and contacted Jack and Paul. He explained what was going on and asked if Paul could play a thirty year old kid.

"No, I can't. Give us that address for that guy Peter Shovello. We'll go over and speak with him. He's another one going into protective custody, as soon as this is over," said Paul.

"If you guys can't replace the kid, let it go. I'll handle it another way."

"You may have to. I don't see how we could replace that kid and get away with it."

"Great, I'll leave it to you guys to handle from here, I'm bushed," stated Eddie.

"We'll talk in the morning," stated Jack.

Eddie hung up the phone and went home for the rest of the night.

***

The next morning, Eddie went to Tony Two Scoops' luncheonette to have breakfast and to talk with Tony.

After breakfast he went over to the club. Ronny was there with Joey Bats. They called Eddie into the office where they met with Wheeze, who was already in the office.

Joey: "Eddie, what's this I hear about you offering to protect this kid?"

Eddie: "Joey, you're the one talking about it; you don't want any more trouble and we have enough heat on us now."

Joey: "Yeah, so what, you don't have the right to guarantee anything here without my permission. This is my family, not yours."

Eddie: "Joey, if I made a mistake, I'm sorry, but listen to what I have to say before you make that decision."

Joey: "OK, talk."

Eddie: "His father just disappeared. You want to do the kid for shooting up the club. Don't you think that the combination of the kid and the father disappearing would bring a lot of heat on us?"

Joey Bats: "You may be right on that point."

Eddie: "I am right and that's why I told Ronny that I think we have plenty of time to take care of him later. We should bring him closer, pay him well and make it look like the guy that did his dad will be dealt with in time. His enemy is our enemy."

Wheeze: "You know, Eddie, you constantly amaze me. You have a leader's mind."

Joey: "You're right, Wheeze. Eddie, you're going to Florida with Ronny, right?"

Eddie: "Yes, that's what Wheeze wanted."

Joey: "Good, you handle the kid. We'll back your play. Wheeze, we need more good men like him."

Wheeze: "I agree and he knows CPR. He helped me out one night."

Joey: "By the way how come you know that shit, Eddie?"

Eddie: "My dad, who was born and raised in Calabria, Italy, had a bad heart and I learned so that I could help him if I was around when he needed help. It turned out that I wasn't around at the right time."

Joey: "Sorry to hear about your father, but it worked out well for Wheeze."

Wheeze: "Sure did. Let's get outta here and leave Joey to his work."

Wheeze, Ronny and Eddie left the office and returned to the card room where they sat at a table and talked for a few minutes.

Tony Two Scoops walked into the club and went over to Ronny's table.

"Ronny, you know that thing we spoke about?" asked Tony.

"Yeah, are we on?" asked Ronny.

"Take care of it. There's a grand in it for each of you," stated Tony.

"It's as good as done. Give me a day or two," replied Ronny.

"Eddie, you're with me on this one. We'll make a fast grand each," stated Ronny.

"On what, what the fuck are we talking about?" asked Eddie.

"Here comes Peter with that kid, Willy. I'll tell you later," replied Ronny.

Ronny got up to meet Peter: "Hi, Peter, glad you came in. This must be Willy."

Peter: "No, not Willy, Wally is his name."

Eddie saw Peter and Wheeze talking. He didn't recognize the kid Wally. The team must have thought better of replacing him with one of the agents.

Ronny: "Sorry, I must have misunderstood. You can go or stay, Peter. Which do you want to do?"

Wally: "I'd prefer that he stays with me."

Ronny: "Fine, your decision."

Wheeze: "We have to go into the boss's office and let him speak with you. Follow us."

Eddie and Ronny led the way to Joey Bats office with Wally and Peter following.

Joey: "Have a seat, guys. I will let Eddie speak on my behalf while we all listen to what he believes is the true story."

Peter: "Wait a minute, Joey, I was there. I saw what happened."

Joey: "We know that, but listen to Eddie before you make any more brash moves."

Joey Bats nodded to Eddie to go ahead and speak. Wheeze and Ronny sat with Peter and Wally to listen to what Eddie had to say.

Eddie: "Peter, I was there as well and I will not try to justify what Nose did. We are just as pissed as you are, but there is nothing that we can do at this point in time.

Sometime down the line Wally will be given the opportunity to get even for his dad."

Wally: "Are you saying that I will get the chance to kill him?"

Eddie: "No one knows exactly what will happen at any time, but I can guarantee you that you will get your revenge, with my help and possibly the entire family. I can't speak for the family, but as I understand it, the family is very unhappy with Nose and do not like his antics."

Wally: "OK, so you guys want him out of the way and to stop causing you unneeded heat."

Eddie: "Basically, that's correct."

Wally: "As of right now there is a contract on Nose that I suspended for this meeting. This contract will be honored by my entire family from my area of Red Hook."

Eddie: "We respectfully request that you withdraw the contract and allow us to clean up our own house."

Wally turned to Peter and they spoke for a few minutes.

Eddie: "Would you guys like to go outside and talk for a few minutes?"

Wally: "Yes, yes we would," said Wally as they got up from their chairs and walked out.

After they left the room, Joey started smiling. "Did you guys hear that bull shit that Eddie gave him?"

Joey: "Eddie, I gotta hand it to you. You're a conniver and a damned good one."

There was a light knock on the door. Ronny opened it and Wally was standing there with Peter.

Wally: "Joey, you have a good reputation for being truthful with your people. Based on that, I'm gonna honor your request. I'm gonna talk with my boss Simon, I think you know him and have the contract canceled. Can I use your phone?"

Joey: "Sure go ahead, do you want privacy?"

Wally: "No, listen to what I say."

Wally dialed the phone and someone answered:

"Simon, I need that contract cancelled for the time being. Joey Bats seems to have the situation in hand and guarantees me that I will do the job myself when he's ready."

The person, Simon, at the other end of the line said something while Wally listened.

Wally: "Joey, he would like to speak with you."

"My pleasure," said Joey as he took the phone.

Joey listened, smiled, then spoke: "Why don't we do that. We can meet in my office to talk further unless you prefer a neutral location?"

Joey hung up the phone and spoke to Wally: "Wally, to guarantee that you are present for the correct moment, you will be coming to work with us for a while. You'll report to Ronny and do odd jobs for a while or until that nail is taken out of your shoe."

Wally: "I'll be happy to."

Joey: "I'll be meeting with Simon Lantigo. He'll let you know exactly when to start after we have our meeting."

Wally: "When will you be meeting?"

Joey: "Wally, don't ask questions. Do what you have to do and you'll work out perfectly while you're here."

Joey: "Wheeze, set up a meeting with all the men for tomorrow morning about ten"

Wheeze: "Will do Boss."

Joey: "OK, we're all set. Everyone get out of here. Wheeze, you stay for a few minutes."

The men left the office and Wheeze sat close to Joey Bats' desk. They whispered softly so that no one standing anywhere near the office could hear them.

Wheeze: "Joey, you don't expect to do Nose, do you?"

Joey: "We may be forced to do him. You don't know this, but I've been speaking with Simon Lantigo for some time now. We're looking at a possible merger between the two families. Many years ago, back in Italy, these two families were one. They split up when they came here after my grandfather and Simon's grandfather had a falling out. It may be time to correct that and get rid of Simon at the same time."

Wheeze: "But, why does Nose have to be thrown into the heap?"

Joey: "I can't tell you everything, but what I decide to do will be done. Nose is only a soldier. I'm not sure how good a one at that, from what I'm hearing. He is expendable."

Wheeze: "I hate to lose his income. He brings in a lot of cash with that airport thing of his."

Joey: "You realize that with the two families as one your income would triple."

Wheeze: "I hadn't considered that. You know you can count on me. I just like to let you know my opinion, that's all."

Joey: "Yes, I know and I count on you for that. One more thing, this guy Eddie, I think he's a big asset. Let's move him up in the family. After the Florida thing is complete, I want to see how he handles the men. Give him more responsibility. He may turn out to be one of our top assets. Now leave me alone so that I can make some calls. "

Wheeze: "I agree I like him, the guys like him and they respect him, which is more important."

Joey: "Yes, I know. Now leave me alone so that I can make some calls."

Wheeze left the office and entered the card room, where he had some coffee and sat alone at his table.

Chapter 18

The Burn

Friday August 11, 1978

Eddie was up late; the last couple of days had been exhausting, running around with Ronny meeting various people and being shown the warehouse, the pickup operation and being introduced to a couple of the pimps that ran the massage parlors.

Eddie had a list that he had to turn over to Jack with names, addresses and locations of all of the operations. He contacted Jack and spoke with a stenographer to get everything down on paper.

Jack read the report as it was being dictated by Ernie and then got on the phone.

Jack: "Ernie, this is gonna be larger than we originally thought. I have some New York detectives here going over this report along with the DEA and they are all amazed at all of the locations that you've uncovered. By the way, you're on a speaker phone."

Ernie: "It appears that these guys are placing some trust in me. All of a sudden I'm told all about the operation that they run. I was asked to go to Florida. It seems that they trust me enough to take on some responsibilities."

Paul: "Yeah, that sounds right, just hold one hand high. Don't trust these guys. They're apt to stab you in the back as soon as look at you."

Ernie: "Yes, I'm aware of that complication."

Jack: "Good, keep one hand high at all times. Do you have anything else?"

Ernie; "There's a job that Ronny has to do. He hasn't told me what it is, but it has something to do with Tony Two Scoops and all I know is that I will be his back up man. As soon as I know what it is, I'll try and let you know."

Paul: "OK, keep us advised. We'll try to stay with you, but as you know, that's not always possible."

Ernie: "I will. Have a great day, guys."

Ernie hung up the phone and drove over to the club.

As he entered the club he observed Ronny. As their eyes met, Ronny waved Eddie over to his table.

"Eddie, we're all set for tonight. I'll meet you here at about eleven."

"You can count on me; I'll be here waiting for you. Can you tell me anything about the job? If not I understand," stated Eddie.

"Yes, I'll tell you, but not here, outside, follow me."

Eddie followed Ronny out to the back alley near the dumpster. Ronny made sure the door was closed behind Eddie so that no one could hear what they were talking about.

"Eddie, do you remember the other day when Tony came in and told me to go ahead with that thing we discussed?"

"Yes, I remember, why?"

"Because that's what we're doing. He owns a run-down building over in Park Slopes and needs it taken care of for him. We get a grand each for the job."

"I see he wants it torched. What about the renters in the building?"

"The building is empty, no one can live there. The Board of Health has condemned it and declared it a dangerous place to live because of all of the problems. When we're done he'll build a new building there. That's a nice area. He'll make a ton of money on this job."

"Then why are we gonna do it for a lousy two grand? Why not demand more money?" asked Eddie

"You must know who Tony Two scoop is by now. If you don't, I'll tell you. He has that name for the ice cream or so he says. Years ago he had that name, before the ice cream shop. When he was much younger, he was a hit man that did everyone with two shots. He was one of the best. All Tony has to do is ask Joey and the job will be done free of charge. He's trying to be friendly with everyone in the family, that's all," stated Ronny.

"Oh, now I understand. OK, I'll meet you here at eleven tonight. Right now I'm gonna get some rest. I'm bushed. I was busy all night with this broad I met," replied Eddie.

"Yeah, be fresh for tonight. I'll see you then."

Eddie left the building and went to his apartment. He telephoned Jack and Paul to advise them of the upcoming burn.

Some of the men were against allowing the building to burn. Others felt that they should close down the operation, thereby eliminating the fire completely. Some of the men felt that as long as they could guarantee that the building was empty, it would be worth the final outcome. The final decision was left to Agent Paul Saunders of the DEA.

Paul thought over all of the prospects. After a lot of discussion, it was agreed that the cover team would check the City of New York property titles. They would find out what building Tony owned in the Park Slopes area. Once they located the building, they could make sure that it was empty before Ronny and Eddie got there. They would allow the building to be burned down.

Paul asked one of the New York Police detectives to contact the insurance company and ask them not to pay out any monies until they were advised differently.

The decision was made. They would all have to live with it.

***

That night at eleven, Eddie met Ronny at the club:

"You ready, Ronny?"

"Yeah, we'll take the truck, let's go."

They walked over to Ronny's pickup truck, which was loaded with two mattresses and a couple of bottles of gin. Eddie looked in the truck and laughed.

"What the hell is all this shit for?"

"Hey, I learned from the best. You'll see."

Eddie got into the truck and Ronny drove off to the Park Slopes section of Brooklyn. He parked the car in front of 802 Union Street a six story building. This building, at one time, contained fourteen separate apartments, including two basement apartments.

"Let's unload this stuff," said Ronny.

Ronny directed Eddie to take one of the mattresses; he took the second one. They went to the center of the first floor apartment, where they placed them one on top of the other.

"Nice bed," said Ronny as he laughed. His laughter seemed to contain a thrill in the making, like you would see in a child, looking forward to going to an exciting amusement park.

"Now what?" asked Eddie.

"This part can be complicated. I'll show you and tell you. You're gonna get one hell of an education. This process comes from the best burner in the business."

"OK, what do we do?"

"First, we wet the top mattress with one bottle of gin. Then we lay the other bottle on its side spilling the gin."

"Yeah, I understand" said Eddie

"Now we take a book of matches and place a small piece of a lit cigarette in it. We close the match book top with the cigarette sticking out. The cover holds the cigarette in place. You take one match and support the weight of the cigarette. This keeps it up and out of the wet area by placing the match, sulfur down in the gin, standing upright holding the end of the cigarette. As the cigarette burns down the matches light up, then the mattresses and then the building. The whole place goes up."

"How long does it take?" asked Eddie

"The whole thing takes no more than five minutes, as long as you don't make the cigarette too long," replied Ronny.

Ronny finished the set up. He and Eddie went out to the truck and waited until they could see some light from the fire in the hallway. Eddie estimated that the whole thing took about six minutes.

"That's burning good, let's get out of here," said Eddie.

"No, one more thing" Ronny got out of the truck and walked up to the building where he closed the door to the hallway. He returned to the truck.

"Now no one will see anything until it's too far gone."

"Oh, I see, you left the door opened so that you could be sure that it all got started properly," stated Eddie.

"That's right. Look at it. Isn't it exciting to watch?" stated Ronny as he sat there is a state of elation that made his face light up with some sort of thrill.

"I guess, if that's your thing," replied Eddie.

"You know, Eddie, I never told anybody this, but sometimes I would rather watch something like this then get laid," stated Ronny.

"Ronny, you are one sick mother fucker," said Eddie as he laughed. Ronny joined in the laughter.

"Fugheddaboudit," replied Ronny.

They left the area and returned to the club. They both went in and played cards for a while.

"Ronny, I'm taking off for the weekend. I'll be back on Monday."

"OK, Eddie, Monday we'll set up our plans for Florida."

Eddie left the club and telephoned Jack, who was already packing.

"How did you know I was planning to head home?" asked Eddie.

"What are you, getting old or just senile? You placed the mini-microphones in that room. We heard the entire conversation. You were loud enough so that everyone heard you. I wish they all spoke that loud. I figured you were giving me a signal to be ready. I'm ready."

"Yeah, I guess I forgot."

"Is the stenographer there?"

"Yeah, you gonna give her the facts?"

"Exactly, and all that was said."

* * *

The weekend went quietly. Ernie and Teresa were happy to be together. They enjoyed each other's company.

Teresa didn't want to nag Ernie, but she felt that she had to ask him how much longer this case would be.

"I'm not sure. I know how you feel and I am sorry, but I'm into it so deep now that I couldn't get out if I wanted to. I have to finish this job. Remember, they killed six innocent men because of my case. I have to do what I can to make up for those deaths."

Teresa replied, "Ernie those men weren't innocent. They were gamblers and one was a major drug dealer, so why do you keep calling them innocent?"

Ernie: "You're right. But they were innocent of what they were killed for. They killed all of those men because one was thought to be my informant. That was not true."

Teresa: "Oh, yes, I forgot about that."

Teresa dropped the questions and was happy to have her husband home with her and safe.

***

Monday
August 14, 1978

Eddie and Jack returned to Brooklyn where they each went back to their own jobs. Paul had been covering all weekend. Jack relieved him so that Paul could have some free time. The New York detectives filled in the other shifts.

The reports read that nothing of any importance had happened, that weekend.

Upon entering the club, Eddie saw Ronny sitting at a table with Wheeze.

Eddie wasn't much of a lip reader, but he could read Wheeze telling Ronny to send Eddie as the man in charge of the group.

Ronny had his back to Eddie. When he got up and turned around, he saw Eddie and called him over to the table.

Ronny explained to Eddie what he wanted him to do and how he wanted the men split up for the job. Ronny gave Eddie a list of five men and the amounts that they owed the family.

This week turned out to be the money week, the week when the Family got paid. Any of their dealers that had outstanding balances on the drugs that they were given to sell had to cough up the money. Eddie was assigned to head up the collections. His partner would be Spitball.

Cheech and Wimp were given two men from the list to collect from.

"Hey, Ronny, do these guys always owe you? I thought that you collected before you gave out the shit."

"Normally we do, but in the case of these five, we front them the shit because they have always been on time with the monies and they can't afford to lay the money out up front. We trust them. You understand that we only trust them once. If they screw with us, they never live long enough to be trusted again."

Everyone was sitting in the card room, waiting for a meeting that had been called by Wheeze for Joey Bats.

Joey walked out of his office and faced the group of men. Wimp, Spitball, Cheech, Eddie, Nose and Tony Two Scoops, along with Wheeze and six other soldiers who rarely show up at the club. They all sat quietly, waiting for the word from the boss.

"Guys, you are all aware of the Red Hook boys, the Simon Lantigo family. Is there anyone here that is not aware of them?"

No reply from the group.

"Good, I want to make sure that everyone knows what's going on. We used to all be one family, many years ago. Now we have the opportunity to create that family again. Discussions are going on, so here's what I want from you guys. No jobs in their part of the city without clearing it through me. No fights in Red Hook. No killings in Red Hook. You do nothing to or against the Red Hook boys or the Lantigo family without checking with me or Wheeze first. I need this from you guys. This will make us all stronger in the end."

"Joey, when is this gonna happen?" asked Spitball.

"Not for a few weeks; maybe in November or December we'll start it. We still have some things to iron out."

"What about Red Hook, they gonna honor our territory?" asked Ronny.

"You know better than that. I wouldn't ask you guys to do this if I didn't already have an agreement that is to our benefit," replied Joey bats.

"Thanks Boss, I was just wondering," replied Ronny.

"OK, go do your thing. Keep those rules in mind. This is for everyone's benefit. You'll all make more money if we pool our resources."

Some of the men got up and left the area while others sat together talking about the deal that Joey laid out. It seemed that they were all happy about it and were making plans already about how to use the extra manpower and what jobs they could do once the merger went through and they had enough help.

"Eddie, let's go over to Tony's place and get some coffee," said Ronny.

They walked across the street to Tony's luncheonette.

"Eddie, we'll be leaving on a flight out of JFK on the twenty-third, a week from Wednesday. Make sure that you keep that date open and a few days after as well."

"Fugheddaboudit, I'm there. You call it and it'll be taken care of," replied Eddie.

"I have the tickets and we'll be staying at my place in Key West on Atlantic Boulevard, a small ranch that I own there."

Ronny was lying to Eddie about owning the house. The house belonged to Joey Bats. Ronny was being himself and wanted to look big in Eddie's eyes, so he lied. Eddie was the first real member of the family that came in after Ronny while Ronny was one of the youngest members.

Eddie: "You must be doing very well with the family to be able to afford a house in Key West."

Ronny: "I do all right and so will you as long as you stay with me and don't team up with one of those idiots that work for us."

Eddie: "I'm here with you now and I'll be here. Do you need anything else from me?"

Ronny: "Yeah, get me some more coffee."

Eddie got up walked over to the counter and took the coffee pot back to the table. "Here, now you can have all you want."

Ronny: "In case I don't see you, remember the date and the time. We'll meet at the club at six in the morning on the twenty-third of the month, next week."

Eddie: "I got it. I will be there. I'm outta here, people to see, places to go, things to do."

Ronny: "You're new here, what the fuck do you have to do?"

Eddie: "Actually, I made a deal to buy some nine millimeter handguns, with sixteen shot clips. I have to make a call and meet the guys. You interested?"

Eddie figured that this would be a good time to inject some strong confidence in himself by faking a gun deal.

Ronny: "Yeah, I'll take a ride."

Eddie: "OK, I'll make the call."

Eddie dialed the telephone and gave the code "Chico" to whoever answered, indicating that he wanted to speak with Jack, who came on the phone. A second phone was picked up, Eddie could hear it. The stenographer would be on that line getting the entire conversation.

"Jack, do you still have that case of nine millimeter guns with the sixteen shell clip?" asked Eddie.

"Can we talk on this line?" asked Jack.

"Sure, I'm alone," as he signaled to Ronny to be quiet. He covered the phone and said, "He's a little shaky. I don't want him to know you're here." Ronny smiled back and signaled OK.

Eddie was putting on a show for Ronny's sake. He knew that Ronny would go back to the club and tell everyone what went down. This would make Eddie look good to the bosses and the men.

"OK, then we are doing a gun deal to impress this guy, right?"

"Yeah, you're right, Jack. Where do you want to meet?"

"How about at our normal meeting area on Cross Bay Blvd. in Rockaway Beach, the parking lot of the Jamaica Bay Wildlife Refuge building, where we have met before."

"Sounds good, say in an hour?"

"That's plenty of time."

Eddie hung up the phone.

"We're all set, we'll meet him at Jamaica Bay Wildlife Refuge building in an hour," Eddie told Ronny, who was in complete agreement.

Eddie and Ronny got into Eddie's car and drove off. "Should we get a couple of guys for cover?" asked Ronny.

"No, we don't need anybody," replied Eddie

They arrived at the location and Jack was there with another agent who he never introduced. They were in a white van.

"Hi, guys, this is my partner Ronny."

"Yeah, OK, get in the van."

Ronny and Eddie entered the van by the back doors. Sitting in the middle of the floor was a case of nine millimeter handguns. Eddie opened the case and grabbed one of the guns. "Nice weapons, how much?"

"We can do a case for three hundred and fifty each."

"That's too much. Twelve at three fifty comes to forty two hundred. Too much money," replied Eddie.

Ronny looked at Eddie like he was crazy, but kept his mouth shut. Ronny knew that three fifty was a fair price for the quality of the weapons.

"I'll give you three hundred each and that's my final offer," stated Eddie.

"You're screwing me, but since you're taking a whole case I can let you have the next one at three hundred each."

"The next one, what do you mean?" asked Eddie.

"This case is sold at three fifty each, so I'll sell you the next case I get, unless you want to offer more for this one," stated Jack.

"How long before the next case comes in?"

"I'll have it within a month," answered Jack.

"OK, I'll wait for the next one. You call me when you have it. You have my number right?" asked Eddie.

"I do and I will call you."

Eddie and Ronny left the van and drove off while Jack drove off in a different direction.

"Man, that was a great deal at their price and you had the balls to cut them down, great job, Eddie."

"Thanks, now we'll put the deal together and sell them for five each on the street or to our own guys."

"I'm in; I'll put up half the cash to make the buy and we'll go from there" said Ronny

"If that's the way you want it, Boss." replied Eddie.

Eddie was building up Ronny's ego. This would help Eddie in the long run.

They drove back to the club where they hung out for a while and played cards.

The next few days went quietly and fast. Everyone knew what was about to happen. Joey was to meet with Simon. This was number one on the list for all the men.

Ronny and Eddie would leave for Florida the following week.

Chapter 19

Lantigo Family

Saturday
August 19, 1978

Eddie arrived at the club in time to see Joey Bats getting ready to leave for his meeting with the Simon Lantigo Family in Red Hook.

"Eddie, I'm glad you're here. You'll be one of my back up men at this meeting. You come along, stay in the background and say nothing. If you have something to say you come to me and speak quietly in my ear. You do not blurt out anything. I will make a decision on whatever it may be that you tell me. Do you understand?"

"Yes sir, I understand."

"Are you packing?" asked Joey Bats.

"Yes, I have a nine with me," replied Eddie.

"It will be taken away before the meeting, allow them to do that. You'll get it back after the meeting," stated Joey Bats.

"Whatever you say, Boss," replied Eddie.

"Let's go. Eddie, you ride with Ronny. Joey will ride with me" stated Wheeze as they all walked out to the cars.

The meeting had been set at a warehouse in Brooklyn on Flatbush Ave., which was located in the center territory between the two organizations. This was known as a neutral area.

Upon arrival, the cars were allowed to enter the truck entrance of the warehouse, placing both cars out of the view of the public and the police.

Eddie and Ronny exited their car and walked over to Wheeze's car. Wheeze was opening the door for Joey Bats.

Eddie and Ronny walked behind Joey and Wheeze as they made their way towards the interior of the warehouse. A table was set up for Joey and Simon to sit opposite each other and talk. There were only two chairs.

Simon: "As agreed, the men will line up and place their weapons on the table."

Joey Bats looked at Eddie, Wheeze and Ronny as he nodded his head in agreement to disarm.

Each of the three men with Joey and each of the three men with Simon placed their weapons on the table.

Joey and Simon sat opposite each other and began speaking to each other as the rest of the men in the area stood around behind their boss, Simon's men on his side of the table and Joey's men on his side. The two men spoke with each other in Italian.

" Buongiorno, Simon."

" Buongiorno. Non ci dovrebbe essere difficoltà dai questi men" Simon risposto.

" Avete un'opinione quanto a come possiamo compire il nostro obiettivo? " blocchi chiesti di Joey.

" Nessun realmente, ho alcune idee che possiamo pensare il about."

" Il Yea, così fa I, che cosa è il vostro? " Joey risposto.

"Entrambi usiamo gli stessi banchieri per prendere la cura dei nostri redditi della famiglia. Perché non faccia uniamo i clienti quindi che conservano una percentuale ai mediatori nella banca e formiamo una famiglia con un nome unito?" Simon suggerito.

"Quello è molto divertente. Stavo pensando la stessa cosa. Tutto altrimenti cadrà nel posto. appena, prende un poco mentre affinchè di tutti gli uomini si trasformi in in funzionamento abituato insieme. Dobbiamo prevedere alcuni problemi, ma dovremmo acconsentire per rivestirli di ferro fuori. Non andare immediatamente alla guerra. Come questo capretto Wally ed il suo papa," ha dichiarato Joey.

"S, che era sfavorevole. Non possiamo permettere che una piccola cosa interferisca nei nostri programmi."

"Abbiamo accosentito, incontrarci diciamo in mese? Possiamo pensare nel frattempo a questo."

"Un mese allora. Una domanda Joey, lo fa però vuole Wally funzionare con i vostri uomini?" a Simon chiesto.

"Dirò che lo voglio lavorare, ma se l'eliminazione è richiesta dovete permetterli che la latitudine,, abbia chiesto Joey

"Un soldato più o meno non lo rovescerà,, Sia i blocchi che Simon di Joey si sono alzati dalle loro sedie hanno agitato le mani ed hanno baciato ogni altre guancie.

ENGLISH TRANSLATION:
"Good morning, Simon."

"Good morning. There should be no trouble from these men," replied Simon.

"Do you have an opinion as to how we can accomplish our goal?" asked Joey Bats.

"Not really. I have some ideas that we can think about."

"Yes, so do I, what are yours?" asked Joey.

"We both use the same bankers to take care of our family incomes. Why don't we combine the accounts, thereby saving a percentage to the brokers in the bank and form a family with a combined name?" suggested Simon.

"That's very funny. I was thinking the same thing. Everything else will fall into place. It will just take a little while for all of the men to become accustomed to working together. We must expect some problems, but we should agree to iron them out, not go to war immediately. Like this kid Wally and his dad," stated Joey.

"Yes, that was unfortunate. We cannot allow a small thing to interfere in our plans," said Simon

"Agreed, shall we meet, say, in a month? We can think about this in the meantime."

"One month then. One question, Joey, do you still want Wally to work with your men?" asked Simon.

"I will say that I do want him to work, but if elimination is required you must allow me that latitude," stated Joey.

"One soldier more or less will not upset me," replied Simon

Both Joey Bats and Simon rose from their chairs, shook hands and kissed each other's cheeks.

Joey turned and faced the men. "Pick up your weapons. We can go."

All of the men, from both sides, approached the table, took their weapons and everyone left in the cars that they came in.

Wheeze: "Joey, I could hear you guys talking. Most of the men don't understand Italian, but I do. That's amazing that he OK'd the hit on Wally."

Joey: "Leave Wally alone. No hit. Not yet. Wally is fairly close to Simon. We may be able to use that knowledge to our advantage at a later time. Contact him and tell him to take a few weeks' vacation, give him some cash. I want him to be happy for now. I do not want him around for the load that's coming in. We have enough problems going on right now without adding Wally to the mix."

Wheeze: "I understand."

They arrived back at the club and went in. Joey went to his office with Wheeze behind him.

Ronny and Eddie took a seat with Spitball, Wimp and Nose at a card table where they all had coffee.

Ronny was asked by Joey Bats to tell the others what was said at the meeting since they didn't speak Italian. In Italian he also told Ronny not to speak of Wally at all.

Ronny explained all that he was allowed to.

All of the men seemed happy about the merger and talked about all their plans for the new family. They even started coming up with future names combining the Borgazino and Lantigo family names, laughing and joking about some of the ideas they came up with, like Bortigo or Langazino. The names were a big game that they enjoyed playing.

Wimp told the guys that he was going to see his girl and that he would see them again tonight. He got up and left the club. The rest of the men kept talking as he left. A few seconds after he walked out the door, they heard gun shots coming from out in front of the lounge.

Everyone cautiously walked toward the front door and stopped. They looked out the front window to see who was shooting at whom. The street was quiet and all they could see was Wimp pulling on the arm of a body that he was trying to drag into the club.

They tried to help Wimp, while two of the men stood lookout for who may be shooting at Wimp and the friend he was dragging.

Wimp: "Guys take him out back, to the alleyway. I'll get my car and pull it around to the alley."

Ronny: "Wimp, this guy is dead."

Wimp: "What a fucken genius. I just shot the prick. He should be dead."

Ronny: "What are you gonna do with him?"

Wimp: "Nose, I was thinking of the junkyard?"

Nose: "Fine with me. I'll give you a hand."

Ronny: "We'll all help you. Get the car."

Wimp brought his car around to the back alley where the body was loaded and then taken to the junkyard.

They went through the same procedure of burying the guy by placing the body under a small car which they turned on its side. This time Nose made a small mistake. He picked a car that was already occupied by a body. They simply loaded this body on top of the one that was already there and placed the car back in its original position, on top of the two bodies.

Nose: "What the fuck. Do you think he gives a fuck anymore?"

Eddie: "No I don't think so. Nose you should have some sort of a procedure so that you know which graves are occupied and you won't make mistakes like this again."

Nose: "Yeah, I guess I could leave a can of paint here and mark the used cars."

Ronny: "Good idea. Do that, Nose."

Nose: "I will."

They left the yard and returned to the club, Ronny spoke to Wimp:

Ronny: "Wimp, not for nothing, but what the hell happened?"

Wimp: "That stupid mother fucker owed me two grand for a small job I did. He paid me two and owed me two. I did one of his single family houses for him and he never paid me. I walked out of here and saw him. I yelled to him, asking where the fuck is my money. He turned towards me, pulled his gun and fired before I could get mine out. I hit the ground and took my gun out as I went down. I fired two shots and hit him in the chest with both. I don't know why he started shooting. He must have been nuts."

Eddie: "You shot him right through the heart."

Wimp; "Hey, not for nothen, but better him than me."

Ronny: "Well, I've had enough excitement for one night. I'm out of here."

Eddie: "I'm gone, also."

Eddie decided to leave the club and return to his apartment where he could contact Jack to advise him of the meeting that all of the men attended and the additional body in the junkyard.

Upon arrival back home, Ernie telephoned Jack, who was all apologies because he and the team decided that it would not be smart to replace Wally with one of the team members.

Ernie told him that it didn't matter because it all worked out for the better and that Wally will probably be going to work for the Borgazino family on a loan basis from the Lantigo family. He further made a report with the stenographer about the Wally incident, the meeting between the two families and then reported the new body, located at the private grave site in the Junkyard.

"These fucken guys think nothing of killing someone," stated Jack.

"In this case, he was assaulted first and simply defended himself. I didn't see it, but that's what he said. Did you pull records on all these people?"

"Yes, as you got to know each of them, we pulled their records. It's like the story of a bunch of monkeys in the zoo. Uncaring for the public and even less caring for each other, they all have extensive records that go back to when they were kids."

"I kind of figured that. It's obvious that they care for each other in one respect, but will screw each other in a minute if given the chance," said Ernie.

"Ernie, what do you think of closing this down with this delivery from Columbia?" asked Jack.

"That sounds good to me, but there is a lot of work that will have to be done. Have you started on the affidavits?"

"We started and these New York District Attorneys are sharp. They have a great way of writing the affidavits. You know me, I would prefer that you and I did them, but we need all the help we can get and they're doing a great job."

"Sorry, this time I have to stay on the job and can't come into the office to help with the paperwork, I am sorry about that."

"Yeah, I'm sure you are. We'll do fine, but if you have any ideas, call me."

"I have one idea. Let's start thinking about my arrest. When you have time, I would like to know your ideas on when I should be arrested, before or after the raid? Put your heads together and let's see what you guys decide is best. Remember we must protect Scar, if he will allow us to protect him. He seems to have confidence in himself for that."

"Your arrest is probably better off taking place during the raid at the warehouse. We'll discuss it and get back to you."

Ernie and Jack hung up the phone and Ernie went to bed.

Eddie worked the weekend in the club covering the card games. It was a quiet weekend and the club took in twelve thousand dollars from the games by cutting the pots. To cut the pot is to take one part of the bet for each hand.

Sunday night, before he locked up the club, he had a conversation with Ronny.

"Hey, Ronny, I placed twelve grand in the safe this weekend. That's not bad."

"Twelve grand, that's all? It must have been slow all weekend. We usually do around twenty grand in a weekend. I know why you did such a low amount, the Feast"

"The Feast?"

"Yeah, we have a feast every August and every June. We run the games and the food, everyone has a great time," stated Ronny.

"That could be it. I have been watching them set up for it, but I've been in here while the fun was going on so I haven't had a chance to look everything over."

"Don't miss the kids climbing the grease pole next Saturday. We nail a couple of sticks across the top of a thirty foot pole and hang Italian meats on the sticks. Then above the sticks we place a fifty dollar bill. We grease the pole down real good. The kids break up into teams. They try to climb to the top of the greased pole to get the meats and money. They have a lot of fun and it is a real sight watching them try. It usually takes all day before they finally get the meats and cash at the top," explained Ronny.

"Then that's why it was so quiet around here we only had four tables going at the most at any one time," stated Eddie.

"That's the reason," replied Ronny.

Chapter 20

Sixty Feet Deep

Monday August 21, 1978

Eddie went over to the luncheonette. He was having breakfast when Tony Two Scoops came over and sat with him.

"Eddie, thanks for helping Ronny with the problem that I had."

"No problem, how did it work out?"

"It went fine. I am discussing numbers with the insurance people now. They claim that some drunk got in there with a bottle of gin, spilled it and while lighting a cigarette the place went up in flames and smoke," stated Tony.

"Are they holding you responsible for leaving the place unlocked?" asked Eddie.

"I don't think so, but they say that they have to conduct their investigation and that may take a while."

"I'm sure you'll come out of it with a bundle," stated Eddie.

"All I want is enough to construct a new building maybe a six unit modern building. I can retire on the income from something like that."

"Retire; you're too young to retire, Tony."

Tony laughed and took Eddie's words as a compliment. "How old do you think I am?"

"I'd say you are about sixty; hell you still have dark hair and very little grey," replied Eddie and thinking to himself that he had to be kind to the guy.

"I'm seventy-five years old, my friend," stated Tony.

"Seventy-five? You'd never know it."

Tony laughed. "That's what they all say."

"I should get going," Eddie said as he got up to leave.

"Here's Wheeze," said Tony.

Wheeze was just entering the luncheonette and saw Eddie, walked over to him and asked him to have a cup of coffee with him.

"Tony, can we have some privacy?"

"Go in the back room, you'll be very private there," suggested Tony.

Eddie followed Wheeze into the back room and Tony brought in a pot of coffee.

Tony left the room and Wheeze looked to make sure that they were alone. He began to speak to Eddie.

"Eddie, you did me a big service and I want you to know that I appreciate it. Joey likes you and the men like you. You have the background for a more important position. We're gonna start moving you into a position like that."

"Thank you, Wheeze, it's always nice to be accepted by one's peers. How is your heart problem going?"

"Oh I'm OK, the doctor sent me to a specialist. I'm on pills now and they told me to watch my intake of sugar and fatty foods."

"Why, are you a diabetic?'

"I guess they call a guy like me a pre-diabetic. I have a blockage in my heart and they're talking surgery if the pills don't work for me."

"Sorry to hear that, Wheeze," stated Eddie.

"Don't worry, I ain't going no place, not yet," Wheeze stated.

"So what do you and Joey have in mind for me Wheeze?"

"When this union of the families takes place, you will be placed in a supervisory position as our representative with the Lantigo family. You will be our eyes and ears."

"Sounds good to me, I'll be happy to do the job, but I may have someone else who is very qualified for the financial end of things."

"Who's that?"

"An accountant that I was in stir with, the guy is a real genius. I don't know if he would be interested, but it's worth a shot."

"When you move over, you can take anyone you like with you as long as our guy in the FBI checks him out first."

"Thanks, Wheeze, that's down the road. We'll talk about it again later. Is that OK?"

"Yes, that's fine. I just wanted you to know what's coming and that we appreciate your work with us."

"Thanks, Wheeze."

The two men left the luncheonette and went over to the club.

When they arrived at the club Spitball and Cheech were sitting alone talking. Wheeze went into his office and Nose walked in behind Eddie and Wheeze.

"Eddie, you ready?"

"Hi, Nose, ready for what?"

"The airport, this is our day."

"It is? OK, I'm ready."

"We have one stop to make. I have to pick up a payment due. We may have to speak with this idiot. He's been a little too private lately."

"You mean he hasn't been paying his bills?"

"You got it," replied Nose.

Spitball, Nose and Eddie left the club and went to a store where Eddie bought a clipboard and a pad with lined note paper, which he placed on the clipboard. This would work as a prop to give him a reason for hanging around the airport area with the guard that he spoke to before. Eddie was to distract the guard again and keep him from asking questions. This procedure worked before and should work again.

After they left the store they went to # 9820 Prospect Place in Brooklyn, which was a Chinese laundry. They entered the building. Nose locked the door behind them. They went into the back area of the store where women were working on machines for cleaning and pressing the clothes.

Nose walked over to a small office where the owner was sitting. The owner observed, through the office window, the three men walk in. He did not move from his desk chair. He watched the three men walk into his office.

"Nose, what's up?" asked the proprietor of the business. Mr. Gui Peng was a slight man about 5'6" tall, with a thin 130 pound body, balding head, dark brown eyes and a slight mustache.

"I know why you're here, Nose," stated Gui Peng in a nasally voice that cracked with a sign of fear while trying to seem firm and confident.

"Where is my money, Gui?" asked Nose.

"You know Nose, you sound like your gonna kill me over a few thousand bucks."

"No, I ain't gonna kill you, but I will take eighty percent of your business in exchange for the payments that you owe me."

"You're out of your mind. This business is worth over a million and you expect me to just sign it over?" asked Peng.

"It's either that or give me the ten thousand dollars that you owe me," Nose demanded.

"What ten thousand? I owe you five thousand from the card game, that's all," replied Peng.

"No, you forgot the vigorish. That's a thirty day vig which is twenty percent a week plus twenty percent for being late. So you now owe me ten thousand dollars.

"You guys back him up on this stealing?" Peng asked of Eddie and Spitball who did not answer him.

"That's the way it is? OK, here's your money, get out! You just lost one of the best customers you ever had," stated Peng as he reached behind him into a draw and took out a stack of cash from which he paid Nose the money owed.

Nose picked up the cash and signaled for Eddie and Spitball to leave with him.

As they walked out Spitball asked, "Nose, you gonna let him get away with calling you a thief?"

"Don't worry, that asshole will get his. Take a good look around. Some time in a month or so we'll do this joint. Then we'll see if he still needs our help or not, after his unfortunate fire and damage," said Nose

"Not for nothing, but do you really want that laundry business, Nose?" asked Eddie.

"Why not? He's a douche bag and I can take it from him without much trouble. The family will make a substantial percentage off of the profits after we get paid."

The next stop was the airport. Eddie went over to talk with the security guard while he held his clipboard.

"I see you found your clipboard?" asked the guard.

"No, I never found it. I had to go and buy another one and redo all the work that I did counting the runway lights, checking to be sure that they are all on and making sure the measurements between the runway lines are correct. It all has to be done regularly."

"What the hell are they afraid of, someone moving the lines or stealing the lights? I don't understand these rules sometimes," stated the guard.

"Who the hell knows? All I know is that I receive a decent week's pay to walk around with this stupid clipboard," stated Eddie to the guard. He looked over the guard's shoulder and could see that the men were loaded and ready to leave the area.

Eddie told the guard that he had to leave and get some work done and he walked off around the corner where he met with Nose and Spitball who were in the van. The van was loaded with stolen bags from the luggage lost and found room at the airport.

They left the airport and drove to the dock where the 22 foot boat was docked and waiting. They loaded the boat with the stolen luggage and took off for the deep water.

The sight of three men on the water in that boat opening luggage and going through it made Eddie laugh to himself as he looked at it through his mind's eye.

Eddie could not understand why no one said anything or asked anything although it was hard to see over the gunnels to view the luggage down on the deck. They threw the luggage overboard after they went through it.

This was not only a violation of state law they were also in violation of local law and federal law. They made sure that they covered all the police agencies. All Eddie could think of was that when the IQ of these men reached 50 they should sell, something he heard somewhere which seemed to apply now. In some ways he felt bad for these guys since he knew what they were facing. They were oblivious to it. Outwardly he was joining them to fit in.

They went through twenty three bags and found a small amount of cash that totaled three hundred dollars.

In another bag they discovered a blue Chavez Regal bag containing several pieces of jewelry worth thousands that they would sell at a later time and split the income.

Another bag had a gold chain that had to be three feet long and as thick as Eddie's pinky. This piece had to be worth several thousand dollars.

Another bag had a crown that was obviously made for a little girl or very small women. It was all gold and had a diamond in the middle of it that was about two Karats in size.

As they finished with each bag they took anything that they wanted including some of the men's jewelry which they shared between them. Eddie was given a pair of cufflinks that he later turned over to the team as evidence. They would then throw the bags overboard locked shut with anything that may float inside them. The bags sunk to the bottom, which Eddie was told was over sixty feet deep.

This job took several hours to go through everything and return to the slip where Nose took all of the booty to his fence. He dropped Eddie and Spitball off at the club.

Eddie made excuses why he couldn't stay, saying that he felt a little sea sick. He wanted to contact Jack and advise both him and Paul of what had happened.

Eddie went to his apartment. He telephoned the team and asked for Jack or Paul.

"Ernie, you're on speaker phone, go ahead," he heard Jack's voice.

"We have a little situation that came up," stated Eddie.

"What's that?" he heard Paul ask.

"Paul, this concerns you. Can you be an accountant?"

"An accountant? I can't even add my bills up at the end of the month."

"Wait until you hear this development: they want to make me a boss. First of all, there's gonna be a merger between the Borgazino and Lantigo families. That's bad enough, they're all nuts in both of those families. Once the merger takes place, Wheeze wants me to go with the Lantigo Family to act as his eyes and ears. I can take anyone I wish. I suggested an accountant that I supposedly did time with. That's you, Paul," stated Ernie

"We better shut this fucken thing down. We can't stay here forever," said Jack.

"Wait a minute, Jack, maybe we can work something out here," stated Paul.

"You guys think about it and let me know. My vote is to close down the operation and convict as many as we can," stated Eddie.

"We'll do that, but first give the stenographer a report that we can look over and everyone can read."

Eddie proceeded to do just that. He reported everything including the airport job and the approximate location where they dropped the bags overboard so that divers could retrieve them in the future. He also discussed the upcoming merger and his recent offer of becoming an underboss

Once he finished giving all of the information Paul told him that they would talk to him in a day or two. They would have a decision at that time.

"I'm going to Florida, remember?"

"Yeah, I remember, we'll talk when you get back," replied Paul.

"OK," Eddie hung up the phone.

Later that night, Eddie decided to go over to the club and play some cards with the guys.

He walked into the lounge and over to the back entrance to the club where he entered the card room. Spitball, Cheech and Nose were there playing cards with an unknown male and George Studs.

George was the man who owned the gun that was used in two murders. The bodies were found by the police some time ago.

They all said hello to Eddie as he entered and asked him to join them which he did.

George: "Eddie this is Currinda Barana, my friend we call him Cure for short. Cure, meet Eddie, you can trust Eddie, he's a good friend."

Eddie: "Nice to meet you, Cure. George, you're not packing, are you?"

George: "Eddie, not after the other night, I learned my lesson. Besides, you threw away my weapon. I have to pick a new one up somewhere."

Spitball: "Good, that's better. The other night I thought that Eddie was gonna do you and we'd have to do another burial. I don't like doing that work."

Cure: "Is there a bathroom in here?"

Cheech: "Yeah, down that hallway, second door on the right."

Cure got up and went to the bathroom.

Eddie: "George, who is this guy?"

George: "Eddie, he's a good guy. He's a little stupid at times. I'll even go as far as to say that any job this man is qualified for should be abolished. The reason I keep him with me is that he is extremely strong and will do whatever I ask of him, no questions asked."

Eddie: "A good type to have around with you."

George: "Now that I told him that you're a good friend, he will do whatever you ask as well, as long as it isn't to hurt me."

Cure walked back to his seat. He was about 6'3" tall and he had to go three hundred pounds, all muscle. He had black hair and brown eyes with the type of personality of a good dog, according to George.

Eddie: "How long have you two been friends, Cure?" He was interested not in their friendship, but in how long they were friends because Cure may be the trigger man between the two of them and the bodies may be his work.

Cure: "We've been together for about five years now, right, George?"

George: "Right, now let's play some cards. I feel lucky tonight."

The men played cards until about two in the morning. The game was friendly and peaceful. No guns. No one got hurt. Everyone was worried that George may flair up at any minute because he was losing over four thousand dollars. He never got upset. He and Cure left the club with everyone else.

Eddie left the club a little early to go to his apartment while Spitball closed up for the night.

Chapter 21

Florida

Wednesday August 23, 1978

Eddie got up and after a shower went down to the luncheonette where he had breakfast with Ronny.

"You ready to go, Eddie?" asked Ronny.

"Yes, I'm ready. I wish I knew more about what we're doing and why. I'm don't like doing things in the blind," stated Eddie.

"We'll talk on the plane, don't worry, it's only a meeting," stated Ronny.

"That's what bothers me, not the meeting," said Eddie.

"What the fuck are you talking about?" asked Ronny.

"When someone tells me not to worry and I'm totally unaware of the circumstances. I begin to worry," explained Eddie.

Ronny laughed, "We're only placing an order; let's get going, the plane in waiting."

They got up from their seats and Tony was walking over to them.

Tony: "Hi guys, what's up?"

Ronny: "Sorry Tony, we have to leave, we have a meeting."

Tony: "You mean Florida. I used to go on that trip years ago."

Ronny: "How do you know about that?"

Tony laughed: "Hey, what the fuck do you think. The world started with you? I did that trip before you were born. During the big war I was running back and forth. Now you kids have it easy. Have a good trip."

Ronny: "Sorry, Tony, I forgot that you were an important part of this family at one time. I wasn't being fair with you."

Tony: "I still am. You asshole, go and do your job. You want to be fair? Listen, fair is a place where you go to ride on rides, eat cotton candy and corn dogs and step in monkey shit. We're not in a fair business. Grow up."

Ronny walked away with his head down and Eddie followed him. As Eddie walked past Tony he said: "Sorry, Tony, no disrespect intended. I don't know what I'm gonna do with these kids."

Tony laughed and Ronny started to laugh along with Eddie. They left the luncheonette. Ronny drove to the airport where they boarded a small jet that took them to Key West, Florida.

Upon arrival in Florida, they got into a cab and went directly to 1010 Atlantic Boulevard the house that Ronny claimed to be his home at the beach.

"Tonight we can go for dinner, look around the town and relax. Our guy will be here in the morning," said Ronny

During the plane ride Ronny had explained what he and Eddie were here to do and who they were meeting. Eddie saw this as an opportunity to meet one of the men behind the card game massacre.

That night they went to dinner at the El Siboney Restaurant located at Catherine Street in Key West, Florida. This was a five star restaurant where they enjoyed some of the local cuisine and drank a bottle of wine.

"This is the life, Eddie. I could do this every night."

"Yeah, but even this can become boring after a while."

"I guess so," replied Ronny.

They left the restaurant and walked the streets for a while looking at some of the sights and passing bar after bar. At one location, girls were grabbing them by the arm and asking them to join the party that was going on inside the bar.

The two men were dressed in suits with open collars. Ronny was wearing a gold chain with a gold horn and hand hanging on it. These are Italian superstition artifacts. Eddie had the open shirt with a thin gold chain and a gold crucifix hanging on the chain, which was very different for this area of the Keys. It appeared that the women they observed on the strip liked their looks and wanted their company. Ronny and Eddie kidded around about that point, but business was more important.

"They just want to have some fun, you can't blame them. Next time we come here we wear shorts and polo shirts," stated Eddie.

"Agreed, let's get back and get some rest so we'll be bright and cheery for the meeting in the morning," stated Ronny.

They went back to the house and each picked a bedroom. They watched some TV and went to bed.

At eleven o'clock that night, Ronny got out of bed and went over to Eddie's room and woke him.

Ronny told Eddie that he couldn't sleep. He asked if Eddie would like to run across to the beach and have a swim. Eddie agreed. They both got dressed in swim trunks and headed across the street to the sand and the beach.

They walked across the street and laid their towels down on the sand. They started towards the water and as soon as their toes reached the warm water Ronny stepped back.

As they walked to the water, Eddie could see the bullet scar on Ronny's back. He would try to get him into a talkative mood.

"This water is warmer then the air," stated Ronny

"What do you expect? We're almost at the equator. Nice place, but the shore water is always very warm this time of year."

"Yeah, I guess I wasn't thinking," stated Ronny.

"If we get a boat and go out a ways, the water will be refreshing."

"I don't want to get a boat now. It's too late," said Ronny.

"OK, then let's go back to the house and go to sleep. I thought you knew this place and owned it. How come you didn't know about the water temperature at this time of year?"

"I call it my place, but it belongs to Joey Bats and his family. I'm part of the family."

"Then you've never been here before?" asked Eddie.

"No, this is my first real large job."

Eddie laughed, "And here you are trying to make me think you're my boss when we're equally in place within the organization."

Ronny's eye opened as though he was a little upset, "No, no you work for me Wheeze said so."

Eddie smiled at him: "I could tell you that he told me, that you work for me."

Ronny: "I don't believe it."

Eddie: "He didn't, but he did tell me that he has a special job for me."

Ronny: "What's that?"

Eddie: "I can't say right now, but I have to pick my own men for the job."

Ronny: I'm gonna ask him about that when we get back. I should be moving up with you if not before you."

Eddie: "That's basically what I said to him."

Ronny: "What did he say?"

Eddie: "He simply told me that you would be taken care of and I was to worry about myself."

Ronny: "Good, I'm glad they'll probably place me as your boss."

Eddie: "You know, Ronny, since we're talking. I was wondering about the time that you got shot. How did that happen?"

Ronny: "That was my own stupidity. There was a ton of cash sitting on the table and I got distracted."

Eddie: A ton of cash, where was this ton of cash?"

Ronny: "You know this guy Paolo Cristino that we're meeting?"

Eddie: "I don't know him, but yeah, go ahead." Eddie saw this as an opportunity to get the story on the Card Game Massacre from the horse's mouth, if Ronny had been there.

Ronny: "I don't really know him either this is our first meeting. He represents the Soldado family of Columbia. They hired Joey Bats Family to take care of a guy for them. In order to do the job right they had to kill everyone at a card game. I was the cover and got distracted by the cash and one of the guys wasn't dead. He shot me."

Eddie: "Oh, so that's how you got shot, now I understand. What happened to the guy that shot you?"

Ronny: "I was with Wheeze doing the cover when I got shot. The hit man was some guy from California. You may know him, Louie, Louie the Lark. Louie made sure they were all dead after that. You should have seen him going from body to body pumping shells into them like his best friend just got shot. He was pissed."

Eddie: "That's really something. I assume that Wheeze and this guy Louie took you to a hospital."

Ronny: "No, you should know better than that. They took me to our doc who took care of me. He did a good job."

Eddie: "I'm gonna get some sleep. I'll see you in the morning."

Eddie went into his room; he couldn't get a pen and paper out of his bag fast enough. He wrote down everything that Ronny told him. He now knew the entire story of the card game massacre and would relay it to the team as soon as he got back. His job was done as far as the card game went. Now he would have to clean up the rest of the case.

Eddie's only worry was that there may be questions on how this information was drawn out of Ronny. A smart defense attorney could make it look like accusatory statement during questioning. The prosecutor would have to present the statements in a way to indicate that Ronny simply blurted it out, a self incriminating statement during an innocent conversation.

Eddie would have to leave these discussions to the district attorney; for now, he was satisfied that he had the people that he went after for the card game massacre. He was pleased that the families of the victims would have some closure, although they may never know exactly how it all came about.

Eddie fell off to sleep thinking about the case and what should be the next move for the entire team.

**

Thursday August 24, 1978

Eddie woke up early and checked the spot in his bag where he placed the information that he wrote the night before. As he was entering the shower he heard a knock on the door.

"Come on in, Ronny. I'm just gonna go into the shower, I'll be ready in three minutes."

"It's eight o'clock. We have time to get some breakfast. I'll call a cab."

"OK. I'll be right out."

They left the house, went to breakfast and returned by nine-thirty that morning. Eddie made some coffee while they waited for the connection to arrive.

"Eddie, this is a mutual situation between you and me. If you have anything to add or say, feel free to jump in. Otherwise, I'll handle the conversation," stated Ronny.

"Thanks Ronny. I wasn't sure if I should say anything, or not."

"I was thinking about what you said last night about what Wheeze told you. I think, it looks like he and Joey Bats would like to put us together. We may as well learn to work together. I think we can make a good team."

"Yes, that may be. We'll see how things go," stated Eddie as he looked at Ronny to see his reaction.

Ronny just put his head down. This action could be a sign of inferiority to Eddie.

The doorbell rang. Eddie looked at Ronny who walked over to the door to open it. Standing there was a 5'7" man, about 40 years of age, weighing about 165 pounds with black hair and dark brown eyes. He was dressed in a blue suit, white shirt and tie.

"Ronny?" asked the man, with a big smile as he stood in the door way.

"Yes and you must be Paolo."

"I knew it was you. Wheeze described you perfectly and he told me that you have another man with you named Eddie."

"Yes, I do, come on in and meet him," Paolo entered the house and walked into the living room with Ronny.

"Eddie, meet Paolo who represents the Soldado family. He's from Columbia and our main man in this area."

"Paolo, you guys really got those assholes at that card game. It's too bad that Ronny had to take a hit for you," stated Eddie.

"You're not supposed to talk about that at all. That is past business, it is finished" said Paolo

"Sorry, I was only trying to make friendly conversation. I did not mean to offend you. I'm very sorry. May I get you something to drink, coffee or something?" asked Eddie.

"No, thank you, I'm fine. You didn't offend me and I understand. Yes, I am sorry about Ronny taking a hit, but he did a great service for my family and for its honor, which is an important thing. We paid him well and owe him for his sacrifice. Let's not discuss this again," stated Paolo.

"Agreed, and thank you for understanding," replied Eddie.

Paolo asked if they should get down to business; Ronny was in agreement.

"What does your family need delivered?" asked Paolo.

Ronny replied by giving Paolo the order as it was given to him by Wheeze, "We need fifteen hundred bricks of marijuana at your wholesale price of two hundred dollars per brick. We also need three thousand keys of blow at your wholesale price of fifteen hundred dollars each, making a total amount due to you of four million, eight hundred thousand dollars American."

Paolo: "That's fine and I see that you increased your order. This is a good sign for future business."

Ronny: "What about delivery?"

Paolo: "The last time we needed three ships because we had several deliveries to make. This time it will be the same. Three ships with a diversionary ship to hold off the police in your area. I have two other diversionary boats; small ones for two other deliveries, they belong to people that work for us here in the United States. All of the extra ships and the men who will be jailed need to be paid for and that will increase the bill by one hundred thousand dollars. Do you have a problem with that?"

Eddie: "I have only one problem and it may be a problem with understanding your plan. We don't mind paying for one ship's crew to be arrested and the loss of that ship. However, you said you have other deliveries. You made it sound like we are paying for all of the loss boats and men while we are only one third of the delivery."

Paolo: "I am very sorry for the misunderstanding. You are one half of the amount being delivered and the total bill is two hundred thousand dollars. You are only paying for your half, I assure you. We would never cheat you, Eddie. We expect that you would have the same respect for us."

Eddie: "Paolo, please do not take it as any offence just because I question your moves. This is our first time on this job and we will learn to trust each other. As of now our bosses trust you and therefore, so do we. With all due respect to you and your family, please understand that with me respect is something that is earned and I have confidence that you are due all the respect that we can muster."

Paolo: "Thank you. Now let's get back to business. The ships shall be unloaded at the same location in New Jersey."

Ronny: "Where is that exactly?"

Paolo: "Wheeze didn't tell you? He knows the location. It worked well for us. The place that you meet the ships is at Cape May, New Jersey."

Ronny: "OK, when?"

Paolo, looking through his paperwork and at his calendar answered, "According to my understanding, your load can leave Columbia by tomorrow morning. The delivery will be at that location on Friday, September first, next week. There should be an almost full moon that will give plenty of light to your men."

Eddie: "Since you're speaking of the full moon, I take it that the delivery will be at night?"

Paolo: "That's correct. They should be there between eleven and twelve midnight on the first of September."

Eddie: "Do we have a way of contacting you for confirmation prior to the delivery?"

Paolo: "Wheeze has all of my contact numbers. I'm sure he will give you what you need. Wait a minute; here, I'll give you the contact numbers now, so that you have them, too."

Eddie: "Thank you Paolo. Have we covered everything?"

Paolo: "Yes, I think so. If there are any problems, give me a call. As I understand it, the first half of the payment will be delivered this week. The rest is due upon delivery. All will go through the standard electronic procedure."

Ronny: "Yes, that's exactly how I understand it. Wheeze will handle that part of the job"

Paolo: "That's fine. If there are no more questions, I'll leave. It's been a pleasure speaking with you men."

Eddie: "No, it has been our pleasure to have this dealing. I am in hopes that it will lead to a long friendship stretching across the United States and into Columbia."

Paolo: "I am sure that it will."

Paolo left the house and Ronny was ready to head home. He was talking about all the things that had to be done, arrange the men, set up the warehouse, arrange for trucks, make sure Wheeze makes the payments. His mind was going faster than a race horse and he was sweating with the thoughts of all the work.

Eddie: "Ronny, slow down, take a breath. We will get everything done. Remember, you're not alone, we are a team. We can do anything and everything that needs to be done. Don't worry."

Ronny: "Yeah you're right; we'll get everything done together. Thanks, I think I was getting a little crazy there for a minute."

Eddie: "You'll be OK. Let's get packed."

They packed their suitcases, called a cab and returned to Brooklyn. Eddie and Ronny went home for the night, agreeing to meet Monday morning at the club.

***

That evening, upon arrival at his apartment, Eddie contacted Jack and Paul to make a report about what had happened in Florida.

He was placed on the speaker phone and the stenographer recorded all of the information that he relayed to the team.

He explained how Ronny got shot, about the drug ships coming in and Paolo's statements on that card game massacre. It was all taken down and they discussed closing down the operation. There was only one problem.

Jack: "Ernie, they keep talking about this guy Eddie that they think works for them and they are serious about finding this guy."

Ernie: "What do you guys suggest?"

Paul: "We can't hear the entire conversations. They speak very softly most of the time. The decision is yours, how do you feel about sticking it out. We have enough to close down right now. We don't have the ships or the hit man that they hired for the card game. The decision has to be yours."

Ernie: "I'll finish this job. By the way, thanks for reminding me of the hit man. According to Ronny, he is a guy named Louie the Lark from California."

Jack: "No shit, he actually told you that? You better include that as an addendum to your report and how he came to mention it."

Ernie spoke with the stenographer again and gave her the information that they needed about Louie the Lark.

Paul: "New York is in the process of obtaining a warrant for the guy. They have some connections in California and they're confident that they can track this guy down."

Ernie: "Good, your people must have some files did anyone run the name in NCIC?"

Paul: "Yes, we do have some connections, but I don't think we'll need them. As you were asking me they were running his name through NCIC and we got a hit. His name is Louis Mandasa. We have his picture coming in and we'll charge him on the basis of the conversations that you had. The DA may have technical problems with the statements, but at least we'll give it a try."

Ernie: "Great, just one thing, don't touch him until we are ready to close down. Coordinate with the California state police to pick him up."

Jack: "Is there anything else?"

Ernie: "Yes, let me know when the meeting date will be, and make sure everyone knows what I look like so that there are no mistakes in case of a shootout."

Jack: "Don't worry Ernie. I would never make that mistake again. Once is enough."

Ernie: "OK, I'll speak with you in a day or so. You guys will get things started to shut down, do affidavits and warrants."

Paul: "We will start first thing in the morning. I have two DA's coming in to go over everything. Ernie, we appreciate your staying in there this way. We know you don't have to now that you have the people responsible for the card game thing."

Ernie: "Paul, there is no way I can walk away from this now. I'm tempted to stay and build a strong extension to the other family, but my wife would shoot me."

Paul: "Ernie, we appreciate that. I only feel bad about one thing; I won't get to be an accountant. I may have had fun with that one."

Ernie: "Yeah, you may have been killed also. It's better this way."

Everyone within ear shot started kidding Paul and joking about being an accountant.

Ernie, Paul and Jack agreed to start the shutdown of the operation. The plan would include specific times and dates, as soon as Ernie had all of the final information. After the discussion, Ernie was tired and went to bed.

Chapter 22

Mrs. Geraffo

Saturday August 26, 1978

Eddie got out of bed and prepared to leave for the day. After he left the apartment he decided to stop at Tony Two Scoops' luncheonette for some breakfast. He entered and took a table. Tony was helping a customer with some packages that the customer had.

Tony walked over to Eddie's table and sat down.

"Eddie, are you going over to the club?"

"Yeah, Tony, why, do you need something?"

"I got a little problem and as you know, I'm actually retired so I'm away from much of what goes on today on the street."

"I understand what do you need?"

"Would you talk with Wheeze for me and ask him to stop by and see me?"

"I'd be happy to, but here he is now, you can speak with him yourself," stated Eddie as Wheeze walked in the front door.

Wheeze walked over to the table and asked Tony for a cup of coffee to go.

"Wheeze, can you spare a moment to talk?"

"For you, Tony, anytime, what's up?"

"My niece had a break-in and they stole all of her jewelry. Do you think we can find out who did it?" asked Tony.

"Is there anything special about any of the jewelry?" asked Wheeze.

"Gold chains, four diamond rings, some gold rings, gold earrings and one special piece, a gold bracelet with pearls and jade."

"Is there a picture or anything of the stolen jewelry?" asked Wheeze.

"Yeah, here, take a look at this, it's the best piece she had. It was worth several thousand dollars," stated Tony as he handed Wheeze a picture.

Wheeze took the picture from Tony, "Eddie and I will see what we can do. We'll be back in a little while."

Eddie and Wheeze left the luncheonette. They took Eddie's car and Wheeze directed Eddie to drive over to a music store in the Bronx, a borough of New York.

"What's over there, Wheeze?"

"This guy is a top fence. If the jewelry that was taken was good stuff, he'll be the guy that will buy it."

"Who is he?"

"This guy owns a music store. He sells instruments and stuff like that. He's a fence in reality. His name is William (Lips) O'Reilly."

"Lips?"

"Yeah, you'll see he has a large lower lip and he's had that nickname since he was a kid."

Just then they pulled up in front of a store called The Music Note. They exited the car and entered the store.

Wheeze looked around. There was a guy behind the counter about 6' tall, balding brown hair, about fifty years of age with a large lower lip. He was taking care of a customer.

Lips looked up just as Wheeze and Eddie entered the store. He nodded to Wheeze who nodded back and walked into the back room. Eddie followed. They sat at a table and waited for Lips to come in.

After a few minutes, Lips walked in. "Hi, Wheeze, what's doing?"

"Lips, have you taken any decent jewelry lately?"

"Fugheddaboudit, I get jewelry every day, what are you looking for? I have all kinds, anything you need."

"Not for nothing, but that's not what I want. I'm looking for a special piece that you may have taken in."

"What does it look like?"

"Along with some diamonds, rings, earrings and other jewelry, there was a special piece, a gold bracelet with pearls and jade. Here's a picture of that one piece."

Lips took the picture, looked at it, scratched his head then looked at Eddie and Wheeze. "Shit, I knew this was too good to be true. I expected to make a real good profit on that piece."

Wheeze: "Then you have the jewelry?"

Lips: "Look, guys, I don't want no trouble with you. I have all of it. I bought it from a junkie asshole."

Eddie: "No trouble, all we need is a name and an address, if you have it."

Lips: "Very simple, look out the front window. He has a small place in that apartment building across the street. The apartment is over the sub shop."

Wheeze: "What's his name?"

Lips: "He calls himself Bubba, his name is Roberto Median, he's from Mexico and he has a girlfriend that is a real looker, but she's as crazy as he is."

Wheeze: "Thank you for your help, Lips. Keep this under your hat for now. How much did you give him?"

Lips: "Five thousand dollars. This stuff is worth about fifty thousand. Don't worry, I won't say anything."

Wheeze: "Give me the jewelry. I'll make sure that you get your money back."

Lips opened a drawer and took out a small bag which he handed to Wheeze. The bag contained the stolen jewelry. "I haven't had a chance to go through it and separate it yet."

Wheeze and Eddie left the music shop and went back to the club to figure out a strategy.

At the club, Wheeze telephoned and asked for a guy named Sausage.

"Sausage, how's things?"

"Good. Wheeze, what's up?"

"Is the Rock around?" asked Wheeze.

"Yeah, he's here; why, do you need some help?"

"Come down to the office, we have a thing," said Wheeze.

"We'll be there in fifteen minutes."

Wheeze hung up the phone and sat back in his chair.

"What do you have in mind, Wheeze?" asked Eddie.

"That was Sausage and Rock, two men that are specialists in convincing people to agree with their way of thinking. We'll have them speak with this asshole Bubba on Tony's behalf."

"They're coming over?" asked Eddie.

"They'll be here in about fifteen minutes. Run across the street and get Tony for me. Tell him that he should join us."

Eddie left the office and returned a few minutes later with Tony Two Scoops. They both walked into Wheeze's office and observed two other men sitting there. Both men knew Tony well and got up from their seats when he entered the room, out of respect for his retired position within the family.

The two men were known as Sausage and Rock on the streets. Sausage was an Italian male about 5'9" tall, 180 pounds, about 45 years of age with grayish black hair. Rock was also about 5'9" tall, about 170 pounds and about 45 years old with dark brown hair.

Wheeze had updated both of them on the situation and the needs of Tony.

They walked over to Tony and told him that this one would be a gift. No charge to him or the family for the service. Tony smiled and they spoke of old times for a few minutes.

"I'm sorry to break this reminiscing up, but we do have work to do," stated Wheeze

They all got into cars and went over to the apartment of Roberto Bubba Median to talk with him.

As they approached the door they heard voices coming from the apartment. They stopped at the door and listened for a few minutes. Rock kicked in the door and they all ran in and subdued both Bubba and the girl that was in the apartment with him.

Tony stayed back in the hallway. He was the last one to walk in after all of the commotion was over and everything was quiet.

He looked at Bubba and just smiled, knowing in his mind what was in store for the little thief that stole from the wrong people.

He then looked at the girl and suddenly he realized what may have happened.

"Don't I know you, little girl?" asked Tony.

"Yeah, Tony, that's right. I was with him," said the girl.

"You're my niece's friend. You're Nicky Geraffo, right?"

"Yes, that's my name. I remember you."

Tony: "I was there the same day you were, the day my niece placed the jewelry inside that hiding place that I made for her under the clock. You saw her put it there," said Tony.

"Yeah, I remember," said Nicky.

"You bitch; you set up your own friend. You're nothing to us anymore," stated Tony.

The girl did not answer she just sat there while Rock and Sausage sat Bubba down at the kitchen table.

Rock took Bubba's hands and held them while Sausage did a rendition on the human hand.

Sausage: "Now take a look at those hands; the human hand had (14) fourteen bones in the fingers, with (8) eight carpals which make up the palm of the hand. Interesting, isn't it?"

Wheeze looked at Sausage and laughed: "Yes very."

Sausage loved hands and knew all about them, especially how to use someone's hands to get what he wanted.

"Ah, but that's not all. You see, if you take a nail and hammer the nail in the correct position, you can go right through the hand without any serious damage to any of the bones. Of course, it will hurt like hell," stated Sausage as he opened a small box that he had brought with him and took out a nail and a small hammer.

Bubba: "Wait a minute, what do you guys want?"

With that question, Wheeze placed the bag of jewelry on the table: "Remember this stuff?"

Bubba: "Yeah, I sold that stuff to Lips. Was it yours? We just needed to get high, that's all."

Wheeze: "No, it is a friend's property. I have the jewelry. I want the money that you were paid returned to Lips."

Bubba: "I'll get it."

Wheeze nodded his head at Sausage who in turn hammered a nail through Bubba's right hand, nailing him to the table. He held a second nail in position over Bubba's left hand as Rock held his hand in position.

Wheeze: "You say you can get me the money?"

Bubba was still yelling from the pain, "Yes, yes, I'll get it, please don't hurt me anymore!"

Wheeze nodded his head again at Sausage, giving the OK to pull the nail out.

Sausage: "Young man what are you doing with my nail? I need that nail back" He stated, as he removed the nail from Bubbas hand.

Wheeze: "Bubba, you have twenty four hours to get the money or I will tell Sausage to finish the job."

Bubba: "I'll get it, I promise. I'll have it tonight."

Wheeze: "Tony, here's the jewelry. I'll take care of the rest."

Tony took the jewelry, turned his back on the girl and walked out. He thanked Wheeze. He didn't care what Wheeze did or how he did it.

Wheeze took the girl by the hand. He looked closely at it, then at her. "You have very pretty hands. I may like the skin for an ornament in my den."

"Look, we'll get you what you want, leave us alone," stated Nicky.

"I'm sure that you will," answered Wheeze.

"Let's go men. Bubba and Nicky, I want that cash back within twenty four hours or I may be forced to allow Sausage here to get back into this operation and finish it. You see Sausage got his name from the way he treats the hands that he takes as trophies"

Wheeze, Eddie, Sausage and Rock all left the apartment.

Nicky went over to Bubba to help him with his hand. Bubba was worried about where they would get the five thousand dollars to pay Wheeze.

"What are we gonna do? We only have three thousand left from the cash that we had."

"We'll get it from my mother, don't worry," stated Nicky.

***

After wrapping his hand, they left and went over to Mrs. Geraffos' home, Nicky's mother. They asked her mother for the money that they needed.

"I can't give him that much money, I'll be broke. You two are junkies and need to pay for what you do. You keep hurting me and now you want me to bail you out. No, I can't afford to do it, I don't have the money."

"Yes, you do, you have those negotiable bonds that Dad left you when he died."

"I can't sell them. I live off of the interest that they pay. That's the only money that I have."

They were all standing in the kitchen when Bubba grabbed her with his good hand and shook the old lady, yelling at her that she had to help them.

Nicky was standing behind her mother, leaning against the stove. Her hand touched a black steel frying pan that was on the stove. Nicky instinctively looked at the pan, picked it up and hit her mother on top of her head. The blow was so hard that she could hear the thud of the pan literally cracking the scull. Nicky leans over and hits her again and begins laughing. Then sees her mother lying on the ground her demeanor changes to sorrow. She kneels down and brushes her mother's hair away from her face, her demeanor immediately changes and she gets up and joins Bubba, laughing with satisfaction that they will get the bonds.

"Come on, I'll get the bonds," stated Nicky.

Nicky and Bubba went into the bedroom, opened the closet and opened a small safe that contained the bonds. They took the bonds and left the apartment, leaving Mrs. Geraffo lying on the kitchen floor.

They went over to the Calabria's Club and handed the bonds to Wheeze, who took them while saying to Bubba and Nicky, "You two assholes had better not let me see you in the area again. You fucked with the wrong people this time. I'm giving you a break because you are a couple of pieces of shit and not worth the trouble of burying you."

***

The next day, Mrs. Geraffo's body was discovered by a neighbor who contacted the police.

When the police found the body, they also found the frying pan. It had blood on it with hair mixed in with the blood. They printed the pan and found a set of fingerprints. They also found a fingernail broken in Mrs. Geraffo's arm where Bubba held her. When they ran the prints they came up as Nicky Geraffo's prints in the NCIC as well as her criminal record which was substantial.

Nicky was arrested for the murder of Mrs. Geraffo and Bubba was with her at the time. The detectives noticed that his fingernail was broken at the same angle as the one they found on the dead women. The police were able to verify that the nail found on the body was the nail that was missing from Bubba's hand. The broken nail matched in texture as well as in the break location and angle to the fingernail that was found imbedded in the dead arm of Mrs. Geraffo.

Bubba was arrested and after a trial they both received a sentence of 20 years to life.

Chapter 23

NOSE

Monday August 28, 1978

Ernie got out of bed and got ready to go for breakfast. He walked out of the building where his apartment was located and stopped on the stoop. He looked around and remembered his childhood in Brooklyn. Flashes of kick the can, stick ball, pitching pennies, the feasts, the grease poles and other games were all running through his mind as he sat down on the steps.

He heard a familiar whistle; he looked in the direction of that sound and saw his friend the mockingbird sitting on a wire, singing.

Ernie joined the song by whistling a song of his own. The bird tried to repeat the song that Ernie whistled. He took a few tries and finally nailed Ernie's song. Ernie stood there for a few minutes and enjoyed watching and listening to the mockingbird sing.

Ernie left the stoop and headed over to the luncheonette. He walked in and sat down. Tony came over with some coffee.

"How did it go in Florida?" asked Tony.

"Everything went fine; why, is there a problem that I don't know about?"

"No, not really, I'm sure that Joey will discuss it with you."

"What the fuck is wrong now?"

"You know, Eddie, everyone likes you. I can't say what I don't know. All I know is that you have to be careful. Joey is a little crazy sometimes. He is better since he got older, but he's apt to jump before he thinks, so be careful."

"OK, Tony, thanks for letting me know."

Tony walked off to take care of some other customers. Eddie sat there wondering what Tony was talking about. Could it be that Joey had decided that Eddie was the bad guy in this entire situation? He didn't know. He decided to wait and see.

Eddie finished his breakfast and started to leave when Tony told him to be safe and remember what he had said.

Eddie felt as though Tony was trying to tell him something. What it was he didn't know for sure. The only thing he could think of was the information that Joey Bats received from his federal connection.

Eddie walked into the club and saw Spitball and Cheech standing by Joey's office, talking. They waved to him as he entered. Spitball leaned into the office and Eddie could hear him tell Joey that Eddie just walked in.

Joey Bats walked out of his office with Wheeze and asked Eddie to join them.

Eddie walked into the office. Spitball and Cheech followed and closed the door after they were in.

Wheeze was standing behind the desk and behind Joey Bats. Joey looked at all of the men and asked where Nose was.

"He'll be here in a minute or two, Joey. I left a message for him," replied Spitball.

"OK, everyone, take a seat and we'll wait," ordered Joey.

A few minutes later Nose walked in. "Sorry I'm late. I just got your message Spitball."

Spitball nodded to Nose.

"Nose, have a seat, right here in front of me," stated Joey.

"Men, we have someone here that is talking to the fed's, giving them information about our operations. We must stop this leak and stop it now," stated Wheeze.

Eddie: "Who is it, Wheeze, can you tell us for sure?"

Joey answered: "We've been analyzing all of the information that we received from our contact and tying it in to locations and places, as well as who was in on what job."

Spitball: "So what did you come up with?"

Joey: "We'll get to that, but first we have some business to conduct."

Nose: "OK, what do you need?"

Joey: "I'm happy that you asked that, Nose. I want you to sign this document."

Nose took the document and read it. At one point he read out loud: "....shall convey any and all properties owned by Mr. Edward Haronetti, who does business as Eddie the Nose, to Mr. Joey (Bats) Borgazino '.....Mumble, mumble...' in exchange for one thousand dollars in US currency."

Nose looked at Joey: "Hey, Joey, this says that I'm selling you my junkyard. What the hell should I do that for?"

Joey: "Because we need you to do that. I can't explain now. I'll give it back to you in a couple of months. That's why the cash amount is so small."

Nose: "Not for nothing, but what if something happens?"

Joey: "How long do you know me?"

Nose: "Most of my life."

Joey: "Knowing that we have been friends for so long, you still don't trust my word?"

Nose: "No, I trust you, but I'm just not sure that this is the right thing to do. Maybe if I knew more about what you're doing I would agree easier."

Joey: "No, I can't tell you anything, just sign it and it will all work out."

Nose: "Eddie, do you know what's going on here?"

Eddie: "No, I have no idea."

Nose: "Any of you guys know what's going on?"

There was no reply from anyone.

Joey: "Nose, that's OK, if you don't want to sign it we'll go another way."

Nose: "I'll sign it. I think I can put my trust in you after all these years."

Joey: "Good, I'm glad to hear it."

Nose signed the paper and Spitball, Wheeze and Cheech signed as witnesses.

Joey: "Now that that's over, follow me."

Everyone started to follow Joey out of the office when he turned to the men, "No not you guys, just Nose, Eddie and Ronny."

Eddie had no idea what was going on. He was beginning to worry that his true identity had been uncovered.

Joey walked out into the back alley, a bad sign in Eddie's mind.

Once they were in the alley, Joey walked over to Eddie the Nose, kissed him on the check, turned his back on him and began walking inside.

Nose knew what that meant and began to yell: "What did I do?"

Joey never turned back towards him and Ronny, who was standing behind him, took out his gun and fired two shots into the head of Nose. Nose fell to the ground. "He's one of our fucken rats," stated Ronny.

"Are you sure Ronny?" asked Eddie.

"Hey, all I can do is follow our orders. Joey said it's him and we were to handle it. Go and get the car."

It was too late, it all happened so fast Eddie had no time to intervene. All he could do now was follow directions. He went and brought the car into the alley way. When he returned, Spitball, Cheech and Ronny were together waiting for him. They loaded Nose into the car.

Ronny: "Grab his keys, we need to make some copies of the junkyard key and give them to the guys. We'll take him there first."

Eddie did as directed by Ronny. All he could think of was that he would make sure that this would be looked at as a cold blooded murder in the first degree, which called for life for every one of these men.

They took Nose to the junkyard. They placed him under one of the cars after digging a shallow grave and covering him with some lime and dirt.

When they were done, they went to a locksmith that Ronny knew and made several copies of the junkyard key.

There was very little talk, mostly because everyone liked Nose.

Eddie: "Guys, that was hard. I liked Nose." Eddie was fishing for information

Spitball: "Eddie, we all liked the guy. Business is business, he could have put us all in jail and then where would we be? He's better off where he is and so are we."

Eddie: "I guess that answers my question."

Ronny: "I'm not so sure. That may be one part of the problem. I get the feeling that there may be more going on. We'll see, I'm sure of that"

They returned to the club where Eddie let everyone off.

"Eddie, where are you going?" asked Ronny.

"I was thinking about a sandwich, you want one?"

"No, come right back, we have a lot of work to do."

"I will, give me a half hour," replied Eddie.

Eddie went to the luncheonette and picked up a sandwich to go. He then drove to a pay phone to call Jack.

He told Jack what happened. In one way they were relieved that Ernie was never identified and on the other hand they all felt very bad that Nose was killed. Ernie could do nothing to stop it. He didn't even know it was going to happen.

Ernie: "We have to get this fucken case closed before these mad men kill the entire family."

Jack: "I doubt that they would do that."

Ernie: "Really, if they get an idea that they made a mistake, they will do whatever it takes for protection."

Jack: "We're working on the paperwork. We have a team working on the closing plan. This case is all over the place. New York, New Jersey, California and Massachusetts and we have to coordinate all of these locations and people."

Ernie: "Good, I have to go, they need me back there. I assume they want to set up for the delivery and the diversion. Hey, don't forget the Coast Guard on this. We're gonna need them."

Jack: "Don't worry, we have it all covered. I think we should have you in here before we close if that's possible so that everyone can get a good look at you. There's bound to be trouble somewhere and you may be in the middle."

Ernie: "You set it up and I'll be there, even if it's only for a few minutes."

Jack agreed and Ernie hung up the phone. He ate his sandwich as he drove to the club where he was to meet with Ronny.

Ronny asked Eddie to leave the club with him.

"Where are we going?" asked Eddie.

"I'll show you our storage facility and introduce you to our preparation and cutting man," stated Ronny.

They drove to the Sheepshead Bay warehouse which was located at 2659 Knapp St in Brooklyn. Eddie made a mental note of the address for the warrants.

They entered the building and Ronny introduced Eddie as his partner, assigned by Wheeze and Joey to the most important man in the narcotics operation, Mr. Alfonso Durangani. He was an old Capo who was now in charge of the drugs once they reached the warehouse. He and his team would cut and package the drugs for distribution to the dealers that worked for the Family.

Eddie: "Is there a piss room here?"

Alfonso: "Right over in that corner. Don't drown," he replied with a smile.

Eddie smiled and walked over to the toilet. He took a match book out of his pocket and wrote down the address and the name of Alfonso for his report.

Eddie returned as Ronny was telling Alfonso when he would arrive with the trucks.

Alfonso: "Remember, your guys have to unload everything and then I take charge."

Ronny: "Understood."

Eddie: "Nice to meet you Alfonso. We'll see you next week."

Alfonso: "I will be here with my team and all the needed equipment and cutting agents."

Ronny and Eddie left the building.

***

Back with Jack and the team

Jack: "Paul, Ernie will probably have some additional information as he gets closer to how they do their cutting and transporting. We have to be ready to move on those things fast."

Paul: "You're right. I just spoke with the California State Police. They are willing and able to pick up The Lark as soon as we let them know our time frame."

Jack: "Great. I'll call the Coast Guard."

Jack contacted the Coast Guard who were more than willing to cooperate. He filled them in on the case and they stated that they would be ready when the team was ready.

They had to contact the New Jersey State Police and they did not expect any problems. They have always co-operated with New York in the past.

"How are you guys doing on those search warrants?" asked Jack of one group of men doing the paperwork. They had everything under control.

He checked with the men doing the arrest warrants and that was all under control.

The next move was to set up a time and date for all the people to meet. That's when Jack, Paul and the New York detectives would distribute the work. They needed to pick a special team that would do the cover at the pickup point for the ships.

They had to be ready in the event that Ernie came in with more information that would change any part of the plan.

***

Brooklyn with Ronny and Eddie

"Eddie, the day is shot. Let's order the trucks tomorrow. We'll have some fun tonight."

"Sounds good to me; I want to head home and take a shower before I go to the club."

"Yes, that's a good idea. I'll see you at the club tonight."

"See you then," Eddie stated as he left Ronny's car. He returned to his car and drove off.

Ernie drove to his apartment and the first thing he did upon entering was dial the team to make a report.

"Jack?"

"Ernie, where the hell have you been? The teams are looking for you. They can never find you anymore. They expected you back yesterday."

"I'm a busy man and I have additional information for you. Let me speak with the stenographer."

"OK, go ahead."

Ernie relayed all of the information about the warehouse and Alfonso and the fact that they would be arranging for the trucks the next day. When he was finished making his report, Paul asked about Alfonso.

Paul: "Ernie, his name wouldn't be Alfonso Durangani, would it?"

Ernie: "Yes, it is, that's how he was introduced to me. Why do you ask?"

Paul: "I assumed he was dead. I knew of him when I was a new agent. He was a big man in his day."

Ernie: "Yes, he was a Capo and had his own team of soldiers. They were a small family within the larger family."

Paul: "Yes, that's him. He was a dangerous man as I remember, but we were never able to pin anything on him. He was smart and cautious."

Ernie: "Well, you have him now. He's the cutter. You have him big time."

Paul: "That will be a feather in our cap. Actually, this whole case will be a feather in your cap."

Ernie: "I don't give a fuck about feathers or credit. I just want to get the guys that killed all of those people without cause. Not that, maybe, they didn't deserve to be killed, but they had nothing to do with my case and that's why they were killed. I want them behind bars and I think we'll get most of them in the roundup."

Jack: "Going over these reports seems to indicate that you got them all, Ernie."

Ernie: "Not me, we got them, but we don't have the boss of the Columbian family who actually gave the order and paid for the hit."

Jack: "No, we don't, but the Fed's are working on that and this case will be a great assistance to them."

Ernie: "I'm happy to hear that. I have to go; I have to meet Ronny at the club. I guess I'll play some cards tonight."

Jack: "OK, be careful."

Ernie hung up the phone and went in to take a shower and dress for a night at the club.

Ernie arrived at the club at eight o'clock that evening and saw Ronny playing cards with Spitball and a few other men that he had seen around the club.

Ronny saw him and signaled Eddie to join the game, which he did.

Eddie: "Hi, guys, what's new?"

Ronny: "Eddie, you know everybody here, don't you?"

Eddie: "I've seen them around and I've been introduced, but I can't remember everyone's name."

Ronny: "That's understandable. Guys, this is my partner Eddie in case you don't know him."

Spitball smiled and replied: "Fugataboutit, everybody knows Eddie by now. He's becoming a big man in this area."

The men all laughed and agreed that they all knew who he was and how he was respected by the bosses.

One man known as Freddie (Freddie the Clam) Amarolt told Ronny that he should be careful because Eddie may take over in his place and become the next Capo instead of Ronny.

Ronny: "I ain't worried about that. Eddie and I are buddies, we look out for each other."

Eddie: "Who knows, maybe I'll send Ronny to jail." as he laughed. Everyone froze and waited for Ronny to laugh. It took a long twenty seconds as he thought about the statement and then started laughing and talking: "Eddie, not for nothing, but you gotta stop that joking around, that kind of fucking around scares people."

Eddie: "That's why I say it, for effect."

Spitball: "Fugheddaboudit, we have too much work coming up. I hate hard work."

About an hour later, a lady pushed through the door and ran to the club. Everyone turned and looked at her. Her right hand was inside her pocketbook and you could tell that she was holding onto something that she didn't want everyone to see.

Unknown women: "Who's in charge here?" she asked.

Ronny stood up: "I guess, for the moment, I am. Who are you? What are you doing here? What's wrong?"

"I'm Mrs. Jonathan Rowden, my husband you call "Rower" for a nickname. He keeps giving you guys all of the money he makes and my kids and I go without." She pulled a gun from her purse.

Ronny: "Wait a minute, what does that have to do with us?"

Eddie: "Mrs. Rowder, how much has he lost?"

"He lost three hundred a week for the last two months. I have three kids to feed."

Eddie: "He's addicted to gambling and you have to feed your kids, right?"

"Yes."

Eddie: "Mrs. Rowder, you will never feed them from a jail cell; put the gun away and we can fix things for you."

By this time, Wheeze had stepped out of his office and was listening to the entire conversation. Eddie had his back to him and did not see him.

Mrs. Rowder placed the gun back in her purse, stating that she guessed he was right. She was at her wits end and didn't know what to do." She burst out in tears.

Eddie signaled her to walk over and sit with him, which she did.

Eddie: "Spitball, get her a glass of water, unless you want something stronger, Mrs. Rowder?"

"No, no, that will be fine, thank you."

Spitball went and got the water. He handed it to her and looked at Eddie as if to ask, "What the hell are you gonna do now?"

Eddie: "Mrs. Rowder, please try to relax. We don't like to see men do this anymore than you, so we would like to help you."

"I don't want anything except to make sure he stops gambling. My kids have to eat. I take in wash, I work as a waitress and I still can't make ends meet as long as he gambles."

Eddie: "The first thing that I will do is bar him from the club, but that won't stop him from going to other clubs that we have no control over his actions."

"No, I know that. I have to get him some help," replied Mrs. Rowder

Eddie: "The second thing we will do is have a talk with him. The first chance I get. I will talk to him about his family."

"Please, don't hurt him."

Eddie: "No Ma'am. I promise that he will not be injured by us. We would never injure anyone."

"Thank you, Mr., I'm sorry for this, but my kids are my life."

Eddie: "You can call me Eddie." as he reached onto the table and counted out three hundred dollars. He handed Mrs. Rowder the cash.

"No, I don't want your money. I need your cooperation to stop my husband from doing this every week."

Eddie: "Listen to me. We were totally unaware of what was going on. We want to help you and your children. Take the money, go home and leave it to us."

Mrs. Rowder took the money, thanked Eddie, and left the club.

Wheeze: "Eddie, come in here."

Eddie looked at Ronny. He walked over to Wheeze's door and walked in.

"Wheeze, you wanted me?"

Wheeze walked over from behind his desk and shook hands with Eddie. "Eddie you did that like a pro. Perfect. Here's the three hundred you gave her. Put it back on the table."

"Thanks Wheeze."

"I noticed that Ronny pulled a blank and didn't know what to do. We'll discuss him at a later date. You stepped in perfectly. You may become a capo around here yet."

"That's nice of you to say," replied Eddie.

"Follow through with your promise to that women and talk to her husband. I'll make sure he's banned from the club. We don't need that kind of attention. I still can't get over how well you handled it. I gotta tell Joey this one."

"Thanks again. We'll take care of it as soon as we see him," said Eddie.

"Good"

"Look, Wheeze, I'm tired, it's very late, I'm gonna head home and get some sleep."

"OK, see you when I see you."

Eddie left the office and Ronny stopped him as he was leaving the club.

"Eddie, thanks. I didn't know exactly what to do. When she came out with that gun, I froze. You handled it the best way possible."

"Thanks, Ronny. I'm out of here. I need my beauty rest."

"OK. I'll meet you here around noon and we can set up the trucks."

"See you then," stated Eddie as he left the building.

Ernie was driving through the city, thinking and preparing himself for shutting down the operation, when he realized that he needed some sort of a diversion to take his mind off of the case for a while.

He found himself in the Red Hook section of Brooklyn on Seventh Avenue. He saw Sackett Street and remembered his Uncle Fredo. Fredo was a tractor trailer driver most of his life and had recently passed away.

**

Brooklyn, Red Hook Section 1971

Fredo was a 65 year old Italian male, 5'8" tall. He was a well built man who still had an appearance of authority and strength when he walked down the street. This appearance was left over from his days as a United States Marine.

Ernie had not seen him for over a year. In 1971, Ernie lived in Massachusetts and had only been on the job as patrolman for a short time.

Ernie parked his car near his uncle's old home on Sackett Street in Brooklyn. He exited his car and looked up. He saw Uncle Fredo coming out of his home.

Fredo, saw Ernie. You could see the happiness in his face; it lit up when he saw Ernie, his brother's son and first nephew.

"Ernie, it's so wonderful to see you. I'm glad you're here."

"Uncle Fredo, the same goes for me. I know I don't get down to these parts very often. I'm sorry that it isn't more often, but I was hoping that we could spend some time together today."

"That's wonderful. You're a cop now, I hear?"

"Yeah, I'll always be a cop, Uncle. Sorry if that bothers you."

"Never, I'm happy that you went legit instead of joining the local family. Can you come with me to my club?

"Sure, I would love to. What club?" asked Ernie.

"A little gambling club with a few tables, I have to open up the place. Some of the guys are from the old neighborhood. They'll love to see you and say hello. Just keep it under your hat that you're a cop and let's call today a day off, OK?"

"Uncle, I'm off for a few days, but why do you say that? You never did anything that would interest a cop. Besides I'm not a cop in Brooklyn, I am a patrolman for the Transit Police in Boston."

"No, I don't do anything serious, I run a card game, that's all. I even have some officials that play there along with the old neighborhood crowd. We serve food and beverages and it's a nice clean place."

Ernie agreed to go with his uncle for a couple of hours.

Fredo drove and they spoke of old times, when Ernie used to ride in the tractor with him to keep him company. Fredo would give Ernie a couple of bucks in appreciation for the company. Ernie was only twelve years old in those days. They spoke of fishing trips they went on and family gatherings as they pulled up to Fredo's club.

They parked the car and Fredo directed Ernie up an alley to the club. He unlocked the door. Fredo, Ernie and the two employees that were waiting for him, entered the club.

Four tables were quickly busy and remained so the entire time that Ernie was in the club. Ernie was reintroduced to old friends from his past who knew him as a child.

These were honest hard-working men who obviously enjoyed gambling, but held steady jobs, had families, homes and loving children. This was their relaxation and time to themselves.

There were men at other tables that clearly were there for business; this was how they made their living, or at least it seemed so. They were the guys who preyed on the losers.

As Ernie talked small-talk with his uncle, he watched the tables. He could see that the "pros" would build a pile of money on the table and win. This was their game. The old men were their prey and the pros were the vultures.

Two males walked through the door and entered the room. These two were different from the rest of the people in the club. The first man walked towards Fredo with a certain bold confidence. He approached the table.

Fredo got up and immediately greeted him with an outstretched hand. Everyone else stayed planted in their seats.

The stranger was a major presence. He was about 5' 7, slim, had dark blond hair, starting to grey, sported a large mustache and was wearing an expensive tailored silver-gray, shark-skinned suit with a matching gray Fedora hat. Ernie looked at his shoes; they were made from alligator skin and very expensive, he guessed. This guy was someone; but who? As Fredo and the stranger were talking, Ernie tried his best to eavesdrop on the conversation out of curiosity.

The second man had to be a bodyguard, Ernie thought. He was about 6'6" tall and weighed near three hundred pounds. This man never said a word, he simply sat down and watched the strangers every move.

Ernie's experiences with organized crime as a kid growing up in Brooklyn told him that this was an important man by virtue of the way he handled himself, at the very least, a representative of an important person within the families of the various organizations.

The stranger turned to Fredo: "Who's this guy?" He was asking about Ernie, whom he did not recognize.

Fredo: "Hi, Sonny, meet my nephew Ernie. You remember my brother Peppi. This is his son. He is not involved with my operation, just so you know."

Sonny: "Ernie, nice to meet you kid. I was sorry to hear about your dad's passing. He was a good guy and a great fighter as a kid and a hero during the war. I knew him well, from the old country as kids" said Sonny.

Ernie: "Thank you, He never spoke, much, of his days with the golden gloves."

Sonny: "At least he made it to the top, not like your uncle Fredo who fought professionally and only won six out of twelve fights. I lost a lot of cash betting on him, but he has always been a good friend," stated Sonny.

Ernie: "Great meeting you, Sonny," said Ernie.

Fredo: "Sonny, how's your brother Paulie doing?"

Sonny: "He's fine, busy as always. I'm covering this end of the business for him. How much do you need for this week?"

Fredo whispered as Ernie strained to listen. "I figure I need about ten large." Fredo, reached into his coat pocket and pulled out a sheet of paper and handed it to Sonny. "Here's the list of funds and whom I loaned out to last week."

Sonny took the paper, reached in his pocket and pulled out a fist full of rolled up bills that could choke a horse. Ernie's eyes opened like saucers as he stared. He had never seen a roll of bills that big come out of any man's pocket. Sonny placed the roll in his two hands, licked his right hand thumb and ripped off one hundred, hundred -dollar bills without a blink. He put the remaining roll of bills back in his pocket. Fredo took them and nodded a thank you and stuffed them quickly in his pocket. Transaction done! Ernie was stunned with the ease of this exchange and quickly looked away.

Sonny and Fredo walked away with the guidance of Sonny and spoke for a few moments, then Fredo walked back to the table as Sonny exited the club. Ernie's instincts and inquiring mind got the best of him and he had to ask: "Uncle Fredo, that Sonny, you asked him about his brother Paulie. Is he from the neighborhood?"

Fredo bent over and softly said to Ernie, "No, I don't think you know him. He's a top dog in the city, he's got a nickname, but you can't repeat it. He's got lots of dough. I don't know where from, but when my gamblers need some help, he's always there. Ya know, we don't always have the cash to play with." Ernie nodded with questions in his mind as he listened to his uncle.

"What's the guy's nickname?" Ernie asked. "They call him the 'Judge' out of respect and because of his authority within the families," Fredo softly responded so no one could hear.

"The Judge" replied Ernie: "A criminal court judge?" asked Ernie.

"No, not the criminal courts as you would know them. He holds a special position within the families that credit him with decision making when there is a problem to be solved," ,stated Fredo.

"So, he solves problems?" asked Ernie.

"You don't need to know more than this. You're beginning to sound like a cop. Shut up for Christ's sake," answered Fredo.

Ernie quickly jumped in, "Sorry, Uncle, I know the rules. Omerta!"

Fredo put his hands up to silence Ernie. Ernie stopped, reflected and said, "Sorry, I know the rules."

Fredo showed that he was uncomfortable and Ernie quickly picked up on it and He extended his hand to say goodbye. He promised to visit more often and said that he would call for a cab, despite his uncle's insistence that he would drive.

Fredo then took out of his pocket two of the hundred dollar bills given to him by Sonny and handed them to Ernie. "For Christ's sake, this will pay for your cab and you'll have some extra to make sure you visit more often."

Ernie gave his uncle a huge Italian hug, kissed his cheek and as he left, heard the sound of a honking horn from a cab, obviously waiting outside. The cabs were always in the area of the club, Ernie later found out.

The club may have been a secret, but the cab drivers knew about it. They were always around for the left over victims needing to get from place to place after they were finished being preyed upon.

***

Back in Ernie's Car

Ernie woke up from his daydream and drove back to his apartment feeling as though he had actually been visiting with his uncle again. Tomorrow would be a long day.

Chapter 24

The Team

Tuesday August 29, 1978

Back at the team office, the men were divided up into separate teams. Each team was assigned a different task. Some were assigned to do search warrants others to do body warrants while still others were assigned to contact the various agencies to be included in the closing roundup of all of the evidence and bodies. The biggest problem with this was that Ernie would be without cover for a while.

Paul: "Jack, I wouldn't worry about that too much. He can take care of himself. After all, we can't even find him most of the time. We never really covered him because he moved around so much that we couldn't keep up with him. I have confidence he'll be OK."

Jack: "Yes, you're right, he moves when he has to and can't be worried about whether or not he has coverage. I guess we have been friends and partners for so long that I worry about his welfare even though I know he's OK. I'll tell you one thing; he would be the same way with me if I were out there."

Paul: "Yes, I can see that, you guys seem to know what the other is thinking sometimes."

Jack: "That comes from spending so much time together. I bet I see him as much as his wife does and at times, when we're on a case, I see him more than she does."

Paul: "She must be quite a woman to put up with all of this."

Jack: "They love each other and that's what counts. Where are we with the DA?"

Paul: He doesn't have any questions right now. He says he will when it comes to the court case, but as far as he's concerned, we have fantastic evidentiary support for the case."

Jack: "Great, what about the location of our meeting? Are we all set with that?"

Paul: "That will be here in the federal building. We have an auditorium down in the basement that will serve us well."

Jack: "How many men will we have?"

Paul: "We'll have my team from the DEA, then we'll have an ATF team. The New York P.D. is sending a hundred men and New Jersey State police are sending about seventy-five men. In all we should have about three hundred men. We will be spread thin because of all of the targets that we have, but we'll handle it.

Jack: "Everything looks like it's coming together. We have to divide the men and send them out. We'll do the primary sites first and then, as the men come in from those, we'll send them out on the secondary sites."

Paul: "Exactly my thoughts. I figure that we'll need about seventy men to cover the ships being unloaded. We'll need men high on this cliff for cover; they have to be careful because the family may have cover men there also. We shouldn't have to worry about Ernie until we hit the warehouse and then we'll take him into custody, just like everyone else"

Jack: "Yes and when they leave the area, the Coast Guard can take down the ships, board them and arrest everyone as well as confiscate the drugs still aboard."

Paul: "Then you want to take the people with Ernie out at the warehouse in Sheepshead Bay?"

Jack: "Exactly"

Paul: "Why wait until then?"

Jack: "Because we can't hit the warehouse unless they have the drugs on the premises. If we do, the warehouse people may have a loophole to jump through."

Paul: "Yes, I think you're right. OK, we'll talk and put a plan together that should work to our benefit."

They went on making plans and decisions that would protect the officers and civilians at the same time by causing what they felt would be the least chance of any shooting taking place or anyone getting hurt.

***

Same Day Back at the Luncheonette

Eddie was having breakfast when Ronny walked in, sat down and ordered pancakes.

"We'll do the trucks today. Wait till you meet this guy; he owes us big time. So whatever Wheeze wants, he gets from this guy."

"Who is this guy?" asked Eddie.

"His name is Adolpho Granolini, owner of the Venus Trucking Company in Brooklyn. Wheeze saved his ass a few years back. He feels that he can never pay us back; it's a nice way to get our trucks for nothing."

"Are you sure that he didn't see what happened to the guy he had a problem with and now he's afraid to say no to the family?" asked Eddie.

"Fugheddaboudit, who gives a fuck, as long as we get the trucks," stated Ronny.

"True," said Eddie.

Tony Two Scoops came over to the table to say hi and speak with Ronny and Eddie.

Eddie: "Tony, I heard a story the other day about you."

Tony: "What's that?"

Eddie: "I was told that you were a Capo and took on specialty jobs years ago which led to your nickname, not scoops of ice cream. Is that true?"

Ronny: "Eddie you shouldn't bring up the past like that. He sells ice cream."

Tony: "No, it's all right. He should know the history of our family. Yes, Eddie, I was a capo and I was a specialty man. I eliminated the problems in those days. Back then it wasn't like it is today, where we can sit down and discuss. In the old days, people started shooting if you looked at them the wrong way."

Eddie: "Thanks, Tony, I like to know who can be counted on in a pinch and it's obvious that we can count on you."

Tony: "Always, Eddie, always."

Eddie and Ronny left the luncheonette and drove over to the Venus Trucking Company in Brooklyn, where Ronny introduced Eddie to the owner. They made arrangements for the trucks and returned to the club where they reported to Wheeze.

Ronny: "Wheeze, we're all ready for the delivery."

Wheeze: "You ordered the trucks?"

Eddie: "Yes, we did."

Wheeze: "You arranged everything at the warehouse?"

Ronny: "All done."

Wheeze: "Then you spoke to the men and had them keep the night free?"

Ronny: "Oh, shit I knew there was something I forgot to do."

Eddie: "We didn't forget, we have to call a meeting tonight or tomorrow morning, as long as it's OK with you, Wheeze."

Wheeze: "That's what makes you two a good team. You seem to cover each other's errors. We need more of that type of team work."

Eddie: "Thanks, Wheeze. When should we call the meeting?"

Wheeze: "Most of the guys are here now. Tell them you'll meet in the morning."

Eddie walked out to the card room and announced that everyone was to be in the club tomorrow morning at ten.

Eddie: "Spitball and Cheech, please contact those men that are not here."

Spitball: "Will do, can you give us an idea of what's up?"

Eddie: "We'll talk in the morning.

Spitball: "OK, Eddie, you're the boss."

Eddie's eyes opened and he turned away from the men. He returned to the office, thinking about what Spitball had said, "Ok, Eddie, you're the boss". He felt kind of bad about what he was about to do.

His mind switched to all the thousands of lives that would be saved from this action, the people that would not have the drugs to become addicted, the hot shots or overdoses that would not be used, the children in grammar school, high school and colleges that he and his team were preventing from becoming addicted. The confiscation of heroin, marijuana and the blow would keep people from becoming addicted; these were the things he was fighting for. The fact that some people went to jail was only deserved peripheral damage.

Eddie entered the office: "I took care of it, Wheeze."

Wheeze: "Good, now get your thoughts together and run them by me before the meeting. You guys are learning and will do very well when you have your own groups after our expansion."

Eddie: "Expansion?"

Wheeze: "Yes, in case you don't know it, we're gonna take over the Lantigo family and all of the soldiers."

Ronny: "He's not gonna sit quietly for that."

Eddie: "No, and you're right, Ronny. I assume that Wheeze and Joey have a plan?"

Wheeze: "You assume right Eddie. You're going over there and so is Ronny. We'll be in constant touch. Eventually we will bring in Louie the Lark, you remember Louie don't you, Ronny?"

Ronny: "Yeah, he did the card game with us."

Wheeze: "Right. He'll take care of a couple of situations for us, the first of which is Mr. Simon Lantigo. If he's not available, we'll give the contract to Tony Two Scoops."

Eddie: "Does Tony know?"

Wheeze: "Yeah, he surprised me when he said that he actually missed the old days. He said that he would love to help out. In that case I think Eddie should back him up, but only if it comes to him taking the job."

Eddie: "What about the hard nose soldiers that Lantigo has?"

Wheeze: "That will be one of your jobs, finding out who they are so that we can eliminate them when the time comes."

Eddie: "We're talking months down the road, right?"

Wheeze: "Maybe a year down the road. I don't usually talk about our plans this much, but you two guys are important to the entire plan."

Eddie: "Thanks for the opportunity, Wheeze."

Wheeze: "You guys, get out of here. I know that I don't have to tell you to keep that information under your hat. By the way, Ronny, you and Eddie will be joining Joey and me after the unloading of the ships. One of the men will take your car. We have a special job to clean up and we want you two with us."

Ronny and Eddie agreed and said they would not say a word to anyone.

They left the building. Ronny went his way and Eddie went back to the apartment to make a call to his team.

"Jack?"

"Yeah, Ernie, what's up?"

Ernie relayed the information that he had and the fact that everyone would be meeting the next morning and that he and Ronny would be holding the meeting.

Jack: "Ernie, let me put the stenographer on."

Ernie spoke to the typist who put the report together as he dictated it. He also included the information that Wheeze told them about taking over the Lantigo family and some special job that had to be done after they finished unloading the ships, which he knew nothing about.

Jack: "Ernie, I was listening. These guys have some big ambitions and what's this special job?"

Ernie: "Yes, and I'm glad that we will be in a position to stop this expansion, or at least hold it up for a while. Make sure that the report shows that the Borgazino family plans to eliminate the heads of the Lantigo family. When the lawyers read that, they will relay it to the appropriate heads of the families. As far as the special job is concerned, I wouldn't worry about it. They probably want to go for drinks and celebrate, since this is the first big job that Ronny and I did alone."

Jack: "OK, as long as you feel secure, we won't worry about that special job. I have some other news. The bankers that are used by both of the families are well known by a member of the team and he has been interviewed. He will be giving us all of the banking information of both families, including the off-shore accounts which will tie into the Columbian family. We'll freeze all the accounts in time. The DEA wants to keep that information quiet until they are ready to close down that operation after they speak with the Columbian government."

Ernie: "That's amazing. Did you ever think that this shitty case would get so widespread?"

Jack: "No one did. We all thought that it would be a quickie, but the investigating of this case will go on for years after we're done."

Ernie: "OK, Jack, I'll let you know what happens at the meet in the morning."

Jack: "Speak with you then. We'll hear the conversation. At those meetings everyone speaks nice and loud, we can hear almost everything through the mikes that were planted."

***

Wednesday August 30, 1978

It was ten in the morning when Eddie walked through the lounge and into the club room out back. The bartender said "Hi" as he passed through and he returned the gesture.

He entered the club card room; most of the men were sitting talking. They looked up at him and some said "Hi," while others kept talking to the group that they were sitting with.

Ronny was at one end of the room at what appeared to be a head table. He waved to Eddie, making a gesture for Eddie to join him.

Eddie: "Are we all set?"

Ronny: "Yeah, I have this list of things to cover that Wheeze gave me. He's in the office."

Eddie: "Oh, I figured he would run this meeting and we would learn from him."

Ronny: "Fugheddaboudit, I have it. He'll listen in and say something if we miss some point."

Eddie: "OK, I'm here to learn from the master, you take it."

Ronny called the meeting to order and looked around. He saw that all the men were present and began with the explanation of what was being done. He assigned men to the ships, the trucks the warehouse and assigned the different men to the different locations.

He set up the meeting for the warehouse after the trucks were unloaded and explained to the men that it would take a few days to cut and package the product before they could pick up their needs.

Ronny: "We've all been through this before, so there shouldn't be any surprises. Are there any questions?"

Spitball: "I know you two are new at running this so if you don't mind, I really would appreciate you giving us some cover while we unload the ships."

Ronny looked at his notes on the slip of paper: "Oh, yes, thanks Spitball, I almost forgot. Who covered the last deal from the top of that hill?"

Two men stood up and stated that they covered the last three deliveries.

Eddie: "Just so we know, where exactly do you cover the deliveries from?"

One of the men explained that about one hundred and fifty feet behind the delivery area, there is a small hill that overlooks the entire area. There is a sandy road that goes up there and that they cover from on top of that hill.

Eddie: "Thank you. It's nice to know where everyone will be. Once we are finished with unloading the ships, you two guys can leave the area."

At the meeting they all agreed to meet at the club on Friday night at six for a preliminary briefing before they took off for the delivery. After the meeting, some of the men stayed and played cards while Spitball asked Eddie if he wanted to take a run out to the airport with him and Cheech.

Eddie told Spitball that he had some things to do, that he would appreciate it if he could put the airport thing off until this delivery was over.

Spitball agreed.

Eddie left the club and went home where he made another report to the team, letting them know exactly where the cover team would be for the delivery.

Chapter 25

Delivery

Friday September 1, 1978

Early that morning Ernie contacted the team office. Ernie was told to meet Jack at their usual meeting area. Jack said that he could leave his car and ride into the meeting with him. Ernie was told to meet Jack at two thirty in the afternoon.

Ernie agreed and advised them of the cover team that was set up by Ronny and what the locations will be for that team. He advised that Scar would no longer be needed and could return to Massachusetts unless the team needed him for some other reason.

"Jack, make sure you tell Scar to stay out of trouble and stay away from the drugs and all the connected people, until this case is cleaned up. He should be home in Massachusetts late this morning."

"I'll take care of it," replied Jack. "I don't know how much good it will do to tell him, but I'll do it."

"Hasn't he been helpful to you guys?" asked Ernie.

"Oh, yes he's been helpful, especially with the tapes that we got with those microphones. He's been helpful in other areas as well, but he is as nervous as a cat and you can see his needs coming through his facade every so often."

"Did you offer him some help with his drug struggle?"

"Yes, we offered many things, including medical assistance, but all we can do is lead a horse to water," replied Jack.

"Please, make sure you offer our help again before he leaves and goes back to Massachusetts," asked Ernie.

"Believe me, I will do all I can to help him, but he has to want help, you know that."

"Yes, I know. I'll see you later this afternoon."

Ernie hung up the phone and went over to the luncheonette where he had breakfast with Tony Two Scoops.

After breakfast, he ran by the club to make sure that there had not been any changes in any of the plans. There were no changes.

That afternoon, he drove over to meet Jack. Jack drove to the main police meeting area with Ernie in the car.

"It's nice to be together again," stated Ernie.

"You're right, I'm very happy with this case, Ernie."

"What amazes me is how large it became is such a short time. I think we owe Scar for that. He did a good job of cutting me into his cousin," replied Ernie.

As they spoke, Jack drove into the federal parking garage under the federal building and parked.

"The meeting hall is on the third floor; wait till you see this place," stated Jack.

Ernie entered a large room something like a university lecture hall with rows of seats and a front stage. In one corner were several large coffee pots and next to them were three trays of donuts to go with the coffee.

"This is some room. What is it, a lecture hall?"

"Yes, they do all their training here. Let's get you introduced," answered Jack.

There were about two hundred men roaming around, looking at all the photos hanging on the wall, reading the notes and waiting to be given their assignments.

"Let's get started, men," said Jack.

They all sat down and waited.

"I want to make sure that you know who this man is" He pointed to Ernie, standing just a few feet away from him.

"A few cases back we had a miscommunication. No one on the cover and closing teams seemed to know who the cover man was. This was very bad because they wound up shooting at our deep cover man, Det. Ernie Lijoi Sr. I want to make sure that we never have a situation like that again. Take a good look at him. This is our cover man, Det. Ernie Lijoi Sr. Do not shoot him unless you have to," Jack stated as he laughed.

Everyone in the room chuckled over the statement.

"Ernie, do you want to say anything?"

"Yes, Jack, thanks. You men have not been assigned to any particular location, but please be very careful. These men all carry guns and they do not have any regard for human life. Another point, I don't know who is covering the ships, but there is a hill off to the left and there will be two men on top of that hill covering the unloading of the ships. Be careful of them. Other than those two situations, the only thing that I will be concerned about is that we handle this in a way so that they do not suspect me. This suspicion may compromise two other men, so if you come in contact with me, make the arrest. Remember, you do not know me."

Ernie thanked the men for their help and attention to the instructions; he thanked Jack, Paul and the entire team for all of their help. He wished everyone good luck on the closing of the case and asked everyone to please be careful and take no chances. Ernie excused himself and said that he had to leave. Jack, Paul and a few other men came over to shake his hand and wish him luck, while others tried to talk with him as he left the area.

Jack drove Ernie back to his car. Ernie drove off to the club for the meeting with the family and the soldiers.

Once Jack returned to the federal building, Paul decided to contact the Coast Guard to advise them of exactly what will happen and what the team will do. They spoke with a Lt. Robert MacDaniel via telephone and told him that they would be receiving a call about a small boat with drugs -and further, that this would be a diversionary tactic. Paul advised the Coast Guard to listen in on the police radio channel and that he would be contacted once the ship was unloaded. The Coast Guard was ready and willing to assist.

The next step was to release William (Scar) Surelo and advise him to stay clean. He was told that Eddie and Jack would do all that they could for him, but he must keep himself out of the business. "Scar, get a job and settle down, it will look better for you when it comes time to address the court," said Jack.

Scar replied: "Don't worry about me; I can take care of myself. As long as you guys help me out with my case, I'll be OK. Nobody is gonna fuck with me, I'm golden"

"You're free to go back to Massachusetts, Scar," said Jack.

Scar left the office and was driven to the bus station where he took the bus for home. The officers watched him get on the bus and then left the station.

Two men were assigned to the hill where the cover men were being placed by the family. These two men left the area to make sure that they were in position before the cover team for the family got there.

They began to assign all of the men to teams that would cover the various search warrants, arrest warrants and the cover teams for the drugs. Paul and Jack would assist in the command center with the New York Police.

They were all set and ready to go.

***

At the Club

Eddie walked into the club and all of the soldiers were there waiting for everyone to show up. One at a time the men drifted in from the lounge until they were all present.

Wheeze started the meeting, "The trucks have left for the area where the ships will dock. We will all get into cars, with three and four men in each and head down to the Cape in New Jersey. The cover team will ride together and go directly to the hill and cover the entire unloading of the ships. Eddie and Ronny, you can ride with me and Joey, if you like, since we have that thing to do later. Any question?"

The men got up from their seats and left the club. They were all on the way.

***

The Cover Team

The Mafia families cover team, two men nick named Bushels and Shield, arrived at the top of the hill, parked their car and walked over to an area where they could view the unloading of the ships. This was a wooded area with plenty of cover if needed.

Bushels: "Did you hear something?"

Shields: "Yeah, I think I did. There may be someone else here."

The two men looked around and saw a man dressed in dirty street clothes sitting next to a tree, sleeping off a drunk, with a bottle of wine in his lap and two other empty bottles on the ground.

Then they noticed a second man. "Shields, I guess we have a couple of drunks here. What do you wanna do?" asked Bushels

"Fugheddaboudit, they won't bother us. They'll probably never know we were here," stated Shields.

As they spoke, they had their backs to the two drunks that were passed out against the trees when suddenly they heard someone say, "You two are under arrest. Drop your weapons, walk away from the edge of the hill and place your hands on your head."

Shields and Bushels turned quickly, to be confronted by the two drunks standing and holding handguns on them.

Shields dropped his weapon. Bushels didn't drop his rifle, but said: "Who the fuck are you guys?"

"I am agent Joey Watts and this is agent Groupo. We are Federal agents. Drop that weapon"

Bushels dropped his weapon and placed his hands on his head as directed.

They were both cuffed and placed in their own car to wait until the agents were ready to leave. The agents then took on the position of the guards.

Someone waved to them from the area were the cars were parked. One of the agents waved back. They set up a camera to record the entire unloading of the ships, which would become evidence in the case later.

Shortly thereafter, Agents Watts and Groupo could see the ships in the distance, coming up the inlet to the docking area. They also saw a long vehicle driving into the area. This car was a long black limousine that was not with the original bunch of cars. It pulled up as the agents watched through their binoculars which they had hidden in the bushes earlier, as the movie camera took in the entire scene.

A Spanish-looking male exited the limousine and as that happened; agent Watts contacted Jack via two way radios.

"Watts to Paul or Jack."

"Jack on."

"Jack, there is a limo here with a Spanish-looking male. Can this be the representative from the Columbian family that I read about in the reports?"

"Most probably; let me know when he leaves."

"Will do."

***

Coast Guard

As the three ships turned up into the inlet a fourth boat that was about three miles away, with two crew men on board, called the Coast Guard via radio. They told the Coast Guard that there was a small ship floating and that it was loaded with drugs. They gave the location of the ship and were thanked. The Coast Guard was expecting a call like this and followed through by going after the ship.

A second call came into the Coast Guard from Agent Paul Saunders of the New York DEA: "Lt. MacDaniel, did you get a call on a ship with drugs?"

"Yes, Saunders, we did and we're on our way to intercept it."

"Good. We'll need a ship to block the exit to the inlet, can you set that up?"

"We can and we will take care of it."

"Good, one and a half ships will unload and then leave the area. They are all yours once they sail away from the dock."

"How many ships will there be?"

"Sorry, I thought that you knew. There should be a total of three ships coming out of the inlet. One and one half should be loaded with drugs. You stop them and confiscate the ships. All of the paperwork will be ready by morning."

"We'll take care of our end. I'll see you tomorrow morning."

"Thanks, after this conversation we will go silent until the morning when I contact you Lieutenant."

"Agreed."

The Coast Guard went into action. As the ships left the inlet they would be stopped, boarded and confiscated. The crews would be placed under arrest and held for trial. Eventually they could get as much as ten year's jail time before the deportation.

***

Back at the Inlet

The ships pulled up to the dock one at a time. They were unloaded into the waiting trucks.

Ronny: "Everything looks good, Eddie. We're gonna make a ton of cash on this deal."

Eddie: "Yes, I think we're all gonna get a lot out of this."

They finished unloading the ships. The truck drivers were all instructed to take different routes to the warehouse.

Ronny, Eddie, Wheeze and Joey Bats joined Paolo Cristino, the representative from the Soldado family in Columbia. They spoke for a while and Paolo was satisfied that Ronny was happy with the product that he took from the ships.

Wheeze and Ronny confirmed that the money would be sent electronically as soon as he spoke with Wheeze. Paolo was happy with the arrangements and left the area.

Once the shipments of drugs were on the trucks, Wheeze, Joey, Ronny and Eddie got into Wheeze's car. Wheeze told Eddie to drive out of the area via the normal route.

***

Paolo Cristino, Columbian Representative

A team was assigned to stop Paolo after he was out of view of all of the trucks and cars and place him into custody. Paolo was stopped and the officers asked him to exit the vehicle. He did and they placed him under arrest.

"You can't arrest me," exclaimed Paolo.

"Why not?" asked one of the agents.

"I am a diplomatic currier and protected under diplomatic law."

"You can discuss that with the courts," the agents replied as they transported Paolo for booking.

***

The trucks

Another team was assigned to stop one of the trucks once it was out of view of the docking area and all of the other vehicles.

The truck was pulled over and the driver asked what the problem was?

"Step out of the truck, sir," replied the New Jersey state trooper.

"What's going on, is there something wrong, guys?" asked the driver.

They looked into the back of the truck and observed that the truck was loaded with bails of marijuana and boxes of other drugs.

"You're under arrest for narcotics violations."

So far, the strategy was working well; the next step would be the one to worry about.

The New Jersey officers contacted agent Paul Saunders via radio. Paul asked them to hold at their location until he and Jack drove over to them with several additional men and another truck.

Upon arrival with two other cars and a truck, they transferred the load of drugs to the spare truck. While the unloading was going on, Jack and Paul spoke with the driver.

"What's your name?" asked Paul.

"William Roundara," answered the driver.

"Oh, you're Willy the Wimp, right?" asked Jack.

"That's what they call me sometimes, you're pretty well informed."

"Willy, we don't have a lot of time. We want you to drive the truck into the warehouse for us and we'll advise the court that you cooperated. That should save you a few years."

"To what warehouse, where is it?"

"OK, fuck you. I'll make sure you get forty years for this," stated Jack.

"For what? I was just asked to drive a truck. I don't know what's in it."

"We watched you unload the ship and load the truck. Need I say more?" stated Paul.

"What do you want me to do?"

"Now you're being reasonable. We want you to drive the truck into the warehouse. Our men will take over from there," said Paul.

"OK, I'll do it. You'll tell the court that I was cooperative, right?"

"I'll take care of it," stated Paul.

Paul loaded several men into the truck which he saw as his own private "Trojan Horse" and gave Willy the Wimp instructions. They were on their way.

***

Back in Wheeze's Car

Eddie was driving up a country road when Wheeze asked him to pull into a dirt road on the right side, about two hundred feet ahead.

Eddie did as instructed and asked where they were going.

Joey Bats: "We have something to take care of that has been waiting until today, it's very important. I'll explain it all in a little while."

Ronny became curious and began asking questions when Eddie looked at him and said: "Ronny, you heard them, let's wait and see"

Wheeze: "That's what we like about you, Eddie, your trusting those that matter."

Eddie: "Thanks Wheeze, you deserve the trust."

Wheeze directed Eddie up some back roads and into a small clearing, where he told Eddie to pull over.

Joey: "Eddie, you and Ronny stay in the car until we call you"

Joey and Wheeze exited the car and went to the trunk. They took out a shovel and a large bag. Eddie was watching as best he could, but was unable to make out what was in the bag.

Joey: "Ronny, Eddie come on out and join us."

Wheeze: "You guys take these shovels and dig a hole in that area." He pointed to an area about twenty feet away under a large oak tree.

Eddie and Ronny looked at each other and just shrugged their shoulders, then proceeded to follow directions.

About fifteen minutes later, the hole was dug and Ronny was standing at the foot of the hole facing Wheeze and Joey Bats, while Eddie was in the hole finishing up the digging.

Suddenly, Eddie heard a shotgun go off. He looked up from the hole and saw Ronny fall back into it and land on top of him.

In that first few seconds, a million things ran through Eddie's mind all at once. *They know who I am, I'm next to be shot, this grave was for me and Ronny*. He figured he was dead.

Eddie, feeling Ronny's blood dripping down on his head and face, pulled out his gun and pushed Ronny's body off of himself. Still standing in the hole, he turned towards Wheeze and Joey in an effort to defend himself. Eddie was ready to kill.

Eddie looked over the top of the grave, towards Wheeze and Joey Bats, expecting them to fire at him. He saw that Wheeze was standing there with a double barreled, sawed off shotgun in his right hand. The shotgun was pointed at the ground. There were no more shots fired. They were standing there looking at Eddie and smiling.

"Why the fuck do you want to kill us?"

Joey Bats: "Not you, Eddie, just Ronny. Sorry that he fell on you. You can clean up at the warehouse."

Eddie: "I still don't understand; why did you kill him?"

Wheeze looked at Joey, waiting for him to say something.

Joey: "Wheeze, you tell him"

Wheeze: "Eddie, do you remember when we told you that we had a connection in the FBI?"

Eddie: "Yes, I do"

Wheeze: "We sent you to Boston to nose around and you told us about that ship that Scar was involved with."

Eddie: "Yeah, I remember, but how does that connect?"

Wheeze: "Here is what we found out. You were correct when you said that Scar was involved with the ships in Boston and got busted. What we found out later was that Scars' cousin Ronny set up the whole drug buy behind our backs. We were supposed to get a twenty percent commission on all of those transactions; Ronny and Scar were cheating us. They had a plan to undermine our operation. They were slowly turning us into the federal agencies as Ronny moved closer to the top. They would eventually take over the entire operation. The best part of this entire plan was you."

Many ideas where running through Eddies mind as he listened to Wheeze.

Eddie: "What do you mean me? What do I have to do with it?"

Wheeze: "You were their cover. They used your name, the code name of Eddie to contact the feds. They figured that if anything went wrong they would point to you or we would figure that you were the bad guy in this scenario. You're lucky that we figured that out, because we were looking at you for a while."

Eddie: "That's amazing, so I'm clear as far as you guys are concerned?"

Joey Bats: "You are our next capo, Eddie. You're aces with us. Now, cover that piece of shit with some dirt and let's get out of here. I want to get to the warehouse before the trucks arrive."

Eddie: "Shit, you're cutting it close, Joey."

Wheeze: "We have plenty of time, they're very slow. I told them, no speeding, no wild driving. We should beat them there."

Eddie was relieved that he was in one piece. He agreed with Wheeze's estimate of time. He finished covering Ronny's body with some dirt and then the three men drove off toward the warehouse together.

Eddie: "One question. What about Scar? What do you plan to do about him?"

Joey Bats: "He is being taken care of as we speak. I called California the other day and made the arrangements."

Eddie: "Thanks, that's good to know."

Eddie wanted to get to a telephone so that he could try and secure Scar, but he was not able to do it. He had to go along with Wheeze and Joey for the moment.

***

Warehouse:

Wimp drove the truck, loaded not with drugs, but with police officers who were determined to close this case without any injury to themselves or any of the suspects.

This may not be so easy to do, Jack thought.

"Let's take our time, we want to be the last truck to arrive at the warehouse," stated Jack.

The warehouse was surrounded by police officers and federal agents. They were hiding in the area and waiting for the trucks to arrive and the signal to close in.

The trucks started to arrive, one at a time until they were all in the warehouse.

Jack looked at Paul and asked if he thought that they should start closing in on the warehouse.

Jack: "No, I haven't seen Ernie, Ronny, Wheeze or Joey Bats yet. Here they come. That's Joey's Cadillac coming down the street now".

Paul: "Shall we shut this thing down?" He looked at Jack, who simply smiled back and said good luck.

Jack notified two cruisers via radio to stop Joey Bat's car and arrest the occupants. They then started out towards a side door to enter the Warehouse.

Jack and Paul entered the warehouse just as the truck carrying the police officers and detectives pulled in and parked.

One of the Borgazino family saw Jack and Paul enter. He picked up his gun and began shooting, hitting Paul in the shoulder. Jack stood over him to protect Paul who was lying on the ground injured.

The men from the truck exited the truck and took up positions while returning fire from the Borgazino family soldiers.

Jack observed one of the men up high on a scaffold taking aim at Paul. Jack fired and the subject fell from the scaffold to the ground.

The shooting continued. Several men were hit including one police officer besides Paul. Finally the Borgazino family decided that they were beat. One man put his gun down and placed his hands on top of his head. The others, seeing that, followed suit.

Everyone was taken into custody and booked at the police station. All of the evidence was loaded onto the trucks and placed in the police garage for safe keeping overnight with guards on duty.

Ernie was taken into custody and booked at the police station as Eddie Pannoni. He was placed in a holding cell with Wheeze and Joey Bats.

***

Back at the station house

About an hour later an officer approached the cell that Ernie was in. This cell now had about eight men in it. The officer called out: "Which of you guys is Eddie Pannoni?" as he read from the slip of paper in his hand.

Ernie: "I am, why? What the fuck are you gonna do, bust my balls some more?"

Wheeze and Joey Bats laughed as Eddie harassed the police officer.

The officer replied with a smile: "No, asshole, you're wanted in Boston on a felony rap and they decided to come and get you."

Eddie looked at Joey and Wheeze and said: "This is what I was afraid of."

Wheeze: "Eddie, don't worry, when you get out, come and see us. You always have a job with us." He shook Eddie's hand.

Joey Bats: "Eddie, I kind of expected this. Once I was sure of Ronny I didn't have time to stop the ships so I let it happen. We have contingencies for this; if you need a lawyer or anything let me know. Your job is always open to you with my family. I'm glad we took care of those guys." He winked at Eddie.

Eddie was taken out of the cell and into an office where Jack and the federal agents were sitting around waiting for him.

As Ernie entered the room they all cheered, clapped and congratulated him on doing a great job.

Ernie: "No, don't do that. I think Scar is dead. Joey sent Louie the Lark after him and Wheeze killed Ronny while I was there".

Jack: "Ernie, in an effort to keep Scar safe I put two guys on him. They were on the scene when a white male, who turned out to be Louie the Lark, tried to kill him. The cover men shot and killed Louie. We are sorry to hear about Ronny. Where is the body?"

Ernie: "In a grave that I'll have to point out."

***

They left the office and Ernie took them to the grave site. Jack went down into the hole and felt Ronny's neck to confirm that he was dead.

"Ernie, I feel a slight pulse" said Jack

"Impossible, look at the wound in his chest" replied Ernie as he called, via radio for an ambulance.

The ambulance arrived and the men worked on Ronny trying to revive him. Ronny finally died in their arms.

Ernie and Jack were finished with this operation and would return to Boston the next morning.

***

Ernie drove the car and did not go to the highway north.

"Where are you going, Ernie?"

"Do you remember when I told you about diving from the bridges in Sheepshead Bay?"

"Don't tell me you want to stop there?"

"Yeah, I want you to witness it and I would like to be the one throwing the change."

"Do you have any change?" asked Jack.

Ernie reached into his pocket and took out a roll of half dollars. "This should be enough."

***

They arrived at the three bridges in Sheepshead Bay. The kids are diving for change just as Ernie did as a little boy.

The two men threw change, the kids dove and they both laughed. This little bit of distraction helped them to accept the numerous deaths that they had observed over the past few weeks. They stayed there a while and then left for home.

***

During the ride home

"Hey, Jack, you know we have an opening to come back and do the back side of this case. Joey Bats invited me to return. He also offered me legal assistance if I need it. He said that I could have my position back at any time."

"Yeah, Ernie, we all figured that if your real identity was kept hidden, they may want you back. It's definitely something to think about."

Ernie turned the car down a side street:

"Where are you going now? This isn't the way home."

Jack looked out the front window of the car: "Ernie, is that who I think it is?"

Ernie pulled over to the side of the road and Don Badi got in the back seat.

Badi: "This must be your partner that I heard so much about."

Ernie: "Don, meet my good friend and partner Jack."

The End

Other books by
Ernie Lijoi, Sr.

Chasing Snow
Destructive Obsession
Meth or Myth
Street Business
Street Business II (with Larry Matthews)
Shoveling the Tide
The Cash Mule
The Preyers".

About our Author

Ernie Lijoi, Sr.

My name is Ernesto Lijoi, I write under the name Ernie Lijoi Sr., my site is http://www.erniesr.com. I was born and raised in Brooklyn, NY on St. Marks Ave in 1943 of Italian decent. If I may I would like to tell you a brief story about how I recently became a writer, after retirement. I was a Police Patrolman for the Transit Authority back in the 1970's in Boston, Massachusetts. After a specific arrest of a suspect for narcotics, I was asked to take a 30 day job as a Deep Cover Investigator for a larger City in Massachusetts. This job required a new identity, Eddie Pannoni. Because of the expertise that I acquired, I was still doing the same job under the guise of Eddie Pannoni 18 years later and had a very interesting and exciting career. In 1980 Sonny Grasso and Eddie Eagan came to see me (Known for the French Connection Movie and others). They wanted to do a book about my career. By that time I had the two contracts on my life. I refused the book because of the never ending work that I had to finish. Since my retirement people are always asking about my experiences throughout my career as a DCI. I have been told, many times, that I should write them down. At age 65, I decided to write the first book named "Street Business" with Mr. Larry Matthews. We were published a few months after it was written. I began another book and Larry suggested that I send it in without any help from him. I did and it was published. I am now 71 years of age and have several books published, namely: *Meth ore Myth, Destructive Obsession, the Cash Mule, Street Business II, The Tunnel, The Butcher of Boston,* and now *The Preyers,* along with movie and TV scripts as well as numerous poems. The movie project called *The* Preyers is well on its way to fruition. The books are based on fact although told in a fictional manner with everything, including locations which, in most cases are changed along with names and dates. You may read more about me at http://www.erniesr.com In the event that you would like to talk, I am, now a Florida resident although this work took place in many states. I should mention that I worked with The FBI, ATF and DEA as a deep cover detective. I have enough material (newspaper clipping, reports, etc.) for at least a hundred or more books. I worked narcotics, murders, robberies and more. I was always on the inside of these jobs as a deep cover operative. PUBLISHING CREDITS: Can be found at my site with reviews news articles to back up my stories

www.ingramcontent.com/pod-product-compliance
Lightning Source LLC
Chambersburg PA
CBHW071525260626
47170CB00002B/505